ECHOES FROM THE PAST

Grace Brannigan

P.O. Box 100
East Jewett, New York, 12424 USA

Echoes from the Past

Women of Character Contemporary Series
Echoes From The Past
Once and Always
Heartstealer
Wishing on a Rodeo Moon

Women of Strength Time Travel Series
Once Upon A Remembrance
Soulmates Through Time
Treasure So Rare

Romantic Short Stories
Two Babies, a Cowboy and Sara
Deception

Website: www.GraceBrannigan.com

All Characters, places and events are fictitious and are not associated or inspired by any person living or dead.

Echoes from the Past
Cover Art By: Stephanie White of Steph's Cover Design: paranormal, fantasy, horror & more
By Grace Brannigan
Copyright 2013   Elaine Warfield

ISBN: 978-1-939061-28-7

∞ Chapter One ∞

CHRISTIE JENKINS ONCE AGAIN counted the bills in her pocket. Seventeen dollars. The gnawing hunger in her stomach attested to the fact that she hadn't had a decent meal in two days.

Shading her eyes against the bright sun, she let her duffel bag slide to the cracked pavement and stared at the royal blue sign beside the road, at the beginning of a long, curved driveway.

Winding Creek Farms, Emerson, Kentucky

The same address as her sister Judith's letter. Christie stuffed the crumpled bills back in her pocket and looked up the curved driveway lined with dusky pink Dogwood trees. Various barns and sheds sat at the top of the drive where gently rolling hills and ribbons of white fence seemed to go on forever. Horses grazed lazily in fenced paddocks and a short distance from the barns stood a house, the midnight blue roof and cupolas lending it a fairytale look. Pure heaven. The sharp nag of pain in Christie's gut cut such thoughts short. Given the events of this year, she was certain there was no heaven on earth.

As she reached for her bag Christie suddenly noticed a movement in the tall grass beside the driveway. A child of about eight or nine, creeping on her hands and knees, pushed her way through the grass. Long blond ponytails fell across her pink shirt. When the child's feet cleared the grass, Christie smiled to see that red cowgirl boots peeked beneath denim overalls.

"Here, Albert." The child's voice was coaxing. "Come on, now."

That's when Christie noticed the small gray kitten near the driveway's edge. A sudden swipe of the little girl's hand as she tried to grab the kitten sent the animal darting out onto the dirt driveway. With the unpredictability of cats, it just as quickly stopped in the middle of the driveway and hunched its back upward. Cautious again, the child slowly rose to her feet to follow the kitten.

Christie heard a new sound and noticed a large hay truck pull away from one of the barns and start down the driveway. The child didn't seem aware of the vehicle as she continued to coax the kitten toward her.

"Hey!" Christie waved her arm at the child.

The little girl stopped abruptly and looked toward Christie, her eyes wide with alarm.

"Get out of there!" Christie called. The hay-laden truck sounded like it was slowing down, but it didn't stop moving toward them. The little girl finally looked at the truck, staying almost frozen in the driveway. Afraid, Christie raced toward the little girl.

¤ ¤

Garrett McIntyre heard his daughter's scream and spun from the barn doorway. *Hannah*! He ran toward the driveway, fear a tight fist gripping his throat when the sound of grinding metal followed Hannah's scream. The hay wagon that had just loaded up at the barn veered off the driveway. He saw a dark-haired woman pull Hannah into the grass. Garrett ran hard. The truck rolled past the woman and Hannah into the small gully beside the driveway. It rocked to a drunken stop.

A trail of smoke. The little sports car tilted nose down into the ditch. The unending blare of the horn.

When he reached Hannah, the woman had her arms around his little girl. Hannah's eyes were closed, her skin stark white. Terror pulled his breath away and he dropped to his knees in the tall grass. He couldn't pass out.

Garrett met the woman's dark eyes, reflecting the terror he was sure was in his own. His gaze jerked immediately to his child, then the truck sitting at an angle behind them.

The knot in his throat restricted his voice, but he tried again, his first fear for his daughter. He touched her cheek, then the dark blond hair that was so much like his own. "Hannah, are you all right?"

She gave a quick nod as a tremor shook her

body.

"She was suddenly in front of me, Boss!" Emmet blurted, dropping from the driver's seat to the ground. "I couldn't stop. The brakes!" Emmet was barely out of his teens and right now his face was drained of all color. Droplets of sweat beaded his forehead as he rushed on, "This woman pulled Hannah out of the road — God Almighty! I thought I was gonna hit 'em both."

"Sit down, Emmet." Garrett thought the young man looked ready to fall down.

Emmett pushed his lank dark hair from his forehead and dropped to the grass. "Yeah. I feel sick." He put his head against his up-drawn knees.

"Come here, Hannah."

The dark haired woman removed her arms from around his daughter. Hannah leaned toward him, her deep blue eyes awash with tears. "I'm sorry, Daddy. I know I'm not supposed to be down here. I was trying to catch Albert. I didn't want him lost."

Garrett sucked in a deep draft of air. "Albert the cat? He's long gone." The animal was nowhere in sight.

"Oh! Albert is gone!" Hannah launched herself into Garrett's arms and began crying loudly. Garrett quickly checked her legs and arms for injury, all too aware of how his hands shook.

"You could have been hurt bad." His jaw hurt from holding it clenched. "It's a good thing you're so tough. Dammit, Hannah, I couldn't take it if something happened to you, too."

"I'm not hurt Daddy, but Albert's gone forever!" Hannah wailed, tears now streaming down her face.

Garrett felt the back of her head carefully, making himself stay calm for her benefit. No blood, no bumps. "Hannah, barn cats aren't used to being carried around. Anyway, he takes better care of himself than you seem to be doing lately. Come on, we'll go to the house and have Ruth check you and this young lady out." He stood and held his hand out to the woman who'd saved his daughter. "Thank you." Quickly, he added, "Are you all right?"

She nodded, taking the hand he held out, letting him help her to her feet. She pushed the hair back from her forehead. "I'm okay. At least nothing hurts."

Taking stock, he noted she wasn't very big, maybe five feet six inches, well under his six-one height. She looked to be in her mid-twenties and had a slim, athletic build. He knew most of the people in Emerson, so she wasn't a local. Deep brown eyes framed by dark lashes watched him warily, and he muttered a curse when he suddenly noticed a slight purplish bruising over her eye.

"You've hurt yourself." Concern made him gently touch the slight swelling about the size of a quarter. She gently moved his hand and explored the bruise with her own fingers.

"It's nothing." She dismissed the injury with a lift of one shoulder as she stared at Hannah. "I don't think your little girl got hurt, a bit shaken maybe. I'd definitely have her checked out."

"I intend to," he said. "It's inadequate as hell but I'm sorry you're hurt but darn happy you were on the spot." How had this happened? Garrett hated the unaccustomed moment of helplessness. She was a stranger on his property and she'd been hurt because of Hannah. For a brief moment he thought of the ramifications of a lawsuit.

"I didn't see Hannah until the last minute," Emmet muttered, still sitting on the grass. He lifted his head. "I'm sorry Miss, for the scare you had."

"It appears no one's hurt seriously. Thank God," the woman said. Looking into Hannah's red, tear-streaked face, she asked gently, "Are you okay, honey?"

"I had my cat and now he's gone," the child muttered. "You scared him away."

Garrett sighed with impatience. "Hannah, I can't believe you were down here by the road." He kept a tight rein on the worry riding him. "This woman very likely saved your life. Don't you think you should say something to her?"

Hannah jutted her lower lip and hunched a shoulder. "I was going to get out of the way by myself," she muttered sullenly, but not before Garrett had seen the flash of fear. "I wasn't going to die!" Hannah pulled her hand from his and ran several feet up the driveway.

"Hannah!"

She stopped in her tracks but did not come back toward him. "Albert is gone." Her voice rose in pitch. "I'll never see him again!" She pointed her finger at the woman. "It's her fault!" Hannah turned and ran toward the house, ponytails flying out behind her. Garrett resisted ordering her back, knowing it would make the growing rift between them worse. But dammit, he couldn't let her ride roughshod over him, either.

"Wait for me in your room!" he barked. Hannah hunched her shoulders and continued toward the house at a fast walk. Garrett closed his eyes and muttered, "Sometimes I wonder what the hell I know about raising a child."

Shaking his head, he looked over at the woman. "Sorry," he said ruefully. It wasn't this woman's fault she'd witnessed his apparent lack of control over a sixty-pound, eight-year old, but he hated like hell that she'd seen it anyway. "I'm Garrett McIntyre." He held his hand out again.

"Christie Jenkins." She took his hand in a firm shake, then released it and brushed at her jeans.

"My housekeeper is a retired emergency room nurse. I'd feel better if she took a look at that bruise before you leave."

Frowning, the woman — Christie — suddenly looked around. "My bag!" She twisted around. "Where's my duffel bag?"

Garrett spotted it in the ditch, partly under the front wheel of the truck. His guts churned thinking of his daughter or this young woman in that ditch instead of the bag. "It's right here."

Her apparent distress surprised him a bit. Warily, he said, "It looks okay. You're not going to cry, are you?" Hannah's mother had been a woman who lived solely on emotion. Life had been a constant in emotional highs and lows.

Christie sighed. "Of course not. I was surprised to see it under the wheel. Hopefully, nothing is crushed."

She pulled at the heavy canvas. Garrett gently urged her aside. "Let me get it."

Garrett signaled to Emmet to get on the opposite side of the front bumper. "If we rock this you can probably pull the bag free."

It only took a few rocks of the truck back and forth before the bag came free. Christie lifted the bag and loosened the drawstring to look inside. She didn't say anything but he saw her shoulders relax.

"That bag must be mighty important."

"It is, but no harm's been done." She lifted her head, giving him a half smile. "Thank you."

"Yeah." He turned his attention to his hired hand and the hay wagon. "Emmet, see if you can find Sam. Have him bring the tractor with the winch and pull this thing out. I'll call my mechanic."

"Sure, boss." Emmet scuffed his boots in the dirt, his face working. Finally, he said, "The brakes were a little spongy. I should have told you." Emmet swallowed. "Do you want me outta here?"

Garrett looked at the young man's closed expression and realized Emmet expected to be fired. "I realize you've only been here a month, but I need any problems brought to my attention right away."

The woman stepped closer.

"This wasn't anyone's fault," she said quickly.

Pushing his hat back, Garrett studied her worried expression. Mildly, he said, "I don't plan to fire Emmet."

He looked at Emmet. "Take care of the truck. The hay will have to be unloaded if they need to work on it. I'll talk to the mechanic and let you know."

Emmet tipped his hat, appearing relieved. "Okay, boss." He looked at the woman. "I'm glad you weren't hurt, Ma'am." He left, walking up the drive toward the house and barns.

Garrett turned back to Christie, took in her dark, dusty jeans and what looked like once-white sneakers. Her blue T-shirt had pulled out of her jeans, exposing a small section of pale skin. She couldn't weigh more than one-thirty, soaking wet. He rubbed his forehead with the back of his wrist. "It's been a heck of a day so far." He looked away from her, toward the house and shook his head. "My daughter ....."

"I'd be worried too," she said. "No one needs that kind of trouble, a child getting hurt."

Garrett allowed himself a rueful smile. "If Hannah's involved, there's always something going on."

Just then his yellow Labrador dog came streaking down the driveway, tail wagging furiously as she moved in eagerly against their legs. In her enthusiasm, she knocked against the woman. Quickly, Garrett said, "Bo Peep, that's enough!" The dog backed up and sat down, then watched him with her head cocked to one side.

Christie knelt down and began to make a fuss of the dog. "Your dog's name is Bo Peep?" she asked, a hint of humor curving her full lips as she looked up at him.

"My daughter's idea. So Christie, tell me, what are you doing out here in the middle of pretty much nowhere?"

Her smile disappeared and she came to her feet once more. "I, uh, was on the road when I saw your daughter in trouble. Actually, I'm looking for Judith Kelly. The last address I have for her is this place."

The hair on the back of Garrett's neck stood up and a band tightened around his chest. "Why?"

"Do you know her?"

Know her? Garrett stared at Christie, searching for God knew what. He saw only honest inquiry on her face. "Why do you ask?" he said instead, knowing there was an edge to his voice.

"She's my sister. I need to find her."

"Christ." Garrett took a deep breath, then another. He cleared his head. "Judith had no family."

Now Christie's eyes widened. "She left home a long time ago, but she had family."

"Can you prove that?"

"I-I can't. At least, not at this moment. I had a letter from her."

"Let me see the letter."

"I don't have it on me."

Beginning to feel annoyed, Garrett half turned away. "I need my housekeeper to look at your head and then I'll call you a taxi." Christie hurried behind him as he walked up the drive to the house.

"Listen, just tell her Christie's here," she said urgently. "It's been a long time but I know she'll see me."

"You can't see her."

She grabbed his arm. "I've come a long way."

Garrett stopped, fighting the dull numbness inside his chest. He faced her squarely. "My wife — Judith, died almost two years ago."

Garrett quickly reached for her arm as she swayed.

"Judith was your wife?" Her voice was barely a whisper.

"If you're really Judith's sister, I'm a real jerk for telling you like that — how come she never mentioned you?"

Christie appeared dazed, but steadier on her feet now. Garrett stepped back.

"We're half-sisters. Judith left home when she was barely fifteen. Our mother threw her out. I don't know why. I got a letter from Judith one day, right out of the blue — said she was thinking about coming for a visit."

"Your name isn't the same."

"Her maiden name was Kelly. My mother's maiden name."

"When did you receive the letter?" he asked tersely.

"A-about two years ago."

"And you're just getting around to looking her up now?" He didn't hide the skepticism in his voice.

Christie hesitated, then admitted, "There were reasons I couldn't come until now."

"So you conveniently tracked her here."

"There was nothing convenient about it." She shook her head and the somber expression on her face made him feel like a mean bastard. She was obviously hurting.

She seemed to shake herself. "I'm sorry for your loss," she added in a low voice. "I had no idea where my sister was, much less that she had married. And I'm sorry for intruding like this. I thought I'd find Judith." She looked up the hill toward the house and went still. "That little girl — Hannah — she's Judith's, isn't she?"

"What is it you really want?" he said, balled fists

on his hips.

She looked up at him, her dark hair falling away from her face. "I don't want anything from you. I told you why I'm here. It seems now like it was a fool's errand." Her voice broke. "But if Hannah is my niece, I have a right to know."

"You're on my property, asking personal questions that I'm still not sure you have a right to ask. I don't give information about my family to anyone."

Christie came to her feet, her hands out beseechingly. "I don't blame you. Please let me get to know Hannah, even for the short time I'm here. She's my niece."

"If what you say is true."

"I understand your suspicions. Someone shows up out of the blue claiming to be related to your child." She looked away from him. "Judith left when I was so young I barely remember her."

"I'm asking again, why come now?"

Her expression closed. "That's my business, Garrett." She drew a deep breath. "I'd like to your cooperation in letting me get to know Hannah. It's not every day you find out you have a niece."

Garrett felt torn. She obviously had information that wasn't easy to come by, Judith's maiden name for one. "Until I check your story out, you're not to tell Hannah who you are."

Christie considered him, her mouth firm, but she nodded. "I don't like it, but if that's the way it has to be, I can live with it. For now," she added, lifting her chin. "I can give you some numbers to call for references. Character references."

"Fine, where are you staying?"

She hitched her duffel bag higher on her shoulder and avoided his eyes. "I'm new to the area. That is, I was hoping to get some work while I was here. I'll do just about anything," she added quickly. "I'm not picky. I can cook and clean." She paused, her glance shifting to the barn and house. "I'd be happy to work in the barns, but I'm also handy at gardening or house cleaning."

"I have someone tending my garden." He found himself grinning. "Ruth would skin my hide if anybody touched her flowers."

She chewed her lip and looked around. "I can push a lawn mower. How about the horses? I'm not afraid to work."

"If you were from around here, you'd know most of the farms hire on extra help well before the spring."

"Does that mean no?"

Garrett stroked his chin thoughtfully, hardly crediting that he was thinking about hiring her. "Actually, I'm a hand short in the barns. One of the girls fell and broke her ankle. She'll be in a cast for at least the next five to six weeks. Maybe I can use you on a short-term basis. Do you have any experience with horses?"

Her face lit up. The sparkle in her eyes caused a tingling across the back of his neck.

"I love horses. I worked one summer at a horseback riding camp. I'm really good around animals."

Mentally, Garrett groaned. "Not exactly the type of experience I had in mind."

"That might not seem like much experience to you, but I'm a quick study." Quickly, as if sensing his hesitation, "You won't regret it. It would give me a chance to get to know Hannah."

"It would be mostly grunt work. I have regulars that handle the horses. I might need someone for a month or so, but I'd rather see how you work out before I promise anything."

"A month?" She hesitated, but then looked up at the house.

He saw a longing in her eyes, which she quickly masked by looking down.

"Okay."

"I'll give you a few days trial, that's all I'm promising," he said brusquely. "Come to the house and we'll get ice on that bump." Garrett sized her up. "You'll have to pull your own weight," he added.

"Don't worry, I always do." She cleared her throat. "Uh, since I've just arrived in town, does this job include room and board?"

Garrett read between the lines. She probably didn't have two cents to rub together, much less money for a room in town. She was old enough to take care of herself and he'd stopped taking in strays a long time ago. For a brief instant, the thought crossed his mind that her arrival here was just like something Judith would do. Reason enough to watch her closely.

"Judith never worried about things like rent or a roof over her head either." The words were almost involuntary, but he couldn't help but make the comparison.

"Maybe we're more alike than you'd think," she

mused.

Garrett had mixed emotions about that. Except for the first year of their marriage where they'd spent most of their time in bed, he and Judith had been oil and water.

"The job includes room and board." He quickened his steps. "The starting pay is a dollar over minimum wage."

"Thanks. I have to admit I'm surprised you're hiring me."

"It's a busy time of year and I am short one hand. Beside that you saved my daughter from being hurt. I've factored in all the variables."

"What if I'm lying?" she asked curiously.

"What do you think?"

"I'm out of here." She shrugged. "That's fair enough."

He looked at his watch. "My housekeeper will have dinner ready. Are you hungry? You can take your dinner over to the worker's cabin."

She rubbed her fingers over her cheeks, causing smudges. "I'm sure I could eat something," she said.

Garrett had the strangest urge to push her hand away and rub the smudge with his thumb. There was an enticing mix of resourcefulness and vulnerability about her. Thinking of Judith and their similarities, Garrett brusquely called the dog and turned away.

"Garrett?" His shoulders stiffened at the hesitation in her voice. "How did she die?"

He continued walking toward the house. "I won't discuss anything personal until I find out you're who you claim to be." And maybe not even then, he told himself silently. Some gut instinct told him Christie was probably telling the truth, but right now he just couldn't even think about delving into Judith's past.

As they neared the barns Garrett saw two of his help, Sue and Buddy as they stood talking beside Sue's new SUV. He looked at his watch. "Hey, you two!" he called. "Go home. It's 5:30 — past quitting time."

"We were in the barn, Boss," Sue called out. "Emmett told us what happened."

"Everything's under control."

They waved at him and Garrett continued toward the house, sparing Christie a glance. "You'll meet Sue and Buddy tomorrow. Sue's my best handler with the foals and Buddy's working during college break."

A vehicle was coming up the drive behind them. They moved to the side of the driveway so the truck could pass. Garrett recognized Les Doyle's red Chevy pickup truck. Les had probably stopped by for his wife Kim's last paycheck. He parked sideways in front of the foaling barn.

Garrett looked at Christie. "That's Kim's husband — she's the one you're filling in for. Give me a minute so I can find out how Kim's doing." He walked across the front of the truck. Christie remained on the passenger side of the vehicle while Garrett approached the driver's side.

"Hello, Les."

"Hey Garrett," Les said loudly, leaning his elbow out the window.

Les didn't look well. He hadn't shaved and his red hair stood on end. Knowing Les' troubled past with alcohol and substances, it wasn't a good sign as far as Garrett was concerned. Garrett wondered if Les had slid back to his old drinking habits.

"You feeling okay, Les? You look under the weather."

"Yeah, fine, fine."

"And how is Kim?"

"You know Kim, she likes to stay busy. She's going stir-crazy."

"Let her know I'll be giving her a call. The girls in the barn were asking if she needed help with the baby. They'll probably come and see her."

Les pushed open his door and climbed out, then slammed the door hard. He stumbled and leaned his bulky six-foot frame against the side of the pickup. "I came for Kim's check." As he heaved himself away from the vehicle the breeze shifted, sending the distinct odor of alcohol toward Garrett.

Garrett sighed. "Les, you've been drinking."

"I only had one."

"The last time you went on a bender, Kim left."

Les held up his right hand. "I swear I'm headed straight home."

"You know I can't let you go back on the highway. One of the boys will run you home."

Les waved away that suggestion. "I'm fine. Kim's waiting dinner on me. By the way, she's itching to get back to work."

Garrett frowned. "I heard she had a bad break and the doctor wanted her to stay off the foot as much as possible."

Les wiped his sleeve across his mouth. "She's worried about losing her job."

"Kim will always have a job when she's ready to come back." Garrett reached in his jeans pocket and pulled out the folded envelope with Kim's check. "I figured you'd stop. Here's Kim's paycheck."

"She wants to come back now," Les insisted. He took the envelope and pocketed it.

Just then Garrett heard a baby's cry. Stunned, he moved closer to the vehicle and looked inside. Les and Kim's seven-month old son Tommy was strapped in a baby seat, and on the truck seat beside him was a six-pack of beer.

"Les," Garrett said.

"Oh, he's okay," Les said. "He must've just woke up." He fumbled behind him and yanked the door open.

Garrett put his palm against the door and pushed it closed. "Les! Don't be stupid. You're getting a ride home and that's it."

Les twisted around toward Garrett, his eyes narrowed in anger. "I'm not hurting anybody. I'm leaving now."

"We'll drop your truck off later."

Les opened his mouth, his face tight with anger.

"Unless you want me calling the Sheriff's office, there are no other options," Garrett said in a hard voice.

¤¤

Tensely, Christie watched the interaction between the two men from the other side of the vehicle. Les was furious, in deep contrast to Garrett's coolly composed stance.

Garrett's dark blond hair was smooth beneath his cowboy hat, and despite the heat his blue cotton shirt looked crisp and fairly clean. Les on the other hand looked like a train wreck about to happen, something she'd seen all too often while growing up. Handsome face, watery blue eyes, faint red spidery lines along his cheeks. He reminded her of her alcoholic father.

"All right, all right," Les was saying now. "I'll take the ride," he said grudgingly.

Garrett indicated Sue. "You know Sue and my new hand, Buddy. I'll see if they can give you that ride." Garrett reached inside the truck and unlatched the car seat with the baby in it.

Carrying both, Garrett crossed back over to Les.

"I'll talk to Sue about taking Tommy."

"In a minute," Les said. "I picked stuff up at the store that I need to get out of the truck."

Garrett motioned with an upraised hand to the tall woman — Sue — who still stood talking with Buddy outside the barn. The pair quickly crossed the yard toward them. Sue, an attractive blond about Garrett's height, appeared to be in her mid thirties while Buddy in contrast was dark haired and about the same height as Christie.

Garrett's introductions were quick. "Sue, Buddy — Christie. We'll do more formal introductions tomorrow. Right now Les needs a ride home. Sue, since Tommy knows you, would you mind running both of them home?"

Sue smiled and unhooked the baby from the car seat. "Of course not. I go right by Kim's place when I drop Buddy off." She cuddled the baby in her arms.

"I'll take the car seat," Buddy said, nodding at Christie as he took the seat from Garrett. Sue and

Buddy crossed the yard and placed the car seat and baby in a dark green SUV.

When Christie turned from watching them, she was startled to find Les a short distance from her, holding a brown grocery bag in his hands. She hadn't realized he'd come around to her side of the vehicle. She was slightly relieved that he stopped three or four feet away. Even so, the smell of alcohol was pretty strong.

Les looked at Christie. "I haven't seen you before."

"I just got here."

He took in her duffel bag. "You working here?" He glared at Garrett. "Is she taking my Kim's place? How the hell is my wife going to get her job back now?"

Christie felt relief when Garrett moved to stand between her and Les.

"Take it easy," Garrett said.

Christie thought he showed tremendous patience.

"No one is taking anything from you or Kim."

"We're ready!" Sue called, pulling the SUV up beside them.

"I'm coming." Les gave Christie one last look, turned on his heel and walked toward the waiting vehicle.

The tension holding Christie in place released when the vehicle pulled away. She crossed her arms, somewhat unsettled by the encounter.

"Is he always like that?" she asked.

Garrett shrugged. "Les used to be a pretty decent guy. When he's drinking, he's totally different."

Garrett turned away and walked toward the house.

Christie fell into step beside him. "What was she like?"

Silence.

"My sister."

"I know who you mean." She sensed reluctance in him to talk about her sister. "Judith wore her heart on her sleeve and took up causes at the slightest whim. She was an emotional woman." He opened a small gate and let her precede him into the yard.

"Let's get to the house for dinner."

∞ Chapter Two ∞

CHRISTIE THOUGHT ABOUT WHAT he'd said. So Judith had been emotional. It hadn't sounded like a compliment.

She took note of wide shoulders stretching the worn cotton shirt before it tapered to a narrow waist and faded blue jeans. She frowned, forcing herself to look away from Garrett McIntyre's backside. He was good looking in a lean, cowboy kind of way. A small shiver raced across her. His eyes seemed to change between blue and gray beneath the brim of that cowboy hat. His hard-planed face could have advertised the old west on billboards and melted a million hearts, but he struck her as a man who didn't have time for any romantic nonsense. He seemed very grounded and she got an uneasy feeling when he spoke of her sister . . . like he was leaving out more than he was saying. Not that he'd said that much.

"I'm not trying to come off as chauvinistic or anything, but don't you have a man or someone traveling with you?"

That made Christie laugh. "No. One thing I've learned is I don't need a man in charge of my life." Garrett was no doubt a man who took charge. "You know, I've seen too many Les's with that same wild look in their eye." Her father's buddies. "I don't care if I ever meet up with that man again." Les' desperate edge repelled her.

Christie hitched her bag higher, reassured by the weight of it against her chest.

Garrett held out his hand. "Let me take that."

Everything she had of value was in the bag. "That's okay, it's not heavy."

"Was Judith the only reason you came here?"

Christie was taken aback by the question. "Yes, what else could there be? I never really knew her, you know. Just vague recollections. . .." she let her voice trail off. How had Judith died? Right now she had no choice but to respect his wish not to talk about it. "I have to admit I still feel out of sync, as if my sister might arrive any moment. I've pictured our reunion all the way down here." She'd traveled to Kentucky to find Judith, and maybe to find herself. "It hurts too much to think about Judith being gone. Can you at least tell me where she's buried?"

Garrett looked at her, not saying anything. Some of her desperation must have showed in her face, because he finally said, "She's buried at a cemetery in town." Almost reluctantly, he added, "If you're here long enough, I'll take you into town one day and show you."

Some of the heaviness eased in Christie's chest. "Thank you."

"We're here," he said, and Christie wondered if that was relief in his voice. They walked around the back of the house and see liked the brand new swing set that had been set up. Hanging from a big tree was an equally new looking tire swing on a rope. Christie looked at the back yard and a knot formed in her chest. A small flower garden behind the swings was enclosed by a white picket fence.

"This is like walking onto a movie set," she murmured, disturbed by a hard ache inside.

"What?" Garrett asked, apparently startled.

Christie struggled to explain. "You know, down home and the average family. The house, yard with flowers, white picket fence, swings in the back yard." She laughed. "I feel completely out of my element. My sister was so lucky. She escaped and found that elusive happiness here." Uneasily, she felt plagued by a sudden uncertain about her wisdom in staying here. Judith's house, Judith's husband.

"Judith never lived here," Garrett said flatly.

He climbed the steps to a small deck at the back of the house and held open a screen door.

"But the address on the envelope —"

"The address is the same. Two years ago this house was in the process of being built. Judith and I lived in the small cottage out back where my foreman Sam lives now. She wanted something bigger — not that I could afford it at the time," he added grimly.

"This house and the barns. . .the horses out in the fields, you look like you're doing so well." She clamped her lips together as his eyes narrowed.

"I can afford it now."

Did he think she was interested in his money?

She hung back. "Er — why don't you just show me where I'll stay tonight? I-I really don't need anything to eat."

"Cabin's out back, but I want you to get ice on that bump first." He held the door open.

Climbing the stairs, Christie walked through the open door into the kitchen. Delicious aromas assaulted her senses. "It smells wonderful in here."

Garrett's smile eased some of the tension lines beside his mouth. "Ruth has a pot roast cooking."

Her mouth watered helplessly. Surreptitiously, she looked around the well-lit kitchen. Garrett might think twice about hiring her if he caught her drooling she thought humorously. She hoped her eyes weren't watering; she'd never felt so hungry.

On Christie's right was a long kitchen counter and cupboards. The light colored oak cabinets had etched glass doors with antiqued pull knobs.

"I really like your dark blue marble countertop," she remarked. "The black appliances give the room an air of sophistication."

He looked at her with one brow raised. "I was trying more for country simplicity."

"Did you design all this?" She looked down at the floor. "I'd say you've achieved country simplicity and more with this slate blue tile. What a great kitchen to work in."

"Ruth seems to like it."

Christie couldn't imagine anyone complaining about a modern kitchen.

Light hued wainscoting coupled with ivory painted walls added to the warm homey look. "Did you do the stenciling over the doorways?"

Garrett laughed. "No, that wasn't me. Actually, Kim tackled that."

"I'm surprised that a man would even think about stenciling." Belatedly realizing how sexist that might sound, she quickly added, "I mean, I don't know many — any men who could single handedly design their own kitchen."

"When I was putting the kitchen together I had some help from the girls who work for me. Truthfully, I didn't think of the stenciling. Kim suggested it and I agreed, as long as she didn't go crazy."

"She's artistic."

"Yeah, well, that's why she took care of it. I can't claim any artistic ability. Now through that door on your left is a pantry, another freezer and the laundry room. The open archway straight ahead, just past the kitchen table, leads to the rest of the house."

Christie looked across the kitchen at the opening Garrett indicated. Through the archway could be seen honey colored oak flooring and a hand woven throw rug in shades of rose and cobalt blue.

Bo Peep trailed behind Christie and then settled with a plop onto a plaid cushion in a corner beside the archway. She found it curious that this big, tough looking man had named his dog after a fairytale character to please his daughter. A smile tugged at her lips. Somewhere under that calm demeanor lurked a sense of humor and perhaps a gentle heart. Christie reined in her wayward thoughts, knowing she had more important things to worry about than her new employer's predilection for kindness. She didn't think she'd ever forget the dread on his face when he'd first knelt beside her and Hannah. It was like he'd seen a ghost. She looked up and found him watching her.

Momentarily caught off guard, Christie blurted, "Your kitchen table is big enough for a small dinner party."

"I like having friends over. I'll be right back." Garrett disappeared through the doorway to the pantry and Christie placed her bag out of the way against one wall. He reappeared moments later with a washcloth and proceeded to open a large upright freezer.

"Here," he said, handing her the washcloth with ice. "Put this on your forehead."

"Probably a smart move," she agreed, taking the cloth and ice. In truth, she had developed a slight headache.

"Sit." He indicated the table behind her.

She pulled out a heavy wooden chair and sat down.

He removed his hat and ran a hand through dark blond hair. It had been combed back from his forehead in a smooth wave, but the hat had flattened it and now his fingers caused further disruption and several strands fell across his forehead.

"Garrett!" A woman called out from somewhere beyond the kitchen. "I hope you're washed up for dinner. I'm almost ready to serve."

The woman who entered the kitchen wore an old-fashioned blue calico dress down over her knees with a pristine white apron in place. She was tall and somewhere in her sixties with tightly curled iron gray hair. Bemused, Christie stared at the running shoes on the woman's feet. When she spotted Christie she stopped short, tossing Garrett what looked like an accusing glance. She picked up a wooden spoon from a spoon rest on the counter and waved it in the air. "You didn't mention you had a guest," she said tartly.

Christie found herself being scrutinized from head to toe. For a moment she wondered if she passed muster, then straightened her shoulders. She was here to work in the barns and get to know Hannah, not worry if the cook/housekeeper found her appearance acceptable.

"And what have you done to her!" The older woman hurried across the kitchen and without ceremony tilted Christie's chin up and moved the washcloth aside.

Warily, Christie watched the spoon waving in front of her eyes. "Just a bump," she murmured, discomfited by the attention. "I've had worse."

"This is Christie," Garrett said. "She's going to be working here temporarily. Christie, meet Ruth, my housekeeper." Garrett lifted a brow. "You'd better put that spoon down before Christie thinks you're going to smack her."

"Hmmph," Ruth said.

Christie didn't know anyone could actually make that sound into a word, but coming from Ruth, it definitely sounded like a statement.

Ruth put the spoon down and with her hands on her hips stared at Garrett. "I knew when I saw

Hannah that something was up. You'd better tell me what's happened."

Garrett ran a hand around the back of his neck. "Hannah was playing out by the road when one of the boys was coming down the drive with the hay truck. Christie got her out of harm's way but hit her head in the process."

Ruth nodded. "Hannah tried to escape into her room, but I chased her down. She wouldn't tell me anything, but she did show me a scratch on her finger," Ruth added. "We put antibiotic on it."

"To make matters worse, Les Doyle showed up."

Ruth reached into an apron pocket and pulled out a pair of glasses. She perched them on the end of her nose and peered at Christie's forehead. "You have to be careful with bumps on the head." She looked directly into Christie's eyes. "Are you feeling dizzy at all? Nauseous?"

"No, just a slight headache."

"A headache?" Garrett jumped in. "You didn't mention your head hurt."

Ruth tsk-tsked. "Of course it hurts, look at the size of that egg." She touched the tender area around Christie's eyebrow gently. "We'll keep a watch over it, though I think with all the worry about head injuries, she should probably go to the hospital." She straightened. "And what's this about Les?"

"He came for Kim's check. He'd been drinking," Garrett said, an edge to his voice.

"If he'd spend as much effort looking for a job and keeping it, that man would make out a lot better," Ruth remarked. "I don't know what Kim was thinking, marrying up with him." Christie saw the sharp look Garrett gave Ruth. "Enough of that," Ruth said briskly. "Right now you two need to get cleaned up and I'll serve dinner. I'll never hear the end of it if it's cold."

"I wouldn't dare complain about anything you serve," Garrett said, grinning.

Christie relaxed. Ruth, for all her gruff manner, reminded her of her own aunt Rose. She wondered if beneath that starched apron beat a big heart. Aunt Rose had been tough, but she'd loved her and her sister Ellen when no one else had cared. Ellen. Christie bit her lip. Two sisters gone. At least she and Ellen had had Aunt Rose. Judith hadn't had anyone.

"Thank you," Christie rushed into speech, "I'm just putting ice on this then I'll go over to the cabin."

Ruth turned to her, then glared at Garrett. "She's staying in that dusty cabin — without dinner?"

Garrett looked at Ruth, but the older woman had turned her back to him, her shoulders stiff.

"There's nothing wrong with the cabin," he said mildly.

Ruth turned, brows raised. "Who stayed in there two nights ago?"

"The boys."

"Exactly, and I haven't had a chance to get in there to clean it up yet. I had other matters pressing for my attention. You know what those young men left it looking like last time."

Christie saw Garrett's grimace. Hurriedly, she said, "I don't mind a little dust and I don't need anything special."

"You can't stay in the cabin," Ruth was adamant. "Sink's over there if you'd like to clean up."

Christie hesitated and looked at Garrett. "I'm sure you'll appreciate the chance to wash up first," she said.

"Garrett, set an extra place for Christie."

Christie thought Garrett might be angry at the housekeeper's highhanded ways, but he seemed to give a philosophical shrug.

"I must say you look like you could do with a few square meals," Ruth added. "You're a bit on the skinny side." Ruth turned away and began to remove pot covers from pans. Christie grimaced. Ruth obviously said whatever was on her mind.

"Don't take Ruth seriously." Christie felt the brush of Garrett's glance. "She likes fattening everyone up."

Christie stared at Garrett's flat stomach. There was nothing fat about him.

"I serve nutritious meals, Garrett McIntyre," Ruth snapped. "A man needs good food after a hard day's work."

"You won't get an argument from me. You're the best cook this side of the Mississippi."

Christie glimpsed the pleased smile on Ruth's face.

"Ruth, where is Hannah?" he asked, drying his hands on a towel. He moved aside from the sink so Christie left the table and joined him.

"While we were patching up her finger your brother rang. He'd called earlier saying he might stop in, but the second call he said he wasn't making it after all, there was a burglary in town he had to check out." Ruth lifted her brows. "After I told Hannah Randy wasn't coming, she ran out of here like a two-minute twister. Right now she's playing one of those video things in her room."

"I'll be right back." Garrett dropped the towel on the counter, his mouth in a straight line.

Christie chewed her lip, watching him stride from the kitchen and through the archway. She kept listening as she washed her hands and face, but she didn't hear any noise coming from the other part of the house. Recalling the grim look on his face, she couldn't help but wonder how he'd discipline his daughter. Christie stared at the wall in front of her, thinking of her father's idea of discipline, and for a moment the old queasiness hit her. She gripped the steel sink, the mess of her own childhood rearing up before her.

"You got any family?" Ruth asked.

Surprised by such a personal question and recalling Garrett's wish to keep her identity quiet, Christie said, "My nephew." She thought of the last time she'd seen Eric. "He's five. He had a birthday last week." She'd missed it, although she had put a card in the mail for him. "I, uh, haven't seen him in a while."

Ruth nodded. "My Mama always used to say when you've got nothing else, there's always family."

Christie hadn't seen Eric since her brother-in-law Darrell took him almost a month ago, the day after the court awarded him custody. Eric had cried, but she'd closed herself off from his pain, the want and need in his face. She'd promised him that she'd return, but that he needed to be with his father now.

At the time she'd been sure it was the right thing to do and she had walked away. After Ellen's death she'd thought she would raise her nephew, but his father's reappearance had changed all that. Emotion bit at her and she drew air into her lungs, slowly and carefully. Reaching blindly forward, she placed the bar of soap on the sink and turned off the water. Eric and Hannah were first cousins.

"I imagine you'll have the cleanest hands at the table," Ruth remarked dryly.

Christie turned. "I was pretty dusty." She ran the damp paper towel over her face and neck. "I guess that will do for now." She looked toward the empty doorway. "Um, what do you think is taking them so long?"

Ruth didn't answer, but ladled gravy over the roast. When she picked up oven mitts, Christie moved closer and lifted the roasting pan for her.

"On the table," Ruth said. "Take a seat, they'll be along shortly. So Hannah wasn't paying attention to the road again? I gathered as much from the little I got out of her."

Christie thought that sounded rather ominous. "She ran after her kitten just as a truck came down the driveway. The driver had all he could do to avoid her. It scared all of us pretty bad."

Ruth's expression softened and she put a hand to her breast. "Poor child and Garrett too." She shook her head. "She's got her father at wit's end. Last week she let Randy's pigeons out, the week before it was the chickens. She just wanted to play."

Christie licked her lips and took a seat. She wondered what kind of mother Judith had been and felt frustrated that she couldn't ask. If Garrett found her asking too many questions before he validated her information. . ..

She looked across the kitchen. What was keeping them?

"We may as well get started." Ruth began filling plates and Christie was left to speculate.

Garrett and his daughter appeared in the kitchen a moment later. Christie's shoulder muscles relaxed when she saw the way the child clung to her father's hand. Hannah cheeks glowed pink and it was obvious she'd just had her face washed. Hannah's gaze met hers across the room and she stopped dead. "You're eating with us?" she asked, the corners of her mouth drooping in obvious disappointment. She gave Christie an angry glare. "Uncle Randy was supposed to eat with us."

"Hannah," Garrett's voice held a warning. "Uncle Randy called and said he had to go back on duty. It had nothing to do with Christie being here." With a hand at her shoulder he urged her forward.

"Sorry," she mumbled, eyebrows drawn together. She slid into the seat across from Christie. Reluctantly, it seemed, she continued, "Thank you for helping me on the driveway. Daddy said the truck could have hit me."

"I'm glad you're okay," Christie said simply, studying this beautiful child who was her niece.

Hannah twisted around in her seat to stare at her father as he stood behind her. The look they exchanged made Christie realize the words had probably been his idea.

"Christie's going to work here until Kim is able to

come back," Garrett said. "We're also going to make sure she doesn't have a problem with the bump on her head."

Christie noticed the slight tremble of the little girl's shoulders and was filled with compassion. She kept her voice matter of fact. "I can tell you I've had much bigger bruises than this little thing."

Hannah watched her warily but made no comment and Christie wondered at the resentment emanating from the child. Had the child decided to dislike her because of the kitten that had gotten away?

Garrett sat beside Christie and Ruth beside Hannah, and the meal began.

As they ate Christie let herself absorb the mellow atmosphere of the kitchen. The table could have held ten people easily, and it sat in a glass enclosed breakfast nook. Christie imagined Garrett sitting here in the morning with his coffee as he looked out over his property. The windows offered a generous view of lush, green meadows and white painted barns. How very lucky he must feel to live in such a beautiful place and to have a healthy child with whom to share it. Poor Judith, to have lost all this.

In the middle of the table was a slender, paper-thin crystal vase with yellow roses. The outer lips of the petals were tinged with red. Christie leaned forward to breathe in their delicate scent. "Breathtaking, I've never seen roses quite that color."

"They're Ruth's secret weapon," Garrett said, passing her a bowl of fluffy mashed potatoes. "They've never taken less than a blue ribbon at the state fair."

"I can understand why."

Throughout dinner Hannah's earlier frowns were gradually replaced by small bursts of chatter. Christie was amused and touched by the way Garrett patiently answered each of his daughter's questions. Christie envied Hannah the opportunity to grow up in a household with such a devoted parent. Her own childhood had been different. . .it would be a stretch to call it a "family life." More often there had been discord than harmony and she rarely recalled her entire family sitting down to an entire meal uninterrupted. Fighting. . .why couldn't she remember the good times?

"Christie, how is your head?" Garrett asked.

She looked up at him with a smile. "Fine."

"Sure you're still interested in the job?"

"I still want the job." She wouldn't get far with the money in her pocket. "Other plans can wait." Did he expect her to back out? "And besides, I feel I owe you for such a wonderful meal." Pointedly, she let her glance rest on Hannah, then returned it to Garrett.

"After the doctor's visit, if he says it's okay, you can start tomorrow." He resumed eating.

"I don't need to go to the doctor," she said firmly. "I'm fine." Christie put her head down and concentrated on the last of her mashed potatoes. She had a feeling it was only a matter of time before Garrett wanted to know more about her plans. Information should flow both ways, but she wasn't used to anyone prying into her business. God knows it had become second nature to guard the truth

about herself and her past. A past she wasn't
particularly proud to claim.

∞ Chapter Three ∞

GARRETT WAS FRANKLY AMAZED at the amount of food Christie managed to consume, considering her slim build. His suspicion that she hadn't eaten in a while might have been on the mark and that troubled him. Plus, she seemed skittish, given the way she'd barely stood for Ruth's examination of the bump on her head.

He was curious about her arrival, traveling over the road. It just didn't fit in with his idea of conventional travel. But then, she didn't fit his idea of someone traveling alone with nothing more than a duffel bag. Every instinct told him nothing added up where she was concerned, and yet her unexpected arrival was similar to something Judith would have done. Inwardly, Garrett sighed. Again, he was back to comparing her with Judith.

During dinner he'd considered all the alternatives as to where she could stay. With two men in the bunkhouse, staying there was out of the question. There was a room over the main barn, but right now that was in a major state of overhaul. He should have thought longer on this when he'd decided to hire her, but given the circumstances, he hadn't felt like he'd had a lot of options. There was the possibility that her story wouldn't check out. . ..

In all fairness, if she was Judith's sister she had a right to know Hannah. But at what cost?

Garrett studied her, the slim nose, full lips, blue-veined lids fanned by thick, sooty lashes. Her skin was light, almost translucent against her dark, dark hair. Judith had been blond and darker skinned and almost on eye level with him.

"The days are pretty hot now," Garrett remarked casually to Christie. "I'll have one of the girls set you up with a hat."

"Thank you, but I don't wear hats."

"I don't need anyone being hit by heat stroke. Not only would it be lost time, but I'll be back to square one and short on help."

"Of course. And I'm here to work." She smiled. "So I'll wear a hat."

"I know you have bingo tonight, Ruth, so I'll take care of the dishes." He knew from past experience that Ruth would grumble for a week if she were late for bingo.

"I do have bingo but Sam has been kind enough to offer me a ride, so I'm not dependent on Myrtle tonight."

Sam? His foreman? Garrett hid his surprise. He couldn't picture Sam, a man of few words, in a bingo hall with his tart-tongued housekeeper. Ruth had definite opinions on every topic imaginable and never hesitated to express those opinions. She'd certainly never held back sharing her wide and varied opinions with him.

"Hannah needs a bath and I'll be glad to see to that before I leave," Ruth added.

Garrett smiled inwardly. Ruth might be cantankerous, but she loved Hannah like her own granddaughter. In that respect alone, she was invaluable to him. She doubled as a sitter when he couldn't be there to take care of his daughter. Lately, he didn't know what type of mischief Hannah might be up to and at times he worried about his childrearing skills, afraid he might make some drastic mistake that might ruin her.

"Come on Hannah, time for a bath." Ruth urged Hannah from her chair.

Hannah rolled her eyes but did as she was bid.

"Ruth, dinner was delicious," Christie said.

Ruth acknowledged the compliment with a slight incline of her head and left the room behind Hannah.

"It's a good thing I won't be here long, I'd put on too much weight in a hurry." Christie sent a smile in his direction.

Garrett lifted a brow and ran a quick glance over her. "You've got a long way to go before you get there," he observed dryly, then picked up his plate. Not really appropriate conversation between employer and employee.

"I can stay in the cabin. I'm not bothered by dust," she told him firmly.

"It's only a one room cabin, and usually the boys stay in there, but they're out of town on business right now." He sighed. "If it's as bad as Ruth thinks it is, I may have to rethink this."

He carried the plates to the dishwasher and then leaned against the counter and crossed his arms.

"So, Christie, where are you headed after stopping here?"

Busy stacking silverware, Christie looked up with a guarded expression. "Nothing set in stone. Just traveling."

"You don't know where?"

"Maybe up north." At his questioning look, she elaborated. "New York." She chewed her lip, a habit he had noticed before. "Didn't Judith ever talk about where she was from?"

"No."

Christie stared at him, speculation in her eyes. "What would you say if I told you it's probably because of the way we grew up? We didn't have a model childhood."

"I gathered that. Judith carried a certain wariness about her too, but she didn't care what people thought. She didn't always guard her words. You do."

"Yes."

"You don't look much alike either."

Christie stared down at the table. Finally, she looked up at him. "Judith had a different father, but I don't know anything about him. My family was never real forthcoming about Judith. You were married to her. Didn't you ever talk about any of her background?"

"She wouldn't talk about anything related to her past." Garrett looked away from her, feeling the stiffness in his shoulders and neck. "She insisted what mattered was the present."

"I've often felt the same way." Christie rose from the table and carried dirty dishes over to the counter, then leaned back against it.

Garrett stared at the darkening sky through the kitchen window. "By the time I met Judith, she'd already been out on her own going on four years."

"She left home and I guess she never looked back." Christie didn't blame her. She moved back to the table, picked up the silverware and carried it to the dishwasher. She proceeded to wipe the table surface with a damp cloth. "You knew my sister a long time before you were married?"

"I met her when she was nineteen and then we lost touch for a few years. When I got heavy into rodeo we met up again and started dating." Garrett leaned back against the counter and crossed his arms over his chest. "Let's talk about you a minute. Do you have a job in New York? For some reason you don't seem like a city girl to me."

"Upstate New York. I took a leave of absence. The job will be there if I want it when I return."

"One day you just decided to come to Kentucky?" His surprise crept into his voice. "It's strange to me that you would just up and leave your life one day."

"That's a simplified version of it, but that's what happened." She shrugged.

"Nothing's that simple. You seem more complicated than that."

She swept her hair back away from her face, the gesture an indication of weariness. Her gaze connected with his. "Haven't you ever done anything impulsive?"

"Not in a long while." He told himself he was crazy. He had too much work to be worrying about Christie's motives for showing up on his place, but he had to protect Hannah. Right now she could fill in at the barn. He needed someone . . . she needed work. Simple. He would be satisfied if she did a decent job in the barns.

"It was time to connect with my sister. There's nothing else I can say. Now if you'll show me that cabin, I'll get settled in."

Resolutely, he turned to the door and Christie followed him outside and across the yard. A small cabin was nestled up against some tall evergreens about a hundred yards beyond the house. He pushed open the door, flicked the light and immediately stepped back as a gray kitten shot out the door.

"Albert." They both said it together as the kitten disappeared in a flash. Garrett took one look inside the cabin, swore, then closed the door.

"Forget it." He leaned back against the door.

"Come on, it can't be that bad."

"I'm going to tear a strip off whoever left a window open. And yes, it can be that bad."

Garrett grabbed her shoulders and turned her back the way they'd come, his expression grim. "You have to stay in the house." He strode back toward the house. Christie hurried to keep up and he ignored her protests as they re-entered the kitchen.

"I'll show you where you can take care of your laundry. You'll have your own room, which is just down the hallway. It has a small bathroom with a shower. You can get settled and start work tomorrow."

He moved across the kitchen and hoisted her duffel bag onto his shoulder. "Are you sure I can't take you into town to the doctor? I think it would be a really good idea."

"No, I'm fine."

"Follow me." He walked to the opposite end of the kitchen and entered the walk-in pantry. Garrett pushed open slatted doors on the right and indicated the washer and dryer inside. "Laundry room." The washer and dryer sat side-by-side, along with detergent and other essentials.

He turned and began to squeeze by Christie, thought better of it and indicated she should go first. Looking slightly flustered, she walked quickly back into the kitchen.

Garrett led the way back into the kitchen and then through the open archway into the hallway. "The living room is through here. There's a terrace off the living room through the glass doors." He continued down the corridor. "Bedrooms are at the end of this corridor."

"Oh, but. . ." Christie looked quickly into the living room, then hurried after him. "I know you said housing was limited, but why couldn't I sleep in one of the bunkhouses, if you have one."

"I do have one and you can't sleep there," he said flatly.

"But I didn't expect —"

Garrett dropped the bag inside the doorway of the spare bedroom and faced her. He knew his voice was hard but there wasn't anything he could do about it. "Whatever you might expect or want,

Christie, you can't share a bunkhouse with my men, as much as they'd probably enjoy that. The other women who work here all live in town. Right now there's nowhere else. Your room isn't fancy, but you should find it comfortable and fairly private." Garrett knew he was taking a leap of faith by allowing her to stay in the house. "There's no other options."

Christie looked inside the room. "I've been on the road awhile and this looks wonderful." She directed a smile at him. "Thank you. You're really very kind."

"No, I'm not," he said, unaccountably annoyed. "I'm too busy to be kind. I'm responsible for a lot of people and countless valuable horses. I will be checking you out."

"I expect nothing less."

"What this job means to you is I expect a fair day's work." Garrett figured that should set her straight. He had never been called kind in his life.

"Whatever you say," she said softly.

Garrett had a sinking sensation as his gut knotted. Her smile indicated she didn't believe him. He backed up a step, questioning the wisdom of letting this woman stay in his house. He also knew it was done. He never went back on his word.

¤ ¤

Garrett jerked awake, tension radiating down his neck as he quickly looked around. Reassured by the sight of Hannah sound asleep on her white bear rug on the living room floor, he rubbed his palm over his face, shaking off the remnants of a bad dream. The incident with Christie and Hannah today must have upset him more than he'd realized. He hadn't had a dream about the car accident in six months or better. Judith . . . her white dress splashed with blood. Her driving had been reckless and she'd taken chances she shouldn't have.

Garrett glanced at his wristwatch. It was way past Hannah's bedtime. It was his fault she'd gotten into the habit of staying up late while he went over his paperwork. It was easier than dealing with her crying fits and temper tantrums. In truth, Garrett had needed to see her at night in the months following Judith's accident. It was a way of reassuring himself that Hannah was okay. Except that now, her late nights were becoming a problem he had to deal with.

Hannah wore a long pink nightgown, her favorite color of the moment, and a small heel poked out from beneath the fabric. Garrett leaned down to brush wisps of baby fine hair back from her face. He was thankful every day that Hannah had survived the car crash, but he had to figure out a way to address her behavior problems.

In the beginning it had been easy to think himself in love with Judith, but the problems from her past had helped to rip them apart. It hadn't been all her fault, but he'd been so busy trying to get his business off the ground it had left little time for Judith and her demands. Her leaving had almost been a relief, but not her death. Never that. And now he had to deal with her sister. Somehow, he knew Christie really was her sister, but he still had to be one hundred percent sure.

"I'm leaving and you're not stopping me,

Garrett!" Judith's voice echoed in his head. There'd been a lot of angry words that last day. Too many.

Garrett tasted again the fear. . . fear that he would lose Hannah too. Judith left him pretty much the way she'd entered his life, in a whirlwind. She'd left in the sports car he'd bought her spitting gravel as she tore from the driveway.

Judith had died an hour later, driving her car too fast; dying the way she lived. It was like she had a rush to experience all life had to offer, and life at the farm hadn't been enough. Hannah had survived, but the eighteen months since the accident had been harrowing. Many times he'd questioned his own wisdom in trying to raise a young girl who might need more than he could give her. However many times he'd had doubts, he also knew he'd never give up on her. No matter how difficult or defiant she was, Hannah was still a part of his heart. She needed him as much as he needed her, but that was something neither one of them might ever admit. Looking down into her face he thought how peculiar it was that she looked more like him than her mother.

Garrett lifted his daughter from the floor and carried her to her room. Carefully, he placed her in the bed shaped like a pumpkin coach. He leaned down to turn off the lamp, his glance falling on the small picture beside Hannah's bed. He, Judith and Hannah in happier times. They had gone to an old-fashioned country fair in town. It had been a great day. Decisively, he switched off the light.

"The covers, Daddy," Hannah murmured. "I like the covers tucked all around me." It was a ritual they'd started from the first, and Garrett continued, trying to keep her on an even keel, though at times it seemed nearly impossible.

"There you go," he said gruffly, touching his finger to her nose. "Warm and tucked in."

Her eyes opened. "I'm still your girl, Daddy?"

Garrett pushed the hair from her cheek, thankful that there were still these tender moments. He leaned down and dropped a kiss on her smooth forehead. "You'll always be my girl, sweetheart."

"I'm sorry, Daddy, for not listening today." Her lower lip trembled ever so slightly. "I try to be good, but I don't seem to have the knack of it."

Garrett couldn't help but smile, recognizing Ruth's words in that statement. "You just forget sometimes. Let's hope the knack will grow on you."

"I like the tire swing you put up for me." She pressed her fingers into the soft pile of the blanket. "And I'm glad you don't make me wear dresses all the time."

"Honey, there's nothing wrong with dresses. All little girls should dress up from time to time. Your mom loved to dress up."

"I know Daddy, but I don't always want to stay clean." Her small fingers gripped his. "One more thing. I saw Albert sunning himself on a rock by the road and I was afraid he would run away. When I saw that truck I was really scared. It felt like my feet were stuck and I couldn't move or anything." She drew a deep, heartfelt sigh. "I always seem to get in trouble. I won't touch the geese pen anymore or Uncle Randy's pigeon cage either. I'm sorry for being so bad, Daddy."

"You're not bad, sweetheart."

"Then why do you get so mad?"

"I worry because I want to keep you safe."

"Then you won't send me away?"

Garrett's heart felt like it was being squeezed. He sat down on the side of her bed and pulled her up into his arms, covers and all. "I'll never send you away. You're mine," he whispered fervently. "My little girl. Now go to sleep."

When Garrett straightened and turned to leave, he saw Christie standing in the hallway. She wore a dark T-shirt and light jeans and her feet were bare. He noticed her dark hair was damp, tendrils clinging to the side of her neck. Caught off guard, he wondered how soft her neck would be if he buried his lips there. Something warm and sympathetic shone in her eyes. Garrett took a deep breath and walked across the shadowed room to where Christie stood in the hallway. The least he could do was say goodnight to his new employee. Carefully, he pulled his daughter's bedroom door half closed and walked toward Christie.

¤¤

Christie knew she should have moved on and given Garrett the private moment with his daughter. How tenderly he'd placed Hannah in her bed, then smoothed the covers and stood back, watching her. She had to wonder what went through his mind, his hard mouth curved in a slight smile.

"I wonder if little girls know how lucky they are to have their dads?" she asked with a smile.

"I'm the lucky one," Garrett said simply.

Christie swallowed. How could she be envious of

a father's love for his child? "I wish I'd had a father like you," she said softly. But her past could never be unwritten. "How fortunate Judith must have felt to have you and Hannah in her life."

An almost painful expression crossed Garrett's face.

"I'm sorry," she said. "Sorry for intruding. You have a right to privacy with your daughter." She pushed her hands into her jeans pockets. "I just happened to see you on my way to the kitchen. She looks sweet lying there. What a unique bed."

Garrett smiled at her, and some of her tension eased as he faced her in the hallway. "She saw a pumpkin coach in a story book and insisted she needed one like it."

"You made the bed?"

"The headboard. I enjoy working with wood and I'm good with my hands."

Christie's thoughts raced as she looked down at his big hands, the palms calloused. She'd seen how tenderly they handled a little girl. She wondered how they would treat a woman. She wondered about his life with her sister.

"Come into the living room." Garrett led the way down the corridor. The ivory painted walls on either side of Christie were hung with framed pictures of horses and racetracks.

"Are these your horses?" She asked curiously.

As Garrett reached the open doorway of the living room he paused and looked back. "Yes. I've been fortunate in the last few years to have several winners." He indicated she should precede him through the glass paneled wood doors into the living room.

The living room was definitely a man's room. Most of the furnishings were dark browns and deep mahogany, yet the overhead lighting kept it from being dreary or too dark. Garrett moved around the room, picking up Hannah's dolls, which were scattered on the couch and chairs. He deposited them in a small wooden box in one corner of the darkly paneled room. A beautiful stone fireplace occupied an entire wall, the mantelshelf holding an assortment of pictures. Family pictures.

"Take a seat, Christie."

She turned from the fireplace and sat on a small blue and mauve loveseat, running her palm over the richly embroidered fabric. Garrett sat opposite her in a large recliner, and behind him Christie saw a glass enclosed wood gun case.

"Are those real guns?" she asked, somewhat awed.

Garrett looked around behind him. "Yes." Seeing the look on her face, he added, "I collect them. They're mostly for sport shooting."

"This room is beautiful."

"Thanks. Let's go over a few things," he went on briskly. "First, you can use the phone any time you need to make a call, in case there's someone you'd like to get in touch with."

Christie shoved a hand in her jeans pocket as she cleared her throat. "Actually, I mentioned to Ruth I do have some family."

"They may worry if they don't hear from you."

"No. For the most part I'm footloose and fancy free." She knew her smile must look forced, but there was no way she could talk normally about her family. From what he'd said about Judith, she hadn't told him much about her life either. Garrett wouldn't understand her screwed up past. At the best of times she even had trouble putting it in proper perspective.

She dug in her pocket and pulled out a piece of paper. Rising quickly, she handed him the paper, then resumed her seat. "That's the number for my boss. He works at the county office in Ulster. He'll vouch for me."

"Thanks. I'll check it out." He carefully folded the paper and stuffed it in his jeans pocket. "So isn't there someone in New York expecting to hear that you arrived safely?"

Christie held perfectly still. As a child she'd yearned for real family ties, but anything approaching normal family life had died with her Aunt Rose, and then Ellen. "No."

"Christie." His voice sounded concerned. "Your face is white. Is your head still bothering you?"

She touched her forehead, feeling its tenderness. "No." She couldn't admit she felt sick, sick in her heart, hurting from loneliness and dwelling on a past she could never make right. Hadn't three years of therapy taught her the tools to survival, to be strong and walk past the hurt? She and Ellen had been fighters, but Ellen hadn't made it and nowadays she didn't feel like much of a fighter.

"Actually, I'm not fine. I'm still having trouble believing Judith is gone. Can't you tell me something about her?" she beseeched him, lifting her hands. "Please understand my confusion. I feel like I'm missing someone I never even knew."

Garrett stood and walked across the room away from her. He stopped beside the fireplace and fiddled with an ornate iron poker. It struck Christie that he might be nervous.

"I'm sorry," Garrett said. "What you're asking is difficult." He paused, then said, "Judith liked a good time. If a party was boring, she'd soon liven it up, whether it was dancing or doing whiskey shots. She had very little inhibition. People liked her. She was that type of person."

"She sounds a lot like my sister Ellen," Christie said softly. "There are — were — three of us."

"Hannah was pretty traumatized when her mom died."

"Of course she would be. H-how did it happen? She was so young."

A resigned expression crossed his face. "It was a car accident. Hannah survived, but still suffers flashbacks. She's only just coming back to the happy kid she was before, but it's been a struggle and sometimes we have setbacks."

Christie's heart went out to him. "Poor Hannah. And you lost a wife."

"We all lost." His guarded expression said he wasn't looking for sympathy. "You should also know Hannah can be temperamental at times. If my daughter's deliberately rude to you, please let me know."

"Is she in the habit of being rude?"

"Yes." Garrett pushed a hand through his hair.

Christie recalled Ruth saying he was almost at wit's end.

"Hannah is testing me. At least that's the psychologist's theory."

Christie felt her respect for Garrett go up another notch. "I think it's important that children get help." Christie clenched her jaw. "Many times people close their eyes to problems."

"With you staying in the house, Hannah may see your proximity as a sign of. . ." he paused, and the silence felt suddenly very heavy.

"Are you saying Hannah may see me as a rival for your attention?"

A hint of color touched his tanned cheeks but his gaze remained level. "Yes. Not that there's any reason for her to think that, but yes."

Christie felt like she'd stepped into a sticky situation. Slowly, she came to her feet. "Well, I certainly won't give her cause to see me as a threat, if that's worrying you. And I won't be here that long anyway."

Garrett looked relieved.

"You know, I still think it would be better if you told her who I am."

"I disagree for now. I think it will upset her."

"I don't want to cause problems but eventually the truth will have to come out. Kids can be amazingly resilient."

Garrett smiled grimly. "How many children do you have, Christie?"

Heat came into her face. "None. But I know children —"

"You don't know my child, so abide by my wishes."

Orders, she wanted to say, but bit her lips

instead. "All right."

Brimming with mixed emotions, Christie murmured goodnight and left Garrett in the living room. She would work at the farm, get to know Hannah, and then go on her way. Emotion raced through Christie. She was an outsider who had no place in this family's life other than a temporary one. Garrett was putting up with her because he had to.

Christie went into the kitchen. Opening cabinet doors she located the drinking glasses and poured herself a glass of water. Rinsing the glass out, she placed it upside down on the dish drainer. Giving Bo Peep a gentle rub under her chin, Christie opened the kitchen door and went outside to sit on the step.

Night had fallen and the air felt warm on her skin. Resting her head against the wood railing, she stared up at the sky. To distract herself from the man she'd just left, Christie thought of all the changes she'd made in her life. . .the bridges she'd burned. Christie wished she could talk to Ellen about how her life had been turned around and upended. Her career and schooling, once so important to her, now seemed a world away. New York was as far removed from this farm as you could get. Whether she was on a fool's errand or not, as her brother-in-law Darrell had accused her, only time would tell.

A flash of light shot across the sky. Christie closed her eyes and made a wish. It had to be right, her coming here. When she reopened her eyes, Christie saw the tail end of the star as it faded into tiny bursts of light. Her faith in her decision grew. She'd made the right choice in coming to Kentucky.

"I hope you made a wish," remarked a deep

voice.

Christie rose to her feet, staring at the shadowy figure just beyond the light at the base of the stairs. "Garrett!"

"Wrong." The man moved closer and she saw his teasing smile. It wasn't Garrett at all, but a similarly tall, broad shouldered male. . .dressed in a dark colored police uniform and wide brimmed hat. At the back of her mind came the thought that Garrett would look exactly like this man if he smiled in such a roguish manner. An interesting, wide smile that touched his eyes.

"I didn't hear you."

"So did you make a wish?" he asked, laughing.

"Of course. No sense in wasting a perfectly good star." She dusted the seat of her jeans. "You must be Randy."

Randy's brow went up as he pulled off his hat. "You're a step ahead of me — I haven't got a clue who you are." His expression turned mock serious. "You're a bit old to be Hannah's playmate. Are you a girl friend of Garrett's?"

Christie hesitated and felt heat seep into her cheeks. "Hardly a girlfriend. I'm going to be working in the barns." She wondered if keeping her identity quiet extended to Garrett's brother. "I just got the job today."

"I didn't realize Garrett was looking for anybody. I don't think I've seen you around town before."

"Are you asking in an official capacity?"

He smiled, but in the dim light from above she could see his penetrating stare. "Old habits die hard, but if there's something you'd like to tell me I'm all ears."

Lightly, Christie said, "The bus I was riding on broke down and I elected not to wait beside the road. I more or less stumbled on the farm and asked about a job."

"So you were on that bus that held up traffic today. The other passengers were content to wait for another bus."

"I'm not most people."

"Sounds like you're the adventurous type," Randy said admiringly. "If you're going to be here any length of time, maybe I could show you around. I'm known as a pretty good guide."

Christie laughed, recognizing Randy as a flirt. "You don't waste any time."

A dimple appeared in his chin. "Life's too short."

"I know," she said dryly, "too many women, too little time."

"Randy." Garrett's voice sounded behind them. Christie turned toward the screen door as it swung open. "I didn't think we'd see you tonight." Garrett stood on the kitchen threshold behind her.

"Hey Garrett," Randy said. "I just got here. Christie and I were getting to know each other." Randy saluted his brother casually, apparently undaunted by Garrett's unsmiling face. Christie wondered if Garrett disapproved of her being out here with Randy. She backed up against the stair railing, feeling awkward under the searching look Garrett was giving her.

Randy lifted his hand and Christie saw he held a six-pack of soda. "How about a soda?"

Garrett's voice sounded mild. "Sure."

Christie knew it was time to make an exit. "Uh, I'm going to pass, so if you'll excuse me," she edged toward the door and Garrett, "it's been a long day. . .."

"Pleasure meeting you, Christie."

Christie smiled at Randy over her shoulder. "Same here. I'll be around a while so we'll meet again."

She ducked under Garrett's arm as he held the door, noticing his barely buttoned shirt and the dusting of hair over a deeply muscled chest. She drew in a deep breath, fighting her curiosity about these two brothers, and fighting a strong urge to linger. "Goodnight."

¤¤

Garrett watched Christie disappear beyond the kitchen then directed his attention to his brother. "So you're hitting on my help again?"

"She's staying in the house? What do you know about her?"

"I know you've been using that infamous charm," he said dryly. "Why don't you tell me what you've managed to learn about her?"

"We only talked a few minutes. She seems like a nice person."

"She's down on her luck and needs a job and I'm a hand short while Kim's out."

"Why do I get the feeling there's more to the story?" Randy asked in a deceptively lazy drawl.

Garrett ignored the question for the moment and gave his brother an assessing glance. "I thought you had plans tonight and that's why you didn't make it for dinner."

Randy lifted a soda and took several gulps. "You know what they say about the best laid plans."

"Melinda stood you up?" Garrett dropped to the top step, reaching for the can Randy held out to him. "Or was it Maggie or Angela?"

"Melinda. She got bent out of shape that I was running late. I didn't even have time to change, and then I had to stop at the office. We ended up stuck there for an hour, so she insisted on going home."

Garrett studied Randy with interest. "Not your usual style. I'm surprised you didn't sweet talk her out of her bad mood and take her dancing."

Randy bit off a short laugh. "Yeah, well, by then the night had lost most of its charm." Leaning against the railing post, he closed his eyes.

"I've never known you to be dateless on a Saturday night." Garrett popped the soda top and took a long swallow of the cold soda.

Randy's expression became guarded as he stared out into the night and unfastened the top buttons of his shirt. "At least I go out on dates. After Judith, you stopped trying."

Instead of taking offense, Garrett just shook his head. "Bringing along a temperamental eight-year old makes short work of conversation. Right now it's simpler to stay home."

"Yeah, keep telling yourself that."

With an impatient sigh, Garrett started to rise to his feet.

Randy gripped his arm. "Sorry. I know how hard it's been to keep Hannah on even ground. She's got to come first, and the rest of it kind of goes to hell."

"We'll get through it." Garrett swatted at a

mosquito. "But don't change the subject. Let's go inside."

Randy sat on the bottom step. "No thanks. I think I'll head home — maybe I'll catch you tomorrow."

"Come on, Randy, something's got you riled. I recognize the look. I figure you're once again in the throes of woman trouble. Come in and talk." Garrett stood and moved over to the door, then pulled it open. Shrugging, Randy followed, taking his time closing the kitchen door and patting the dog.

Garrett sat down at the kitchen table and patiently waited.

Randy dropped into a chair across from him, his shoulders slumped. "Don't you ever get tired of being alone? I mean — coming home to an empty house . . . empty bed?"

"Hell yes, but somehow I don't think we share the same problem." Dryly, Garrett added, "I've heard about your exploits too often."

"I like women, I won't deny it. I hate being alone. Admit it, once Hannah's in bed, that's it Brother, you're on your own."

Garrett thought of earlier that evening when he'd let Hannah stay up late with him. "Sure, but I'm not ready to jump into a relationship unless it feels right."

Randy lifted a brow. "What's right? How do you know it?"

Garrett gave a short laugh and lowered his voice. "You're asking me? I don't have the best track record in that area."

"Neither do I."

"You've got to learn to go out with a woman

more than once. It's called getting to know each other."

"I know, but I just can't seem to help myself. There's so many lovely women in this town."

"Like Ally."

"We'll leave her out of it."

"Randy, let's cut to the chase. Why don't you ask Ally out? That's what this is about, isn't it? You've been hot and heavy after Ally ever since she got rid of her husband. Hell, if it helps, I'll even give her time off from work."

Randy shook his head in resignation. "She'll tell me to get lost. She'd rather work with your horses anyway, than go out with me."

"Have you tried just talking to her?"

"Not in the last month. It gets discouraging being turned down time after time."

Garrett folded his arms. "Is it the chase that you like or the girl? I don't want Ally hurt because you're just trying to scratch an itch."

"How can I know what it is? She won't give me a chance. How can I make her see I'm serious if she won't talk to me?"

"You could start showing her by example — like not taking out a different woman every other night."

"Come on, Garrett, can you imagine me in a one-woman relationship?" But Randy's scoffing didn't wash with Garrett.

"It does stretch the imagination, but if it's what you really want. . .."

Randy ran a hand over the back of his neck. "Hell, right now I'm not sure what I want. All I know is something's missing." He looked at his watch.

"And it's getting late. I'm going to head out. I know you've got an early day tomorrow. I missed Hannah tonight so tell her I'll make it up to her and stop by tomorrow." Randy stepped over to Garrett and slapped him on the shoulder. "Thanks for listening."

"Yeah, for all the good it did. See you tomorrow."

Randy gave him a wink. "If I can't get through to Ally, maybe I can get to know Christie better."

Garrett opened his mouth with a ready retort, but saw the teasing in Randy's face. Mockingly, he said, "I don't know if you'll ever get the idea about monogamous relationships. By the way, I need you to check into Christie Jenkins' background."

Randy stopped cold, his expression turning sober. "What?"

Garrett pulled out the slip of paper Christie had given him. He held it out to Randy. "She claims she's Judith's sister."

"Judith? Are you kidding? Why would she show up now?"

"She said she didn't know Judith died."

Randy whistled. "So that's why you're letting her stay here?"

"What could I do? At least here I can keep an eye on her. She said all she wants is to get to know Hannah."

"Do you believe her?"

Garrett shrugged. "Until I find out otherwise. I told her to keep quiet for now about being Judith's sister or she's out of here."

"Well, if it's true, you can't keep her quiet forever."

"I know. That phone number is her boss in New

York. I have a feeling she's telling the truth. But if she's anything like Judith, she'll tire of this place and leave soon enough."

"You could be asking for trouble, letting her stay. What if she wants Hannah?"

"She'll be in for a hell of a fight," Garrett said grimly, staring out into the inky black night. "Nobody's taking Hannah from me."

¤ ¤

Christie sat in the dark bedroom, her eyes fixated on her duffel bag. She'd placed it in the closet, but the door had not closed entirely and she could see the edge of the bag. She turned on the small bedside lamp and got out of bed. Lifting the duffel bag, she reached inside and lifted out the small wooden box in the shape of a book. Gently, she ran her fingers over the inlaid decoration, then she traced with a fingertip the inscription, *Ellen Jenkins, beloved sister and mother.*

Inside was all that remained of her sister. A tear fell onto the deep, reddish brown wood. Horrified, Christie quickly grabbed a tissue from the bureau, but the tear had already bled into the wood, marking it.

∞ Chapter Four ∞

IN THE EARLY AFTERNOON of the following day Garrett raced across the grass of the southeast pasture. The sun, unbearably hot, caused sweat to drip down his neck. He cursed under his breath the entire length of the paddock. A stallion had managed to get in the broodmare paddock, something that had never happened in all the years he'd owned horses.

He tossed a worried glance at the usually sedate group of mares and foals who now circled wildly. Some of the mares, already bred back to his other stallion, had tried to kick at the stallion invading their pasture. He didn't need a breeder's worst nightmare, an injured breeding stallion.

As he reached the end of the paddock where the stallion pranced, Garrett slowed to a walk and shook the grain pail in his hand. "Come on, Blue Boy," he called softly. "Come on, nice and easy." He circled around the horse. However, with the scent of the mares luring him, Blue Boy continued to move sideways, neck arched and nostrils flared.

"I'm behind you, Boss," said Sam Connors, his barn foreman. Sam sounded winded. "I've got Miranda and she's in a foal heat. We'll use her to lure him into the smaller corral."

Sam's plan to use the young mare worked like a charm. Blue Boy followed the mare as Sam led her at a trot into a smaller corral on one side of the paddock. Garrett pushed the gate closed behind Blue Boy just as Sam and the mare exited a gate on the opposite side of the corral. Still speaking to the stallion, Garrett approached him and snapped a lead line on Blue Boy. He ran his palm soothingly down the horse's trembling neck.

Sam led the mare away from the corral as Sue came running over. "I'll take the mare," she said.

"Let's get everybody inside," Garrett said to Sue. "Have Ally help you get them back inside."

"Sure, Boss." Sue led the mare toward the barn.

Garrett kept a hand on Blue Boy's shoulder. Away from the mares, the horse had already calmed considerably.

Garrett glanced at his foreman, taking in the sweat-streaked gray temples. "Take it easy out in this heat, Sam." Sam was a hard worker but he was pushing seventy. Knowing Sam's pride might take offense, Garrett added, "I'm already sweating my ass off. The humidity's a killer today."

"And it's supposed to stay the same all week. I'll check who put the horses out. Let's hope no one's hurt," he added dourly. "I'm off for half a day and things go to hell."

Garrett restrained a smile. "I'm putting Blue Boy back in his stall while I check the fence. I don't want a repeat performance. I'll let you know when everything's secure."

"I'll come with you."

"Aren't you still off work?"

"Not anymore."

As Garrett led the stallion back across the pasture to the barn he looked thoughtfully at his foreman. "Sam, I've been thinking if you need more personal time off, just say the word. You've got a lot of vacation days stored." Sam hardly ever took time off. If he let him, Garrett knew he'd work seven days a week.

Sam stared at him, his dark gaze direct in his lean, tanned face. "I appreciate that Garrett. I've been thinking about taking a few days." They walked in silence for several moments before Sam cleared his throat. "You know, of course, that I've been helping Ruth out since Vern died."

"Yeah, and I'm really glad you found her for us. I don't know what we'd do without her."

"Well Vern was a good man. He worked hard his whole life." Sam looked uncomfortable. "We grew up together and worked some of the same places here and there."

Garrett stopped and faced the other man, not sure what he was trying to tell him. "Listen Sam, we've known each other since I was a kid. Whatever you tell me will go no further."

Sam pushed his hat back on his heat and scratched his head. "Well, the truth is, Ruth and me have been spending time together lately. No disrespect to Vern, but he didn't leave her real flush, if you know what I mean."

Sam paused again.

"My job here at the farm is sweet, what with the place on the back acres that you let me use. I was wondering if you'd mind if Ruth moved into the cottage." Sam seemed to swallow a few times. "With me, that is."

Garrett looked at the man who had been a good friend to his father, and a steadfast, reliable employee to him. "It's your decision, Sam. I have no problem with that."

Garrett caught a rare glimpse of a smile on his foreman's weathered face.

Just then a movement on the far end of the paddock caught Garrett's eye. He could see Christie sitting on the paddock fence. "Let me check the fence and the gates," he said.

Sam gave him a quick nod and reached for Blue Boy's lead. "I'll get this guy cooled out and catch up with you."

Garrett strode back out to the paddock where he'd spotted Christie, and found her standing beside a steel gate. She swung the gate closed.

"Why is that gate open? Now I understand how the horse got in with the mares."

Christie swung around to face him. "Garrett! You scared me." She bit at her lip and fumbled with the gate latch. Garrett stepped closer and pushed her hands out of the way. He latched it securely and turned to face her. "Why was it open?"

Christie gave him a wary look. "I don't know. I

saw everyone chasing horses and thought maybe it should be closed so they couldn't run out this end."

"It's not okay when a stallion gets in with mares and foals. There's a potential for any of the horses to get seriously kicked."

"It was open when I came out." She pushed her hands in her jean pockets.

Garrett stared at her suspiciously, aware of a curious sinking feeling. "Christie, did you open the gate?"

The hurt surprise on her face made him feel like a heel for asking.

"I wouldn't open any gates unless told otherwise."

Some of the tension eased from his shoulders. "The first hard and fast rule on the farm is that gates are always kept closed. It doesn't matter if there's a horse in the paddock or not."

"I hope the horses are okay," she said. "I would have come to find someone but I didn't realize anything was wrong. Really, I didn't know," she added defensively. "I came out here to eat my lunch."

"Well, next time you'll know. I can't have anyone being careless. These animals are too valuable." Garrett turned away and they walked side-by-side along the small footpath beside the fence. "How's your head? I see that bump looks better."

Christie gave him an amused glance. "I swear I'm fine. No headache, nothing to worry about. I've got a hard head. It's been knocked around more than that little bump."

Garrett looked over his shoulder at Sam as he

joined them. "Christie, this is Sam Connors, my foreman Sam — Christie Jenkins. She's helping while Kim's out."

His hard-edged foreman gave Christie a big smile.

"Welcome aboard, Christie," Sam said. "Ruth told me about you."

"The gate was open," Garrett told him.

Sam scratched his head. "Joey put the horses out and must be he didn't latch the gate securely. He swears he did. There's a mare with a scraped hock but it doesn't look bad."

"I'll take a look. We both know about small scratches that blow up overnight into a big problem."

"Uh, Garrett, what time do you want me at the barn in the mornings?" Christie said. "You never really said."

Garrett turned to her. "Eight is fine."

She hesitated. "I'm usually up by six. Since I'm up early anyway, if you'd like I can help out with Hannah."

Garrett immediately shook his head. "No. Ruth sees to my daughter." Realizing how curt that sounded, he added, "Thanks for asking. I'm sure you'll see Hannah off and on during the day."

"Sure. No problem." She looked away from him and toward the house.

He knew he was protective of Hannah, but he wasn't changing anything just because Christie was here. She'd better understand that now or they'd be at odds from the word go.

He looked at Sam. "Let's go check that mare."

¤ ¤

Several hours later Christie sat at the kitchen table. Sunlight spilled through the windows across the wooden table, the light dancing across her glass of lemonade. Ruth had shown her where to find cold drinks and snacks and then left for parts unknown. The house was incredibly quiet.

Christie thought about the pasture gate that had been left open earlier, and Garrett questioning her as if she'd been responsible. She supposed since she was the new one at the farm he'd question her first, but it was almost as if he expected her to be irresponsible. Sue had told her if Garrett hadn't acted so quickly, the horses could have been badly injured.

Christie hadn't mentioned to anyone that she'd felt like she was being watched as she'd eaten her lunch in the sun. She'd dismissed the notion as paranoia. Later, she'd heard Joey adamantly deny leaving any gates opened. He'd worked for Garrett for two years and knew the routine and Christie believed him. As she thought more about it, she wondered if someone else had opened the gate and watched everything unfold from the trees beyond the paddock. Why mention such a theory though? They'd probably think she was crazy or something.

Looking up at a slight sound, Christie twisted in her chair and found Hannah watching her from the doorway.

"Hi, Hannah. I didn't think there was anyone in the house." Hannah was a beautiful child with her rounded cheeks showing just a hint of pink. Christie wished she could remember her oldest sister. Maybe it would have helped her if she'd ever seen pictures of Judith when she was younger. Judith's death still felt unreal, as if she was missing out on a connection she should be feeling.

Hannah hesitated in the archway, looking ready to bolt back the way she'd come.

"I like your boots," Christie said quietly. "I noticed those red boots the first time I saw you."

Hannah stepped into the kitchen. Christie noticed the toes of her boots were scuffed down to their natural leather color. "If I had boots like those, they'd be my favorite pair."

Hannah's eyes widened in surprise. "Well, these are my favorite." She tucked her white T-shirt into her blue jeans and then looped her thumbs in her pink belt. A small plush rabbit hung half way out of her front jeans pocket. Weighing down the front of her belt was a large silver buckle.

"I didn't see you this morning," Hannah said, her manner offhand. "I thought maybe you left."

"Nope. I'll be here for a month."

Christie suppressed a grin as Hannah rolled her eyes.

"My sister Ellen had a collection of those animals," Christie commented, indicating the stuffed rabbit. When Ellen died, she'd given the animals to her nephew. Idly, Christie wondered if Darrell had let Eric keep them. She shifted her gaze to the roses in a vase in front of her. Reaching out she ran her fingertip along a thorn, testing it sharpness. A tiny drop of blood appeared on her skin.

"Mommy gave me this one," Hannah said, waving the rabbit in the air.

"It's great that you have a keepsake." Casually, she added, "That's a neat buckle."

Hannah rubbed the buckle's shiny surface with her forefinger. "Daddy won it at a rodeo. Now it's mine." She tilted her head so her long blond hair hid her face. "It says 'All Around Roper'." Hannah's gaze met hers. "Daddy quit when him and my mom got married." She frowned and hunched her shoulders. "She was beautiful. She died," she mumbled.

Christie swallowed past the tightness in her throat. "You're lucky you have your dad."

"He's not my dad!" Hannah blurted. "Not really."

Taken back by the vehemence in Hannah's voice, Christie also heard the underlying uncertainty. The words themselves struck Christie like a physical pain in her chest, making it hard to breath.

Taking several breaths, she focused on Hannah and the child's pain. Christie said slowly and carefully, "Anybody can see he's your dad in every way that counts." Inside, she felt sick, her fingers clenching. Something wasn't right. She couldn't question Hannah. She pressed her lips together, feeling a rigid ache through her whole body. Garrett had lied to her. They needed to talk.

Hannah's expression looked hopeful, but then she seemed to crumple and with an angry mutter, ran from the room.

Christie let out a breath. She'd blown that. Everything in her wanted to soothe Hannah's hurt, tell her she was so lucky to have a dad who loved her. Christie knew from her own experience not all dads loved their kids like Garrett.

Christie saw the floppy rabbit on the floor where

Hannah had dropped it. She left the table, washed her glass and leaned down and picked up the stuffed toy. She rubbed its softness between her fingers. A part of her was numb by the truth Hannah had innocently divulged. Garrett was not her biological father.

Turning the rabbit over, Christie could see where someone had repaired one leg with long, uneven stitches. One ear was narrower than the other and it had stitches along the side. Had Judith mended a beloved toy for her daughter?

Christie left the kitchen and walked down the hallway. Looking into the living room, she found Hannah lining her dolls up on the area rug. Christie stepped back out of sight and knocked on the door casing, holding the stuffed toy so all Hannah would see was the rabbit. "Can I come in?" she said in a high, whiney voice. "Somebody dropped me and I hurt my ear. Look, it flops."

A small giggle from Hannah, then silence. Christie wiggled the rabbit sideways. "Please? I want to play with Hannah's dolls."

"You can come in," Hannah said quietly.

Christie stepped around the corner and entered the living room.

Hannah solemnly accepted the proffered rabbit and put it on the floor beside her dolls. Christie noticed the dolls were arranged in order of size and hair color — blondes, then brunettes. "Luckily your rabbit wasn't hurt so you won't have to stitch him up. It looks like you've operated on him a few times."

Hannah nodded. "Daddy sewed his ear here," she

held the rabbit up by the ear, "and on his leg when he broke it. See?"

Impressed, Christie said, "Your dad did that? Wow, I couldn't sew a stitch if you paid me."

Hannah looked down at the rabbit. "Daddy can do all kinds of stuff."

"I believe you. He seems pretty smart." Garrett was mother and father all rolled into one, but he had lied to her. A lie of omission.

"Well," Christie said cheerfully, "now that you and the rabbit are reunited I'm going back to work. Maybe I'll see you later, Hannah."

Hannah didn't say anything, but for once her smile was sweet and unguarded.

¤¤

Hannah stared at her dolls after Christie had left. Carefully, she rearranged them a bit. Christie seemed pretty nice, but Hannah remembered Mommy saying you had to be careful of people. Sometimes they acted all nice because they wanted something. Hannah chewed her lip, wondering if maybe Christie wanted something. No, she'd brought her favorite rabbit to her and she didn't have to do that. Christie was nice. She kept her from getting hurt the other day too, and she never yelled at her for being dumb and standing in the road.

Hannah held the rabbit tightly to her chest and smoothed the soft old fur with one hand. She wondered if she should be friends with Christie. Maybe she'd ask Daddy or she could just wait and see if Christie did anything mean.

"Sometimes people just need a little rope to hang themselves." Hannah put her hands over her ears, but she still heard Mommy's voice. Sometimes it got in her head and wouldn't go away.

She gathered her dolls in her arms and climbed into Daddy's chair. She stuffed the dolls all around her and sat very still. On a table beside her was Daddy's old baseball cap. She picked it up and held it tightly. Daddy called it his lucky hat. As she stared at a picture of Daddy and Uncle Randy on the wall, she began to feel better. Mommy's voice was gone. Hannah relaxed.

¤ ¤

Later that afternoon Garrett stabled his gelding in the barn and strode down the newly raked barn aisle. Another day come and gone. The barn smelled sweetly of hay and clean bedding. He checked each of the box stalls as he passed by them, but most of the horses were busy with their feed and paid him no attention. He'd spent the latter part of the afternoon checking fence in the furthest pastures from the house. Some of his young stock were out in those pastures and he liked to keep a regular eye on them. He made a mental list of the chores he hadn't been able to get to today, and knew they'd still be there tomorrow, and so might the heat.

"Hi, Boss!" called out Sue as he neared the end of the barn. Sue stepped out of the box stall next to the doorway and into the aisle. It was the stall of the mare that had been injured today. Garrett noticed the black jar of ointment in her hand.

"Hi Sue. How's Bridie's leg doing?"

"It's looking good — no swelling so far. I just cleaned it again and put on ointment to keep the flies away."

Garrett entered the large box stall, the crisp shavings stirring underfoot. Birdie was one of his better mares, a sleek gray whose foals were just beginning to prove themselves on the track. "Hello, girl." Her almost black foal approached him in his usual friendly manner. "Hello Speedball. Don't want to forget you." Garrett rubbed under the foal's chin.

Facing Bridie's hindquarters, Garrett ran his hand down the inside of her hind leg. She offered to lift her leg, but he patted her and stepped back.

"Looks good. Go ahead and eat, Bridie." Garrett and Sue exited the stall. Garrett pulled the sliding door closed, pushed the latch home and pulled it down to lock in place. "How did it go today?"

"Fine. I gave Christie the general run down on what we do at the farm. She's a good worker."

"Good. Maybe it'll be easier to get caught up now. Have you seen my daughter?"

Sue looked past him and pointed toward the open doorway. "I saw Hannah a few minutes ago right outside with Christie and Buddy."

"Okay, thanks." Garrett moved from the cool barn interior out to the sun-baked holding and paddock area, batting the dust off his jeans as he walked.

"Hi, Daddy!" he heard Hannah yell.

Garrett veered to the left and spotted his daughter straddling the wooden paddock fence behind Christie and one of his new hires, Buddy Thatcher.

Christie leaned against the wooden rail as she held carrots out to the grazing mares.

Garrett approached them. Christie and Buddy

were talking about the horses. He noticed that Hannah ignored Christie when she turned to talk to her, but as soon as Christie looked away, Hannah watched her again.

Garrett lifted a hand and wiped the dust from his face and mouth. All afternoon the hot, almost sultry wind had blown dirt and grit in his face. He sorely needed a shower, but he figured it could wait a few more minutes. He walked up to his daughter. "Hannah, sweetheart, how did your day go? Do anything interesting?" Because she straddled the top fence rail, Hannah looked down at him.

"Me and Ruth went into town with Sam. He drove us. We got big red tomatoes and corn. I already had some of the corn. It was so sweet."

"I hope you saved me some corn for dinner."

Hannah smiled at him. "Of course, silly."

Christie darted him a glance, and something there made him pause. She turned back to the fence, intent on the horse she was feeding. She put her foot on the bottom rail and hoisted herself higher. Garrett stared at the slender, fine-boned ankles showing above her ragged sneakers. He frowned and jerked his gaze upward. Those exposed ankles made her seem vulnerable, probably because she was all slim arms and legs anyway. Garrett wondered about her life before she'd landed here. Had it been anything like Judith's early life? Any information she'd imparted was sketchy at best.

Buddy nodded his head at Garrett. "Hey Boss. I rode the southern pasture today. Everything checked out just fine and I gave Sam the report."

"Thanks Buddy."

Out of the corner of his eye he saw Christie lean too far out and begin to lose her balance. Garrett quickly stepped forward and grabbed her securely on either side of her hips. He steadied her. "Watch yourself."

Unexpectedly, she leaned against him, and then hopped down from the rail. Garrett stepped back quickly.

"Garrett." Her voice was cool.

"How did your first day go?" he asked, resting his hands on his hips.

"Fine." She shaded her eyes and looked away from him.

"Any problems I should know about?"

"No. Sue showed me the ropes. I spent most of the day in the barn, cleaning tack, raking the aisles and mucking the stalls. After work Buddy introduced himself. We got talking and then he showed me where I could feed the horses." She threw his ranch hand a friendly smile. Garrett envied their easy camaraderie.

"I love watching the foals play," she said. "That's the day's highlight."

Seeing the genuine delight and caring in her face caused an inexplicable twisting in his gut. Garrett reminded himself this was all new to her. She was used to New York and enclosed spaces. A slight breeze swept her dark hair across her eyes. He had the strangest notion to twine its soft texture through his fingers. He dug his hands into his jeans pockets instead.

"You're lucky to live in such a beautiful place, Garrett. Sue told me some of the history of these

Thoroughbreds. You must be so proud of your success."

He nodded.

"Daddy, look at me!" Hannah squealed. She jumped from the fence into his arms. Garrett reacted automatically, catching her as she threw her arms around his neck. He noticed the quick glance she threw Christie's way, as if checking for her reaction. Garrett swung his daughter around and dropped a kiss on her warm neck.

He ignored Hannah's squirming antics and looked at Christie over the top of her head. "Yes, from here my yearlings go on to another trainer at the racetrack."

"But everything starts here with you. I've never seen anything like this place. Buddy kind of showed me around after work."

"Well," Buddy broke in, "I've got to get moving. I promised my dad I'd be home to help him with some chores. I'll see you folks tomorrow." Buddy tipped his hat to Christie and nodded to Garrett. "Garrett, one more thing. I saw Les Doyle earlier. Did he come up to the house?"

Garrett looked at him in surprise. "No. When was this?"

"Oh, I'd say around nine or so. He was out by the main road. I think he was having trouble with his truck but he said he could fix it so I went on."

"I'll give Kim a call at home."

Buddy turned to go.

"Thanks, Buddy," Christie called after him.

Garrett watched Buddy turn, walk backwards several steps and give her a thumbs sign up before continuing on his way.

"He's a nice kid," she said, looking up at Garrett.

Garrett raised a brow. "Kid? He's probably your age."

"He's graduating from college this summer, so I'd guess he's about twenty-two. I'm twenty six." Christie smiled. "That's light years away."

Garrett digested that information. "I'm sorry I didn't get a chance to introduce you around, but it was unavoidable."

"Don't worry about it. I know how busy you are. Besides Sue I met Ally, Buddy and Emmett, again. Sam took me around and introduced me to a teenager named Joey."

Garrett looked at her with surprise. "Sam?" His foreman was getting around these days.

She shaded her eyes and looked up at him. "Yes. I really like Sam. He tells it like it is." She smiled. "You know exactly where you stand with him, don't you? There's no deception."

"Always have," he acknowledged, wondering at her choice of words. "I've known Sam since he worked for my dad doing odd chores. It doesn't sound like you missed anyone. What else did you and Buddy do?" he asked casually. He saw her surprised expression and he wondered if there'd been an edge in his voice.

"Is there a rule against the help socializing?" she asked coolly.

Hannah pulled the hat off his head and put it on her own. Garrett welcomed the slight breeze that cooled his head. "No." He made his voice neutral, knowing it wasn't his business if Buddy and Christie spent time together.

Hannah squirmed restlessly. "Let me down, Daddy. Ally is bringing the puppies out. I want to see them."

Garrett put Hannah on her feet. "You're getting kind of big for me to carry you anyway," he said, retrieving his hat. "We're going to eat soon," he warned. "Don't be long."

"Okay. I'll be real quick."

"Famous last words," he muttered, smiling. Garrett saw Ally carry the cardboard box with the puppies from the barn and place it on the grass beside the barn. His daughter ran over to Ally and dropped to the ground. She fussed over each puppy as she lifted them out of the box.

Christie looked at him and when he met her glance. "Hannah adores you. But of course you know that." Her words seemed measured.

He studied her curiously. "It works both ways."

"Hannah mentioned you and her mom used to go to rodeos." Her voice seemed overly casual.

"That part of my life is over."

"That must have been an exciting time, the hustle of rodeo life, one town after the other."

He stared at her. Something didn't feel right. "I'd rather not dwell on the past." Judith had had a penchant for wheedling the truth out of him, and she hadn't been averse to using that knowledge against him. He wondered how Christie would react if he told her that about Judith. Maybe she'd be the same way.

"If you'll excuse me, I'm going to get cleaned up." He didn't want to talk about personal stuff. Judith had taught him that lesson. When he took a step back, Christie moved to stand in front of him.

"Garrett, you lied to me." Christie's words stopped him dead. Her gaze rested on Hannah. She turned her head, eyes laser sharp on him. "You let me believe you're Hannah's father. Hannah told me about her mother marrying you."

He stepped closer to her again, his entire body now filled with angry tension. "I adopted her," he said in a low voice. "Make no mistake, I am her father. And any court will say the same. My God! If you're thinking of interfering —"

Christie drew a harsh breath and there was pain in her eyes. "You think I'd take her from you?"

"You can't."

"I wouldn't!"

He stared at her grimly. "It remains to be seen why you're even here."

"You don't trust me at all." Her shoulders seemed to slump. "Or maybe it's just women you can't trust. No wonder you won't talk about anything personal."

"It's not your business. Leave it."

"My God!" she exclaimed softly, studying his face. "What did my sister do to you?"

The note of wonder and soft sympathy in her voice caught him off guard. "You don't know what you're talking about."

Her dark eyes seemed to hold a wealth of knowing. "Judith and I are from the same background. I don't know what happened to her after she left at fifteen, but I know about her life before she left. There wasn't much room for normalcy."

Garrett wanted to know what it was she meant. But then he actually felt afraid. Maybe he didn't want to know. Judith was gone, everything they'd had was dead and buried. Did he want to dig up old demons?

"Daddy!" Hannah called. "Come and play with the puppies." She ran over to them and pulled on Garrett's hand. "Come on. They're so cute Daddy. Don't you think?"

"Everything little is cute," he said dryly. "Then they get big and chew my boots and track mud." He squatted down by Hannah. "I'm going to get cleaned up sweetheart. Why don't you show Christie the puppies?"

Hannah threw Christie a look of invitation, obviously happy to show them to anyone. She then ran back toward the puppies. Christie gave him one last glance he couldn't interpret, then followed Hannah to kneel in the grass and lift one of the puppies.

Bemused, Garrett stared at Christie and his daughter, both of them sitting on the grass with eight puppies climbing over them as they laughed with delight. Hannah actually smiled at Christie. Judith, despite living on a farm, had never bothered with any of the animals and he knew darned well she'd never pick up a puppy and kiss the top of its head as Christie was doing.

Judith and Christie looked as different as night and day. His wife had been high maintenance, and in the beginning he'd been proud of it. Somewhere during the time of their marriage she'd accused him of changing, and he knew she'd been right. A woman who needed a lot of attention hadn't meshed well with the long, demanding hours he'd put in to keep the ranch going.

Garrett hoped Christie would work out for the short time she'd be here. Even Hannah seemed to be warming up to her. It would be easier if his daughter decided to be agreeable. One less fight. Garrett still didn't know if he could trust Christie's motives, but for the time being he'd continue to keep a close eye on her.

∞ Chapter Five ∞

GARRETT ENTERED THE KITCHEN late the next afternoon. He had spent most of the day working on the horse exercise walker that had decided to quit. Usually he liked tinkering, but he didn't have the patience for it today. It seemed that every time he turned around he encountered Christie, and for some reason it was disrupting his concentration. He'd finally decided that what he needed first and foremost was a cold beer. As he walked toward the house, he noted his brother Randy's truck parked in the driveway and he wondered how long he'd been here. Randy usually came looking for him. Apparently not today.

As soon as he stepped into the kitchen the smell of baking cookies made his mouth water. Ruth was making his favorite chocolate chip cookies. The screen door bumped against him as he stopped to draw in a deep, appreciative breath. He heard

Hannah's giggles followed by the low murmur of his brother's voice.

He dropped his hat on the hook right next to Randy's dark Stetson. Hannah sat on Randy's lap at the table, armed with a spatula as she removed cookies from a cookie sheet.

Garrett moved toward the refrigerator.

"Hey, Garrett," Randy said.

"Randy, I thought you'd be out keeping the city crime-free today. What brings you to this part of the county?"

Randy smiled. "I do get days off from the Sheriff's department. Hannah called to give me heck for not showing up last night, so I had to make it up to her. In the meantime, I'm renewing my acquaintance with Christie."

Garrett gripped the handle of the refrigerator door. "You'd think you were old friends already," he said dryly, watching his brother closely. Randy's light blond hair and usually immaculate appearance looked a bit the worse for wear. His hair stood partially on end and his black designer T-shirt had been spattered with bits of cookie dough. Garrett allowed himself a smile. Today Randy looked more like the brother he'd grown up with, always ready to have fun, not the sheriff deputy who'd made himself scarce around the farm of late while putting in a load of overtime.

"'Course. I'm going to make sure I stop over this way more often," Randy added, grinning.

"Did you come to see Ally?" he asked bluntly.

Randy cocked a brow. "Maybe."

Garrett looked away from his brother and stared

at the beer in the refrigerator, debating if he should have cookies instead.

The dryness in his throat won out. He grabbed a can of beer, turned to Randy and held it up. "Randy?"

His brother shook his head. "I'm having lemonade."

Garrett laughed. "You're joking."

Randy indicated a tall glass of pink lemonade in front of him.

Garrett toasted him with the beer and took a gulp, then leaned against the counter and crossed his boots. He saw flakes of mud just under his boots. He'd better clean that up or Ruth would tell him about it. He looked around. "Where's Ruth?"

"She's not here," Christie said, surprising him as she walked out of the pantry carrying a large bag of flour.

She wore a dark red T-shirt and blue jeans that were liberally dusted with flour. A large wet spot ran across the front of her shirt. Garrett moved forward and took the flour from her to set it on the counter. His glance dropped to her shirt and the way it clung to her full breasts. He looked at his brother and frowned. By the direction of Randy's glance, his brother hadn't missed the wet spot either and was enjoying every minute of his time here.

"Thanks," Christie said.

Remembering the dirt he'd left on the floor, Garrett reached over the counter and grabbed several paper towels. Running them under the water faucet, he then squeezed them out. "Does Ruth know you're in here using the kitchen?" he asked curiously, picking up the bits of dried mud with the paper towel.

"Well, I did ask permission," Christie said dryly, opening the flour bag.

Garrett noticed two sugar dusted jellyrolls sitting on the counter behind Christie and his sweet tooth kicked into gear. When he looked up he realized Christie was staring fixedly at his can of beer. Deliberately, he lifted the can and took a deep swallow. It felt good going down.

He wiped his sleeve across the corner of his mouth and studied her carefully. "The way you're staring makes me wonder if you want one. You're not working, take one if you want."

She shook her head quickly, her glance sliding away from him. "I don't drink."

"You don't know what you're missing on a day like today." He took another swallow. When he looked at her again she had turned away but Garrett thought her shoulders looked rigid. He finished the beer, moved to the sink to rinse the can and then threw it in the recycle trash bin on the open pantry door. Leaning against the counter, he watched Christie mix ingredients. "I needed that to clear the dust I've been eating all day."

"Well, if you'd like something really scrumptious," Christie said lightly, "try some chocolate jelly roll. The cookies are almost ready too."

"Daddy, I made your favorite," Hannah said cheerfully, holding a cookie in the palm of her hand.

"I see that." He pretended to smack his lips. "So Christie knows how to bake cookies."

"Ruth had to leave," Hannah said. She transferred the cookie to a plate and looked at Christie. "Ruth's cookies are better than anybody's in the whole world. Nobody can make them as good."

"Actually, one of my great loves is baking," Christie supplied, opening the oven door to slide a cookie sheet inside. "My sister's favorite was chocolate chip too."

Garrett went perfectly still.

"You have a sister?" Hannah asked, stuffing a cookie in her mouth, eyes wide on Christie. Garrett stared at Christie, trying to catch her eye so she didn't say anything else but she didn't look up at him.

"I used to." She turned away, her voice muffled as she faced the sink.

Garrett looked at Randy, who in turn was looking at him. Garrett took a step toward Christie.

"Her name was Ellen," Christie said. "She died." She paused with her wet hands suspended over the sink and Garrett stood there stupidly, feeling shock clear to his boots. Ellen? The sister who was so like Judith? Christie hadn't told him she'd died too. Christ.

Christie fumbled for a dry cloth. Garrett reached into a drawer, pulled out a dishtowel and handed it to her.

Briefly, her glance met his. "Thanks."

She wiped the counter.

"I'm sorry," he said quietly. "Why didn't you tell me?"

"She died not too long ago," she said tersely.

Damn. "If you ever need to talk. . ." He cursed his own awkwardness. Two sisters? He swallowed, imagining her pain. No wonder she hadn't wanted to talk about it.

She nodded jerkily and he wanted to offer something, maybe an apology for his earlier gruffness with her.

The sadness in her eyes affected him, as much as he didn't want it to. He could imagine the pain she tried to mask.

Randy cleared his throat, drawing Garrett's attention away from Christie. "Garrett, I wondered if I could borrow your motorcycle? I've got the truck."

Garrett gave him a look of disbelief. "You want to haul my Harley in that junker of yours outside? For what you make as a cop, you should be able to afford something that doesn't belch when you drive it."

"If I break down I can always ride the Harley home," Randy said smugly. He turned to Christie, an invitation in his smile. "Have you ever ridden a motorcycle, Christie? Maybe you'd like to go for a spin with me."

Garrett stiffened, well aware Randy's idea of a spin wasn't limited to a motorcycle ride. He liked women and women liked him. Garrett stared at his brother. "I don't think that's a good idea."

Christie stepped around Garrett and gave his brother a broad smile. "Actually, that sounds like fun."

"I'll have to catch you when we both have time off," Randy said, giving her a wink. "I can show you all the ins and outs of riding."

"Next thing I know, you'll be charging for lessons

on my motorcycle," Garrett said with a hint of irritation. "Maybe I should rescind the offer of a loan."

Randy gave him a narrowed-eyed look, rose to his feet and placed Hannah in the seat he had just vacated. "I guess I should quit while I'm ahead. I don't know anyone else who'd loan out a Harley. It's time for me to go." He dropped a kiss on Hannah's head and turned toward the door. "See you later, Squirt. Christie."

"Uncle Randy, you can't go!" Hannah threw her arms around his neck. With some satisfaction, Garrett saw cookie crumbs rain down the back of Randy's shirt, leaving a dusty trail.

"I have to go." Randy dropped another kiss on Hannah's cheek. "Maybe I'll see you tomorrow."

Garrett followed his brother out the door. "Leaving so soon?"

"I don't want to cramp your style, big brother."

The screen door closed behind them. "What's that supposed to mean?" Garrett growled.

Randy just whistled and Garrett followed him down the steps and across the back yard, a tinge of guilt snaking through him. Maybe he should have kept his mouth shut. Randy had been having a good time with Hannah.

Randy kept walking. "You figure it out."

"My ribbing never bothered you before," Garrett said stubbornly.

Randy stopped and faced him. "That's right, and it doesn't bother me now. I'm just backing out gracefully. I get the idea you're feeling a bit territorial."

"That's crap."

Randy smiled, speculation in his gaze. "Is it?"

Garrett opened his mouth to refute his brother's statement, then closed it. Was he acting territorial? Yeah, he'd been annoyed at the idea of Randy making moves on his new employee.

He pulled open the door to the small shed behind the house. "Yeah, it's crap," he said. He walked into the shed and then pushed his motorcycle outside. "She's been here a few days and you're seeing something that isn't there. Anyway, I know you're really after Ally."

It irritated Garrett when Randy merely shrugged a shoulder.

"You keep bringing Ally up."

"Why don't you bring some honesty into this conversation and admit why you're really here?"

Randy just looked at him. Shaking his head, Garrett put a wooden plank against the lowered tailgate of Randy's truck and together they pushed the Harley onto the truck bed, then tied it securely on both sides with rope and tie-downs.

"By the way," Randy said, "Christie checks out. Her mother got pregnant as a teenager with Judith Kelly, who later was listed as a runaway. Your Judith. Judith's father unknown. Christie has no priors, clean record. She had another sister, Ellen Jenkins, who died about three months ago."

"That's it?"

"Do you want me to go further? I had Melinda at the office do a quick check. I didn't call that number yet to check with her boss."

"No." Garrett felt a mix of relief and new tension.

Christie had been telling him the truth. She had a right to know Hannah. In his gut he'd known it but he had to be certain for Hannah's sake.

Randy slid dark glasses on and clapped him on the shoulder. "Thanks for the loan of the motorcycle. I'll let you know how my hot date goes."

"So you've decided to go back into the game? You can spare me the details."

"I'll give you all the details." Randy gave him a big smile. "I don't want you to forget what a date is all about."

"Very funny," Garrett said sourly. What did it matter if he hadn't been on a date in over three months? It had been his choice. He was happy working his ranch. Hannah needed consistency. He didn't want to shake her world up again, not after the last fiasco when he'd brought a female friend to the ranch. He cringed now just thinking of the temper tantrum.

"I'll probably see you in a couple days — if not before."

"Before you go," Garrett said, "I need another favor. Can you check up on Les Doyle? I'm worried about Kim."

"I heard he got canned at the plant and he's drinking again."

"I know that much."

"I'll keep my ears open. It's nice to have a brother in law enforcement, now isn't it?"

Garrett smiled grudgingly. "Thanks."

Randy opened his truck door with a loud squeal of hinges.

"That seat looks like it's going to fall in the road.

Somebody should give you a ticket."

Randy turned the screwdriver that served as his key. The truck started with a loud backfire and then a roar.

"You need a muffler," Garrett said when the truck backfired again.

Randy smiled. "It needs more than that. I'll write myself a ticket. See ya."

"Randy!" Garrett heard Christie's voice as his brother began to drive away.

Christie ran around the side of the house toward the driveway. "Randy!"

Randy stopped the truck and a swirl of dust rose up around him. Coughing, Garrett stepped back.

Christie gracefully jogged across the driveway, a brown paper bag in her hand. She leaned in the open passenger window of Randy's truck and handed him the bag. She stood waving as Randy drove off.

Christie turned to face him. "I almost forgot to give Randy his cookies. He told me they were his favorite."

"Mine too," he said deliberately. "My mom always made chocolate chip cookies on Sundays. My dad was a chocoholic before we knew what that meant."

"I've always had a weakness for chocolate myself," she admitted with a conspiratorial smile.

Garrett smiled back at her as he led the way back to the house. At the back door he held the screen open for her. Once inside the kitchen, he said musingly, "I'm amazed Ruth turned the kitchen over to you. She's very territorial."

Christie moved to sit at the table across from his

daughter. "Hannah and Ruth were in the midst of making cookies when she had to leave." She lowered her voice. "Hannah was disappointed and said her friend's mom makes them cookies all the time, so I volunteered to fill in."

Stiffly, Garrett leaned down and placed his palms flat on the table, his face very close to Christie's. "I need to see you outside," he said.

"What about your special cookies, Daddy?" Eyes wide, Hannah watched both of them.

"Save them for me," he said. Courteously, he held the door open for Christie and they walked back outside. Almost defiantly, she swung her tail of hair over a shoulder and stomped down the stairs. She didn't stop until she reached Hannah's tire swing under the big old maple tree. She swung to face him and put her hands on slim hips.

Garrett's mouth went suddenly dry. Unaccountably, he had the strongest urge to lean forward and kiss that impertinent mouth until it turned soft and responsive. He shoved away that tempting thought.

Looking up toward the house, Garrett could see his daughter watching them through the kitchen window, but knew she couldn't hear him. He kept his voice low anyway. "I need you to understand Hannah can't get her way all the time, or depend on you to make cookies. That's Ruth's job."

"I happened to be there so I said I'd help finish the cookies they'd started. Hannah wasn't happy, but I guess she really wanted to make the cookies. The other night you warned me about your daughter's possible hostility and now you seem bothered that she might be okay with me. I'll remind you I am her aunt."

Garrett took three steps away and then circled back. "Hannah likes to pretend. She misses her mother, but I don't want anything setting her up for heartache later."

"I'd never hurt a child, especially one as sensitive as Hannah." Christie set her jaw. "And I'm certainly not trying to take my sister's place."

"I'm not saying you'd hurt anyone on purpose." All he had to do was look in her eyes to know that, but he had to protect his daughter. "She was hurt bad when her mom died. She's still pretty breakable."

"I understand your priority, but see it from my point of view. She's my only link with my sister. If Hannah comes looking for me, I won't turn her away."

"Why didn't you tell me your sister Ellen died?"

"What does it matter to you?"

Garrett had no ready answer. "I don't know, but it might have made a difference."

Her lips trembled. "Ellen's passing is something that's so new, I really can't talk about it. First Ellen and now I find out about Judith. How do you expect me to talk about it?" She pushed at the moisture at the corner of her eyes. "Right now I'm battling for some tiny measure of affection from Hannah. That's my priority." Christie took a step toward the house but Garrett grabbed her forearm and kept her still.

"I won't have Hannah hurt. She won't turn out to be a bundle of neuroses like her mother." Resigned, he bit back a sigh. "Judith could never understand how families work together. She hated long-term commitment."

"You keep implying I'm like Judith. Is that what you think about me?"

"I don't know you. But I can say if you're like her, you wouldn't be happy at Winding Creek Farms for the long haul."

"You sound so certain."

"I lived it."

Christie's eyes grew wide and he knew he'd upset her. "I have cookies in the oven," she said. This time, Garrett didn't try to stop her from leaving.

¤ ¤

From the window Christie watched Garrett's quick, hard strides. She picked up a dishrag and vigorously cleaned the table where Hannah was busy stirring batter.

They all had places of blind, tender pain in their lives. With her, it was her family, and in a way she and Garrett shared that pain. Perhaps it was what Garrett left unsaid that was the most telling, but he'd certainly laid the truth out in the open this time.

Before, it was everything he didn't say that made Christie wonder if his relationship with her sister had been less than ideal. There was so much pain in him. Christie thought of when her sister Ellen had died, the empty, echoing apartment and then she'd lost custody of her nephew. God knows it had been more than she could bear. She had taken the easy way out, she'd run.

"These are all for Daddy," Hannah carefully arranged cookies on a separate plate. "And nobody else."

Christie hid a smile. "Your dad will gobble those up."

The wide eyes and hopeful look on Hannah's face was almost too much to see. She looked down at the cookies and pulled the plate closer. "Do you really think so?"

"Of course. Not only are those your dad's favorite cookies, but since you were the one who made them, they're extra special."

A look of pure pleasure stole over Hannah's features. Christie hoped she hadn't overstated Garrett's reaction to Hannah's cookies. Surely he was sensitive enough to make a big deal out of his daughter's baking.

Idly, Christie folded and refolded the wet cloth as she stared out the kitchen window. She could see Garrett and Buddy talking by the barn. Watching them, Christie mused that Garrett was a man in charge of his world. There was nothing wishy-washy about him. For the first time in years she found herself seriously attracted to a man. That was a dangerous thought since he was a man who had loved and married her own sister. A woman full of neuroses, by his own words.

He was the first cowboy she'd ever come in close contact with. He was so masculine, so forthright. He said what was on his mind, yet she sensed caring in his actions. That was a big plus in her mind, but she wasn't discounting the physical aspects either, and she didn't want to be attracted to him. She'd deliberately kept all relationships platonic since the fiasco of her engagement six years ago. But for once, she wanted to throw caution to the wind. She wondered what it would be like to love a man like Garrett, though that wasn't too likely. He kept himself pretty well insulated against getting too personal.

Christie rubbed the goose bumps on her arms. Falling for this man would only mean trouble. Dismay formed a hard knot in her throat. She had not come all this way to be attracted to a tall, soft-spoken cowboy with a hint of steel in his manner. She would not.

Christie chewed her lip, wondering if she could work a deal with Garrett to use one of his vehicles. She needed to look around the area, see if there were any suitable places where her sister Ellen's ashes could be laid to rest. She had wanted to share them with Judith, but now that would never happen.

With determination, she turned from the window, wiped down the last of the counters, then washed and dried the cookie sheets just as Ruth's blue station wagon pulled up outside.

"Ruth's back!" Hannah exclaimed, jumping up from the table. She paused at the back door. "You can leave now," she said abruptly, then ran out the back door.

Christie grimaced, thinking she'd just been firmly put her place by an eight-year old. Christie caught the screen door before it hit the wall and followed the child outside. She walked over to the car as Sam exited the driver's side and opened the back door. Hannah stood beside Ruth's door, talking excitedly about having seen Uncle Randy. "It was the best part of the whole afternoon," she ended.

"Hi Sam," Christie said. She reached inside the

car and began lifting out grocery bags.

"That's not necessary, Miss," Ruth told her, having come around to the back also. Christie looked at her with surprise, noticing her graying head held rather stiffly.

"Oh, I thought I'd help," Christie said, stepping back. She looked inside the car, the bag clutched in her hands. "There's quite a few bags in there. Between the three of us it'll take no time."

Ruth's mouth relaxed just a bit. "Come along inside, then. There's no sense standing out in this sun."

Hannah shouldered past her and ran ahead with a small white bag in one hand.

"Hannah, don't you go through anything until I get these groceries unpacked," Ruth scolded.

It was obvious how much Ruth cared about the child. Children needed to know they were wanted. Not that she expected anything less of Garrett. He was the type of man who would surround his child with people who cared about her. She just wished Hannah didn't dislike her. She'd never had a child act that way to her before and found it unnerving. She wondered what kind of reaction she'd get if she told Hannah she was her aunt, as she wanted to do.

In the kitchen Hannah stood beside the counter with the small bag, watching Ruth with an expectant look on her face.

"How you manage to find the one bag that might be for you, young lady, I'll never know," Ruth said affectionately.

"Probably because you've been bringing her gee-gaws since you started here." Sam deposited two bags on the counter top.

"What is it?" Hannah asked eagerly.

"Look and see," Ruth said with a laugh.

Christie watched Hannah's delight as she opened the bag and pulled out a book. Christie caught a brief glimpse of the cover and recognized it as one of a children's series about a magic tree house. For a moment, tears smarted her eyes. It had been Eric's favorite series of books and she'd been reading them to her nephew just before she'd left. With a pang, she wondered if his father had continued reading to him each night. Running to Ruth, the child looped her arms around the older woman's hips and hugged her.

"Thank you."

The back door swung open and Garrett walked in with several bags in his arms.

Hannah spun around excitedly. "Daddy, look. Can we read this tonight?"

Garrett looked at the book. "Hmm, how did Ruth know you haven't read that book yet?"

"She always knows!" The child exclaimed. "This is even better than making cookies."

"Hannah!" Garrett's obvious disapproval made Hannah dip her head. He softened his voice. "It was nice of Christie to use her free time to help you bake."

"Sorry," she muttered. Surprisingly, she looked up at Christie and said, "Thank you for helping me with the cookies."

"Any time, Hannah," Christie said quietly.

Garrett ran a hand over the top of his daughter's head in an affectionate gesture. Christie saw him eyeing the newly baked cookies on the counter. When she caught his glance, his eyes held a twinkle instead of the residue of irritation she half-expected from their earlier conversation.

Christie, never one to hold a grudge, felt the attraction for this man surge inside her. "Go ahead," she invited. "You look like you can't wait to dive in."

Hannah grabbed her father's hand. "Wait, Daddy." She lifted the plate of cookies she had earlier set aside. "These are yours. I made them all by myself. They have extra chocolate chips."

Garrett reached for a cookie from Hannah's plate, then changed his mind and grabbed three. Christie saw his boyish grin as he bit the first cookie in half. He stopped chewing for a moment, a strange look on his face.

"Are they good?" Christie saw the way Hannah clenched her hands in anticipation of Garrett's response. "Are they, Daddy?"

Garrett nodded vigorously. "Good, great." He chewed faster and then swallowed. "The best I've had today. I had no idea you could bake such good cookies, Hannah. Do you think this batch could be all mine?" he added.

Hannah beamed. "That's why I made them."

Garrett balanced the remaining cookies he had taken in one hand. Christie watched him bite into another cookie, chew and swallow.

Sam carried in the last two grocery bags and placed them on the table. Absently, Christie reached for a small piece of cookie from Garrett's plate that had broken in two. Ruth spoke to Garrett about dinner while Hannah stood leaning against her father's leg, her fingers hooked in one of his belt loops. Hannah watched him closely as he ate the entire cookie. The screen door opened and closed as Sam went back outside. Christie felt enclosed in a silent void, as if imprinting this scene in a corner of her mind.

They were a family. Christie realized, not for the first time, how much she didn't belong here. When the month was up she would be gone, leaving life and the people at Winding Creek Farms undisturbed. Hannah would certainly be happy when she left, Ruth might be indifferent, and Garrett. . ..

Christie stared at Garrett. He was totally involved in the success of his business and his daughter's happiness. Her leaving would impact nothing in his world. He and Hannah were their own little family unit.

Heat pricked at the back of her eyes and she hated her weakness, the emotion rising because she could never have what was here. She had always wanted this while growing up, but she'd never really known for sure that it existed. Parents and children who talked to each other, a sense of love and well-being filling a house. She wondered if she was meant to go through life a shadow, never having an impact on anyone's life.

With a muffled excuse, she left the kitchen and hurried down the back steps. She walked away from the barns, toward the open pasture. Her throat contracted in a tight band. She was afraid she would start bawling right then and there. She felt terrible and shaky deep down inside. God! She was jealous. .

.jealous of the love in that house. How terrible a person did that make her? She and Ellen had been so close, and then she and her nephew Eric, but now they were both gone and she still wanted that warm closeness.

Christie's hands shook. She realized she was furious that it had been snatched away. She drew in a lungful of air, then another, pushing back the thoughts that threatened to bring her to tears. She felt overwhelmed by anger and for a moment, swamped with self-pity.

The world could sometimes be a cold place, but not here, not these people. That thought became a conviction. She almost wished she hadn't gotten this glimpse into life here at the farm. They had troubles, Garrett and his daughter, but they loved each other and that caring was half the battle won. They would make it.

She looked down at the piece of cookie in her hand. She took a bite and chewed it, then almost gagged. The cookies that Hannah had taken such pride in were loaded with salt. She had added too much salt. Lifting her hand, Christie pitched the rest of the cookie as far as she could into the woods.

She smiled, and then she began to laugh. Garrett had known. She put a hand to her mouth to stifle her giggles. Christie walked further from the house, her shoulders shaking uncontrollably. Garrett had known with that first bite that the cookies weren't edible, and yet he hadn't let anyone know. He'd even eaten a second one so as not to hurt his daughter's feelings. Hell, he'd asked for the entire plate! Where do you find a man like that, a man who took such care with a child's feelings? Unaccountably, the thought came: he would cherish a wife. The woman he loved would never doubt he was a man who cared deeply. What then, had happened between him and Judith?

In that moment, Christie realized how lucky she was to have ended up here on Winding Creek property, even if only to see this type of love and trust first hand. Wistfully, she wondered if her life would have been different if she'd grown up in this town, or if she'd met someone like Garrett years ago, when she'd still thought there was a place for love in her life.

∞ Chapter Six ∞

A FEW DAYS LATER, Christie prepared to leave the house for work. She paused on the kitchen threshold when she spotted Garrett climbing out of his pickup truck, a bag hanging from one hand.

Christie backed into the kitchen, not really prepared to face Garrett. Her face felt hot as she recalled the dreams she'd had all night. If dreams were wishes she was in trouble. She'd dreamt she and Garrett had made love and she'd awakened tired and out of sorts. She remembered her sister Judith had yelled at her in the dream that she couldn't have Garrett. After that, she'd tossed for two hours until she'd decided to get up at five thirty.

Watching him out the kitchen window, Christie saw Garrett turn and walk toward the house. A beard shadowed his cheeks, as if he hadn't had time to shave. His unshaven face coupled with his windblown hair, added to his raw appeal. Christie quickly backed away from the window as he mounted the steps outside.

The door opened and Garrett entered the kitchen.

"Morning," Christie said, digging her hands into her pants pockets.

"You're up early." Garrett walked over to the table and placed the package on the table. "These are for you." He opened the plain brown bag and pulled out a pair of high top leather boots and dropped them on the floor with a thump.

Christie looked at them in surprise. "They're for me?"

"Yes." Garrett moved over to the counter, lifted the coffee pot and poured himself a cup of coffee.

Christie followed him as he carried his cup toward the back door. "Hang on a second. Why do I need boots?"

Garrett turned on the threshold and Christie stopped a few feet from him.

"It's a hard and fast rule anyone working around the horses wears steel-toe boots. Yesterday was the first chance I've had to go into town, so I picked you up a pair. They're not much heavier than regular boots, but they'll protect your feet." He looked down at her feet. "If a horse steps on you with those sneakers, you'll have broken toes or a foot."

"Oh." She looked down at the boots. "I didn't think of that. How do you know if they'll fit?"

"I've got an eye for detail. Size seven?"

"Yes."

"If they're not comfortable, let me know right away. I can exchange them."

"Thank you, Garrett. Please take it out of my wages." She pressed her hands together anxiously. "I have a question. I wanted to know if it's possible to borrow a vehicle? I wanted to scout around the area, maybe do some sightseeing." Christie reasoned it wasn't really a lie, she would be looking around the area. "I'll reimburse you for gas."

"Do you have a valid driver's license?"

"Yes."

"Show Sam your license and let him know the morning you need a vehicle. I'll talk to him about freeing one up." He took another swallow from his cup, moved past her and placed the cup in the dishwasher.

"I appreciate that, Garrett. I'll pay you for its use."

He swung back around to her and shook his head. "Not necessary." Clearly on his way to the door, he stopped beside her and frowned. "Are you okay?"

"Yes. Why?"

"You look tired."

"Oh." Being so close to him she could see the fine network of lines beside his eyes. "I, uh, didn't sleep that great. Nothing to worry about." His nostrils flared slightly as he stared down at her.

"It worries me when it might affect your work."

"Oh, yes, of course." Christie nodded with understanding, feeling a bit of a letdown. Surely she hadn't expected some kind of personal interest?

"No falling asleep on the job." She stepped back. "I won't. In fact, I was getting ready to go out to the barn."

Garrett's eyes grew serious and a slight frown appeared. "Wait."

Christie's throat tightened and suddenly it felt like there wasn't enough air coming into her lungs. Garrett had that affect on her. She could smell his aftershave and just being this close to him affected her strongly.

"I'm sorry," he said. "I do care — but — I can't. I won't."

An incomprehensible, crazy yearning seized Christie when instead of moving away, he took a step closer..

Garrett's head dipped slightly, then more. "The way you're looking at me. . .." His mouth hovered over hers. "Maybe you'd better stop me," he murmured, putting one hand on the wall behind her head. She was free to move away, but in that moment she didn't want to.

His mouth touched hers, lightly, briefly, then again, harder and more satisfying. Sensation coursed through her and she pressed her fingers against the front of his shirt.

Christie closed her eyes, totally involved in the taste, feel and scent of Garrett. It felt so right and exciting. He was so big and warm, his clothes carrying the clean scent of hay. She didn't want to reject this closeness, even though part of her knew it was the smart thing to do. The safe thing to do.

Garrett released her and stepped back. Christie opened her eyes, her thoughts jumbled in her head. Blood sang in her veins and her face felt hot.

"That's something I shouldn't have done," he muttered, glaring at her as if it were all her fault he'd kissed her. "You're Judith's sister, for God's sakes!"

Elation leveled out. Christie couldn't find words as he turned away and yanked the door open. Reaching back inside for his hat on the peg, he loped down the stairs and across the yard.

Her mouth stretched into a smile, almost without her thinking about it. Something close to happiness filled her. Garrett had admitted she was Judith's sister. He knew it was true.

Who would have thought there'd be such an explosion of feeling between them, just because of one kiss?

She sat at the kitchen chair, running her fingertips lightly over her lips. She closed her eyes as a momentary hopelessness gripped her. Did she have a right to be happy that this had happened? She liked being kissed by Garrett. It had been too long since she'd been touched intimately or held. Garrett had made her feel special for a few moments.

Christie picked up one of the boots and found a package of new socks inside. The boot leather was supple beneath her fingers, the inside thickly padded. Kicking off her worn sneakers, she pulled on the socks and boots. As she laced them, a wry grin split her face. It was silly to be so happy over a pair of boots. She wondered if it was the gesture that meant so much to her or the fact that it was Garrett McIntyre who had given her the gift. In her heart she knew it had to be the latter, and that's what worried her. Garrett didn't want to feel anything for her, nor did she want to feel anything for him.

¤¤

Christie looked forward to working at the farm each day. She helped Sue or Ally clean stalls and feed the mares and foals each morning. On warm, dry days the horses remained outside until early afternoon.

Once cleaned, fresh sawdust or straw was placed in the stall, all the water buckets were cleaned and refilled. Sweet-smelling Alfalfa and clover hay was placed in the mangers. The last job was to rake the center aisles before the horses were returned to the barns for the evening.

Christie noticed that mostly women worked in the foaling barns and handled the young horses. She didn't mind the manual labor in keeping the barn clean, but she loved the time spent with the foals.

Early in her second week of work Christie returned late to the house one evening. The sky had deepened to a dusky pinkish/gray as she walked tiredly up the back steps to the kitchen. Surprisingly, she hadn't seen Hannah all day. Usually she saw her out with her father or at lunchtime. Although Hannah at first had seemed determined to keep her distance, she seemed to be coming around little by little. Christie had begun to grow fond of the eight-year-old. How could anyone with a heart keep a child at arm's length, especially a child so thirsty for attention and determined not to show it?

Christie entered the kitchen and found a note from Ruth that her dinner was wrapped and in the refrigerator. She felt touched by the older woman's thoughtfulness. They weren't anything near friendship, but Christie knew the older woman had softened toward her to some degree, if not actually warmed up to her.

Christie went to her room and washed up quickly. She had missed lunch and felt quite hungry, and Ruth's cooking was not to be missed.

Exiting her room into the dimly lit hall, a slight movement caught her eye. Garrett walked toward her down the hallway, his only covering a towel. Christie stopped, stared at his wide, hair-dusted chest. Desire clenched hard and fast at her stomach. She met his equally startled gaze.

"Christie." He stood still, one hand on the towel at his right hip, the other hand clutching a pair of jeans. "Sorry, didn't know anyone was in the house." He lifted the jeans. "Dryer."

"Sorry," she mumbled. "Next time I'll make more noise."

He smiled with genuine amusement, then turned sideways and entered his bedroom, closing the door.

Christie took a deep, fortifying breath, her face heated. Quickly, she walked to the kitchen and her dinner. Annoyed with herself, she clenched her shaking hands.

She had tried to deny to herself the attraction she felt for Garrett, but seeing him like that, just now, didn't help.

She had an idea she wanted to put to him. She had been thinking about it all week, once she'd found out about the small apartment above the barn. She also knew the renovations were just about complete. It was too difficult being in the house day after day in such close proximity. It distracted her, filled her head with thoughts about a man she couldn't have. How could she ever forget he'd belonged to her sister?

Christie heard footsteps and braced herself as Garrett entered the kitchen.

"You were out to the barn pretty late."

"Just finishing up."

"Hours are —

"I know — work is over at five." She shrugged easily. "It was my choice to hang around with Ally."

Garrett lifted his cowboy hat from the peg by the back door, pushed the door open, then paused to look over his shoulder at her. "You work hard. You're doing a good job."

"Thanks." She smiled.

"I'm going in to town to get Hannah. See you later." With that he was gone.

Her dinner was delicious, but suddenly she wasn't hungry. Garrett and Hannah drove into town on a regular basis and Christie was curious as to the reason why.

She left the kitchen and walked down the hallway into the living room. Opening the glass doors that led to the terrace she walked outside, the stone cool on her bare feet after the day's unrelenting heat.

She settled in one of the comfortable lounge chairs with a sigh and was content to listen to the muted sounds of the night.

Christie sank further into the cushioned chair, mesmerized by the unrelenting inky darkness. At her old apartment she had shared with Ellen, she never recalled the night having this deep stillness. She lifted her feet and curled into the chair. Lucky man, Garrett appeared to have it all.

She lifted her gaze to the heavens. She wished she could move on with her life. Sometimes she felt as if she was running in place, afraid of what the future might hold or what it might lack. She had always been so strong when Ellen was alive, now, she felt anything but. She wanted someone to lean on, and yet that very idea was foreign to her. She and Ellen had been a team, but in the end she'd made all the decisions. Ellen had been too weak, and the last two weeks of her life, too absorbed in the process of dying.

Christie had used Garrett's vehicle several times in the last week, driving into town and the surrounding area. She was becoming familiar with the roads and outlying towns. She needed to find somewhere special for Ellen's ashes, but she didn't know what that place would be.

Guilt touched her as she wondered about her nephew Eric. She hadn't talked to him in almost three weeks, thinking only of her need to keep moving, her goal to connect with Judith. She had neglected him. With sudden resolve, she knew it was time to call him.

Dropping her feet to the stone floor, Christie rose and walked back into the living room. She found a cordless phone on the table beside the door and brought it out onto the terrace with her.

She stared at the phone keypad for several moments. What if Eric didn't want to talk to her? The last time she'd seen him it hadn't been a happy occasion. She had dropped him off at his father's apartment. She still recalled his silent tears as his father kept him from following her. Christie bit her lip and took a deep breath as she punched in the numbers. Anxiously, she waited as the line rang.

"Hello?"

Christie's hand jerked when she heard Darrell's voice in her ear. In a brief moment of panic she almost hung up on the phone.

"Darrell." She hoped her voice came out calm. She and Darrell had never hit it off, but she had tried for her sister's sake to get along with her husband.

"Christie, is that you? Are you okay?" He sounded surprisingly anxious.

"Yes, it's me." She could hear a child singing in the background. Christie's hands began to tremble. Eric loved to sing. "I'm okay. How is Eric? I can hear him singing." Some of the tension eased from her body.

"Eric's fine. Why haven't you called?" he demanded in a low voice.

She gripped the phone. "I've been traveling."

"You can't say you're going traveling and not tell anyone where you're going."

A bitter laugh left her lips and she felt the pain of it to her toes. "Fancy you saying something like that, Darrell."

"You'll never let me forget, will you?" he muttered. "Ellen understood why I left her. I couldn't stand to see her like that. It was easier for everyone."

"Easier for you." She heard his curse. Christie could imagine Darrell in his and Ellen's old apartment, running a frustrated hand through his almost black hair.

Suddenly ashamed at her own rigidity, she

quickly said, "Listen, I don't want to fight. For Eric's sake, we've got to be civil. Can I say hello to him?"

"Sure, but first tell me where you are in case I need to contact you. You just disappeared one day. Your friends at work didn't know where you had gone and your boss said you took a leave of absence. Geez, Christie, I've been worried out of my mind."

"Why would you worry, Darrell? I told you I was leaving. That last day, I told you I was going to find Judith."

"I thought you were bluffing. You haven't seen your sister Judith since you were a kid. I didn't think you'd pack up and just leave."

I didn't want to, she cried out inside. She tightened her lips against letting the words escape. "You know I couldn't stay. I felt like I was being eaten alive." The memories. Ellen was everywhere she looked. "I told you I had to scatter Ellen's ashes," she said with quiet deliberation. "Ellen asked me to find Judith, to make her a part of our lives once again."

Reluctantly, it seemed, he said. "Did you find her?"

Christie drew a deep breath, and it hurt her to say what she had to say. "Judith died, Darrell. She died right after she sent Ellen that letter."

He swore. "Then come home. There's no reason for you to stay."

"I can't. There are other reasons I can't leave yet."

"Ellen had a memorial service. Let it all go."

"Ellen asked me for more. I made her a promise."

"It's a crazy idea, taking ashes across the

country."

"You could have taken the ashes." Tensely, Christie added, "How can you criticize my choice to honor Ellen's last wish? Can I talk to Eric?" she asked in a measured tone.

"Hang on."

Christie heard voices in the background and then Eric's sweet, innocent voice. "Hello, Aunt Christie."

Relief spread throughout her body, yet she felt as if she wanted to cry. "Eric, it's so good to hear your voice. How are you doing? I could hear you singing just a minute ago. What song was that?"

"Itsy bitsy spider. I learned a new one this week. Mrs. Gardner taught me."

"Which song did you learn?"

"Wee Willie Winkie. Mrs. Gardner said it's the best song she ever heard anyone sing."

"I'll bet she's right. Are you looking forward to school? It's so exciting that you'll be starting in the fall." She had thought she would be there to see him get on the bus that first day of school.

"It's okay, I guess," he said slowly, as if he hadn't made up his mind yet. "Daddy said I'll have new friends."

"Of course you will. I'm very excited for you."

"Aunt Christie, when are you coming home?"

For a moment her mind went blank. When was she coming home? When the heartache lessened, when the memories faded? Where was home? Her apartment had been rented, her furniture sold. With the exception of Eric, she had no reason to go back.

"I'm not sure, Eric. How about if I make you a promise that we'll see each other by the end of the summer?"

"Okay. Then I'll be able to tell you about summer camp," he said, excitement entering his voice.

Christie's heart tripped and then speeded up. "You're going to camp?" Her sister had thought Eric was too young to attend camp.

"Yes, Daddy said I could."

"You'll have to tell me all about it." She tried to keep her voice neutral, but her thoughts raced with worry. What did Darrell know about keeping a five-year old safe?

"I will. Daddy wants to talk to you again. I love you Aunt Christie."

The tightness in her throat threatened to choke her. "I love you too, sweetheart."

"So when are you coming home?" Darrell asked in her ear.

Christie closed her eyes. "I'm not. I-I like it here at Winding Creek. I'm staying awhile."

"Where is Winding Creek?"

"I'm in Kentucky."

"Geez! Christie, don't you think you're carrying this a bit too far? What the hell was your sister doing in Kentucky?"

Darrell's barely concealed anger made her hunch her shoulders. She knew from past experience Darrell would voice his opinion whether she wanted to hear it or not. He used to ride roughshod over Ellen, even though she had to admit he'd made her sister happy. "Eric said he's going to camp?"

"Yes." She heard the steel in his tone.

"Do you think he'll be happy there?" she asked carefully.

"He wants to go, it's a kid's camp. They've got riding and swimming. I did check it out." He was Eric's father and she had nothing to say in the matter.

She persisted anyway. "It's just that Ellen felt he was too young."

"I know what Ellen's thoughts were on camp. I don't agree. He'll have a good time, meet kids of his own age. Besides, it's just a day camp, not overnight."

Relief filtered through her. "Oh, I thought he would be away overnight."

He made an impatient sound. "I'm not an idiot. Eric isn't ready to stay away overnight. We both know I've screwed up in the past," he added bitterly, "but I take good care of my son."

She had questioned Darrell's suitability as a father. Was she so unforgiving she would risk hurting her relationship with her sister's only child? She knew in her heart Darrell had always been a good father, she couldn't take that away from him. That's why she'd been able to leave. She knew Darrell needed time with his son.

"You're right, Darrell. I'm sorry. I know you've always done what was best for Eric." When he walked away from Ellen he had left Eric with her. Losing her son would have devastated her sister.

His tone softened a bit. "You've had a rough time, Christie." He let out a deep breath. "I know we've never gotten along that great, but you're always welcome here when you're ready to come back."

Her throat ached with unshed tears. "That means a lot to me. Eric is my last link with Ellen."

"Christie," he said tiredly, "I'm his father. You know the judge's ruling is the way it should be."

The truth in his words didn't lessen the hurt and loss she felt deep inside. Ellen had asked her to take care of Eric and she had lost him. Christie felt incredibly tired, confused. "I'm going to go now. I'll call again. Goodnight."

"Wait, let me know how to get in touch with you."

She hesitated. "I'll send you the address. Good bye, Darrell." Christie pressed the disconnect button, knowing she wouldn't send him the address. For now, she needed to be on her own.

¤¤

Garrett found Christie sitting alone on the terrace outside the living room. Her bare feet rested on his wicker footstool and her dark silky head rested against the cushioned back of his chair. She held the cordless phone in her lap, one of her hands still curled around it.

He stood in the living room doorway, gripping the wide curved handles of the French doors that stood slightly ajar. Christie hadn't seen him yet. Even in T-shirt and jeans, he realized she was eye catching. It was strange, but he hadn't noticed how truly attractive she had first arrived in town. Of course, with Ruth's good food, she didn't look as tired or thin as that first day either. For a brief moment, he wondered how hungry she had been and knew she'd never tell him. He had a feeling there were a lot of things Christie kept to herself. She had a stoic air that hinted at things better left unsaid. Like Judith. That thought twisted his guts in knots. Judith had always joked about her horrible childhood. Garrett had never really known what stories were truth and what she'd exaggerated.

Garrett studied what he could see of her profile, sensing a certain childlike vulnerability there. But she was no child — there was something undeniably sexy and alluring about her face, the slim nose and full lips.

"Christie." He stepped outside, his boots scraping across the stone floor. She turned her head and looked up at him. Garrett felt a rush of adrenaline. He clenched his fists, then flexed his fingers, wondering at the expectant look on her face. He remembered the last time they'd been close, the kiss they had shared. It had been a simple kiss, but one that had stuck in his memory all week. He wasn't sure why, anymore than he was certain why he'd sought her out after settling Hannah in bed. Something had drawn him out here tonight. Curiosity? Desire? If only it was something as simple as mere desire. Garrett shook that dangerous thought from his head. Desire and sex led to complications.

"Hi, Garrett."

She curled toward him in the chair and he moved closer.

"Hannah and I just got back from town."

"I haven't seen her all day," she said.

"She's been with my mom. I put her to bed since she's not feeling well."

"Have you had her to the doctor?" Her voice tense with concern, her urgency surprised him.

"It's just a cold."

Christie sat up straight. "I know kids get colds all the time. But when I was little I never got sick."

"Never?" he asked with disbelief.

"Not that I remember." She hesitated and then added, "My sister Ellen was always sick. She wasn't real strong. I looked after her. We were a team."

"I'm sorry, Christie. You've had a double loss."

She turned her head away. "I miss her," she said in a low voice. "And Judith. . .I never really got the chance to miss her." She looked back at him. "But you understand how it is when you love someone so much. When they're gone from your life it's a void that can never be filled. At times it's still unreal."

"Christie. . ." Garrett didn't say the words that would disillusion her about his relationship with Judith. He heard the pain in her voice and understood the sense of loss she felt. Judith, however, had squeezed out all the love he'd felt for her long before she had left. Garrett clenched his fists. Judith had almost taken everything away from him. Hannah.

Christie's face held a sweet innocence, similar to the trust in his daughter's face. How could he extinguish that by telling her the ugly truth about his marriage? About her sister. . ..

"I know how you feel," he said simply. "I lost my Dad a few years ago. It seemed like he'd be around forever. Brothers and sisters have a special bond too. It sounds like you and Ellen were really close. Randy and I are pretty tight, most of the time." Garrett grimaced. "I ride him about his carefree lifestyle and he gives me a hard time about working all the time."

"You two must have been some pair while growing up."

"We were inseparable, but things change. Randy's got his life in town and I'm out here."

Garrett pulled up a chair and sat beside her. He lifted his feet onto the footstool, staring at his boots next to her delicately curved bare feet.

Needing some action, he reached over and removed the cell phone from her hands, then placed it on the table beside him.

Christie stared at him blankly for a moment. "I made a long distance call to my nephew. Let me know how much it is so I can reimburse you. Hannah has a first cousin, you know. He's younger than her and his name is Eric."

Carefully, he took her hand. She looked so wrapped up in her thoughts that he had to give her some form of comfort. Maybe to let her know she wasn't alone. "Memories getting to you, huh, Christie?"

Her hands were cool, the fingers slender against his rough and calloused hands. Surely it wouldn't hurt to offer each other friendship and a bit of caring on this quiet Kentucky night.

Christie's fingers moved. No longer passive in his palm, they gripped his fingers with strength.

"The memories are nothing I can't handle." As she looked up at him the soft glow of the overhead lamp showed the smile curving her lips. "You're one heck of a cowboy, Garrett. Running this place, raising a little girl."

He gave an amused laugh. "Honey, cowboys are a dime a dozen out here. Somehow, I don't think you've had much experience with them."

"You're right about that." She threw him a sidelong glance. "I wouldn't mind getting to know at least one of them better while I'm here."

"Since several of my men have lined up to ask you out, I'm sure you'll have plenty of opportunity," he remarked, staring out into the dark night. "You're young, you should go out and have a good time. No reason to sit around on a night like this." If the better part of him didn't feel so scarred he'd even think about asking her out as friends.

Christie shrugged in an offhand manner. "I'm the new face around here so of course they've asked me out," she said simply. "But I wasn't talking about any of your men." She sat forward in the chair and brought her face close to his, her eyes soft and vulnerable.

"Do you want to ask me out Garrett?"

Her question took him by surprise. He breathed in her clean scent. Feminine, something fresh, like flowers and laundry soap. Her dark eyes were so close he felt as if he looked into her heart.

He stared at her warily as she touched his rough-whiskered cheek with tenderness. "I'm not one for games or waiting in line," he said harshly. "I did it once, I'll never do it again."

"I don't play games, Garrett." Her voice was deadly serious. "Life is too short."

It had been a long time since he had tried to read the signals a woman sent out, maybe too long to think he could do it again and get it right. Damn, but Garrett wanted to believe Christie wouldn't mind him kissing her again. But then, maybe she would let one of his ranch hands kiss her too. "Maybe you just want a cowboy experience." His voice was harsh, he knew it.

"No."

Garrett stood, pushing his chair back. Christie stood also and leaned toward him just the slightest bit. Feeling her warmth, drawn in by the quiet, waiting quality in her face, Garrett thought maybe he didn't care if that's all she was after. Maybe he could learn to play that game.

He bent slowly, unable in that moment to deny himself the pleasure of kissing her. He reached out and pulled her up to him until they stood inches apart. Lightly, he brushed her mouth with his. Sensation rocked him. He closed his eyes, repeating the light caress. A groan built inside his chest. He wanted to lift her off her feet, bury his face in her neck, the fragrance of her hair, and maybe take her inside and into his room. It had been a long time. Garrett cupped her face and kissed her again, deeper, and her lips parted to welcome him as her hands gripped his arms.

"Not here," he said, and he took a step toward the living room doors. He hit something with the toe of his boot and looked down. A doll. Hannah's doll.

The sight of that jolted him. He swallowed hard. He wasn't a kid. He had a daughter to think about, a life he was getting back on track. He dropped his hands and clenched his fists. He had only taken a taste of Christie, but that taste made him want more. Iron control kept him still and his arms at his side.

In the next moment Christie's hands crept up his shoulders. The pads of her fingers rubbed the worn fabric of his shirt. His shoulders tensed in anticipation and his body grew tight with wanting but he stiffened his resolve. Better to stop now before things went further.

He put his hands up to push hers away. Their fingers tangled. Of their own volition, his fingers curled around hers, holding them captive, squeezing. He stared at her intently, sending a silent message that he was serious.

Christie watched him. Garrett could almost feel the quick, shallow breaths she drew into her lungs. He heard the sudden intake of her breath as he settled one hand at the small of her back. She arched into him, her breasts against his chest, her eyes half closing.

He groaned. For his own curiosity, for this momentary insanity, he would let her get close to him. He needed to be close to her. It felt as natural as breathing.

She dropped her head back and looked at him through half-closed lids. Garrett tensed as she ran her tongue ran over her lips. He needed to taste those lips.

"Christie." He cupped her face, his calloused hands gentle on her cheeks. With one hand he cradled the nape of her neck. Her skin felt so soft, so warm, her bones fragile under the skin. He lowered his head and touched her mouth. The taste and texture of Christie wound through him, insidious, alarming in its subtlety. Any lingering intentions to step back fled. He wanted this moment and the consequences be damned.

They seemed to breathe together. Slowly,

provocatively, he traced her lips with his tongue. Christie reciprocated, then ran her tongue lightly along the rim of his teeth. Her softness, her willingness to be wooed drew him in further, making him ignore the warnings in his head.

Heat raced across him, swirling around them as the sounds of the night faded away. It was only he and Christie. Garrett moved closer, then gripped her hips and pulled her tightly against him. The groan in his chest rumbled, releasing itself on the night air.

Garrett went still. He stepped back, realizing his good intentions had just bit the dust. What possessed him to reach for her? With a mutter of disgust, Garrett knew what had possessed him. Raw need, the desire to be close to a woman. For a moment, he had let himself be lost. He had forgotten the past, let go of the mistakes he could never undo.

Her lashes fluttered and her eyes opened. Garrett felt like he'd been punched in the gut. Emotion, unspoken want tugged at him. For a moment, he thought he would drown in those eyes. Slowly, he released the breath he was holding and drew in several more. Christie blinked as if she had trouble focusing. Her silky dark brows drew together as she studied him curiously. He knew the moment she regained control of her breathing, her senses. The slightly glazed look in her eyes faded, gave way to that bit of wariness that always seemed to lurk there.

He looked away from her mouth, clenched his teeth, glad of the shadows around them. Damn! He didn't need to complicate his life by acting on a damned impulse.

Garrett stepped back and moved to the edge of the terrace. Somewhere, a wild dog howled. It was a familiar sound, but tonight, it sounded so lonely, so desperate. He shoved his hands in his pockets, aware of his own brand of desperation.

He stared somberly out into the night. "Christ, I seem to be about to apologize again." Garrett knew the gently rolling hills were out there but the darkness hid them from view. "Flings, affairs . . . they're not my style." He laughed. "Hell, I don't have a style. Randy has a style." Randy had dated more women than most, while he was just a rancher with a young daughter trying to make a decent living. He'd learned during his brief marriage he didn't know squat about women.

"Why apologize?" she asked. "I helped the matter along."

"Yeah, well. . ." He stopped. "I don't make a practice of necking with my employees out on the terrace." He needed to say those words baldly. He needed to shock her to create some breathing distance between them.

He had to put what had happened in stark black and white terms, bring it into sharp focus so it would lose some of its potency. He wanted to dispel that damnable sense of magic taking place. Magic and miracles were the stuff of dreams. His boots were firmly on the ground. A failed marriage and the responsibility of an eight year old kept you on terra firma.

"So, I guess I'm the first employee to earn that honor?" she asked dryly.

Garrett turned quickly. He'd expected anger,

maybe chagrin. Not humor.

With one brow raised, she continued calmly, "I'm the first employee that you've honored by necking out here on the terrace?"

"This isn't a joke," he bit out, surprised by the slight smile curving her lips. He crushed the urge to yank her close and kiss her again.

"No, it's not. It's mutual attraction between two people." Her voice grew passionate. "Don't try to take that away, Garrett. One thing I've learned is life's too short to waste it on regrets over what we should have done."

Grimly, he thought of Judith and their married life.

"It gets too short when you follow one impulse after another. Ultimately the impulses break your life apart. They can bring you to the edge of bankruptcy and almost cost you everything you've worked so hard for." He clenched his jaw.

She studied his face. "You sound like you speak from experience."

"Whatever's between us, this shouldn't have happened." He ignored the disappointment that flared in her eyes. "We're too different to think of pursuing a relationship. You're Judith's sister and leaving in a few weeks. Why pursue something that doesn't have a snowball's chance in hell of surviving?" *Would she stay if he asked her?* Garrett discarded that notion. Kim would be ready to return to her job and Christie would have to leave.

"Maybe you're right. Let's pretend this never happened," she said briskly, crossing her arms. "I'm game if you are."

He felt irritated that she agreed so easily.

Christie took several steps away from him. "I was wondering what plans you have for the apartment over the barn?" she said in a sudden change of topic.

Garrett didn't answer right away, trying to mentally switch gears. "I'm not in any rush to decide. Eventually I plan to make it into another office, but that's probably a year down the road."

"Will you rent it to me while I'm here? You could think of it as way to get me out of your hair."

"It sounds like you've thought this out."

"You and Hannah would have the house back to yourselves. You've been really generous to allow me to live here, but I'd feel more comfortable knowing I wasn't in the way."

Garrett knew she was right to put distance between them, but he felt reluctant to agree, which was contrary to his earlier rejection of her closeness. "You're only going to be here for another few weeks," he said, reminding himself also of that fact. It was what she had agreed to from the beginning, but it felt like such a short time now.

"True, but I think living so closely creates tension."

He agreed but why did he feel so reluctant, then?

"I know you were worried about Hannah's reaction to having me in the house, but she's really a great kid. My nephew is five and I really miss him. I know how tough it can be, being mother and father all rolled into one."

Garrett studied the sincerity in her face. "Then you can understand why I worry about Hannah." He pushed a hand through his hair.

Her smile and the caring in her face invited him to confide, but Garrett rejected the notion. He would handle his daughter's problems. He cleared his throat. "Now," he said brusquely, "about that apartment, it's pretty rough. There isn't even any carpet."

"That won't bother me at all."

"There's no substantial heat when the nights get cold."

"I'll use a blanket."

"Well, it is vacant. You're welcome to it."

"Wonderful. Can I make the move this weekend?"

"You don't waste time, do you? I'll see what I can do."

Her smile appeared strained.

"Good night, Garrett."

Garrett forced himself to keep his hands at his sides. "See you tomorrow." He wanted nothing more in that moment than to reach for her again. He watched her walk back through the terrace doors, her bare feet noiseless on floor, and he suddenly felt empty inside, as if he'd let something precious slip away. Foolish. Nothing had slipped away. He'd sent her away.

∞ Chapter Seven ∞

SEVERAL HOURS LATER CHRISTIE skirted a small table on her way to Hannah's room. It was probably unnecessary, but she felt the need to check on her niece. It kept running through her head that her sister's illness had started out with cold-like symptoms also. What most people saw as a simple cold, she had learned to fear something worse. It was a deeply ingrained fear.

The door to Garrett's room stood slightly ajar and the room was dark. She folded her arms around herself, suddenly conscious of her thin nightshirt. The cotton reached the tops of her knees, so it was perfectly decent. Quickly, she slipped past his door and then the next door down the hall was Hannah's room. Silently she entered the room and made her way to the bed.

The room was softly lit by a night-light, and she could see Hannah as she lay sleeping in her unique pumpkin bed with its gold painted wheels.

A soft thumping drew her attention. Bo Peep lay at the foot of the bed, wagging her tail against the floor. The dog's eyes gleamed an eerie gold in the meager light. Christie spoke softly to the dog and gently fondled her head as she slipped by her.

Christie touched Hannah's forehead with her fingertips. Her skin felt cool and her breathing sounded normal. Feeling reassured, realizing she'd worried needlessly she pulled the covers up to Hannah's chest.

Christie noticed the framed picture on Hannah's bedside table and she lifted the picture. She could make out the faces in the glow of the night light. Hannah, Garrett and a dark blond woman with eyes like her sister Ellen. Her memories of Judith were vague, but Christie knew this had to be her. Her breath caught as emotion tightened a band around her chest and her eyes burned. Judith.

The picture showed Garrett beside Judith while Hannah stood in front of him. There was something very possessive about the way his arm rested across Judith's shoulders.

Slowly, Christie replaced the picture. She backed away from the bed and stumbled back against something. She threw her hand back and it slid down a warm leg. Quickly, she pulled her hand back and spun around. Garrett stood behind her. His big hands gripped her arms.

"Why are you in here?" Garrett's warm breath hit her cheek. A shiver ran down her back where she could feel the heat of his chest.

"Garrett." In the meager light she saw he wore

only boxer shorts. His upper torso was tantalizingly close and somehow her hand had come to rest against his chest. She became aware of soft chest hair and flexing muscles. Her breathing quickened and with determination she stepped around him and walked across the room to the door. Once out in the hallway she turned and he was right behind her.

"I saw the picture of Judith."

Garrett's eyes narrowed and he glanced back toward Hannah's room.

"I didn't mean to snoop. But it was there." She swallowed. "She looks like Ellen."

"Why were you in my daughter's room?"

One look at his hard face reminded Christie she was walking around in her sleepwear. She tried not to think about his hard, almost naked body so close to her. Sexual awareness of him made her heart pound and she stared at his boxer shorts again. She rubbed her palms together and sighed, knowing nothing less than the truth would do. "I wanted to check on Hannah. I was worried about her cold."

He looked surprised, then skeptical. "She'll be fine in the morning."

"I know, I know, but sometimes colds escalate into something worse, or other symptoms mask themselves as colds. . ." she let her voice trail off. "I'll just go to bed. Good night. See you in the morning." She knew she was talking way too fast but something was happening inside, making her feel all shivery and shaky. She wasn't sure how to deal with this sexual need. In truth it had never hit her so hard. At least, not when she felt so vulnerable, and . . . needy.

"Are you sure you weren't looking for my room?"

Feeling a sense of shock, Christie said, "Of course not! And I do know which room is yours. I believe you made it clear earlier you don't want to get involved. You're right, of course. Why get involved when we're so very different?"

When his hands came down on her shoulders Christie stiffened. If she tilted her head back she could skim his throat with her lips.

His thumbs moved in a circular motion. Didn't he know what that touch did to her insides. . . that the scent of him was warm in her nostrils? She wanted to lean a bit closer and forget everything. She groaned. "You make me want things I can't have." Christie was mortified to hear the words out loud.

Garrett let out a harsh breath. "Damn, I want to forget everything I said earlier."

She sucked in a startled breath. She had to get out of here before she did something they would both regret, like follow her thoughts with action.

"I...er, better go to bed. I know there's a heavy breeding schedule for tomorrow . . .um, with some outside mares. . ." Christie closed her eyes a moment, biting her lips. Each word out of her mouth invoked silent thoughts of intimacy.

"Yeah, bed," he said, not moving, not releasing her. Seconds passed; thick, waiting, excruciating. "Go to bed, Christie." He sounded angry.

"Yes. G-good night." She spun around and rushed blindly forward, bumping against the small table she'd avoided earlier. Together, they reached for the table as it rocked sideways. Garrett's hand brushed against her leg. Christie drew in a startled breath as heat raced to her stomach.

"Sorry," he muttered, then added, "Ah, hell, I'm not."

Despite the fierceness of his voice, the hand that reached to cup the side of her face was gentle. With a groan, Garrett dipped his head toward her. His mouth took possession, his tongue gliding over hers. How many times had she wanted to do that to him? She reciprocated and fire exploded in her chest. She needed air, but wanted only to breathe in his scent and experience the hardness of his body; mint toothpaste and the scent that was all his. She savored his taste as she explored his mouth with lips and tongue.

"You taste good," she murmured, coming up for breath.

Christie pressed her fingers against his chest, tangling them in the hair. It was erotic, letting her fingertips slide again and again over his chest, aware that his breathing was just as erratic as hers.

Garrett cupped her cheeks and held her still when she would have kissed him again. They stared at each other in the dimly lit hallway. "Time to say goodnight," he said, his voice uneven.

She knew he was right, but the words felt like cold water. He pushed her slightly away. She turned with a muted sound of anguish, need churning a hole in her stomach.

Christie knew she was in trouble, these emotions churned inside her, but she didn't care. It had been worth it, experiencing that kiss, touching Garrett. When he pulled her right up against him, it hadn't been a simple kiss any more. Elation and fear tore through her, but she didn't regret the kiss. Even now her stomach was churning with different emotions, a combination of pleasure and pain. She'd wanted to jump off the deep end and pull Garrett in with her.

She'd probably burn in hell, but given half a chance, Christie would reach out to the fire in Garrett again. She wanted it to burn her and that reckless notion frightened her. Maybe that's why she left him and ran toward her room. It was so mysterious, the way two bodies could ignite when they came together.

Shakily, she climbed into bed. Rolling over she pulled the covers tightly around her body. She couldn't stop thinking about what had happened. . . and her last sight of him, his forehead against the wall as he muttered a string of curses.

What was there about Garrett that drew her to him? She felt complete when she was with him, as if she could tell him anything. A foolish notion, she thought bitterly. She knew men did not want to know everything, no matter how much they professed to love and care about a woman. Garrett certainly didn't love her. Lusted for her maybe, not love. She knew some things were better left unsaid — some action better left undone.

Christie felt equally frightened and exhilarated, and hugged the conflicting emotions to her chest.

¤¤

On Saturday, Christie woke to the warmth of the sun heating her body. It felt so good she was tempted to stay under the covers. Unbidden, thoughts of waking beside a man like Garrett entered her mind. It was crazy to allow her heart to follow this attraction, but she had thought of little else lately.

Guilt flared. She had thought of Ellen only fleetingly in the last two days and of Judith, she'd thought hardly at all. How could she let this attraction consume her thoughts when her first priority was to find a resting place for her sister?

Christie rose quickly and dressed.

Garrett had said she could move into the apartment over the barn today so she stashed her clothes in the duffel bag, straightened the bed and walked to the door. Looking back at the room, she saw the wrapped bundle on the dresser.

Christie crossed the room and lifted the urn, moving to sit on the bed with it clutched in her hands. She unwrapped the cloth and stared at the small wooden book urn with its inlaid running horses. Ellen had loved anything of beauty, and Christie knew she would have cherished the beauty of this keepsake urn. Carefully, she rewrapped it and placed it in her bag.

Christie left the quiet house and walked across the dirt driveway toward the barn. Once inside, she walked to the end of the barn aisle and climbed the narrow stairway to the room upstairs. Two stairways led to the apartment, one of which had access through the barn, and one that went down to the large inside arena on the back side of the barn.

She stepped inside the apartment and came to a standstill in amazement.

The light colored hardwood floors had been scrubbed clean of construction debris and dust. A mattress still in plastic leaned up against one wall, and a single bed frame and box spring had been pushed into a corner beside a small dresser and bed table with a lamp. The sloping ceiling made a cozy little nook by the windows and Garrett had already placed a dresser and night stand there.

Blankets, sheets, pillows and a colorful quilt lay folded on top of the dresser. On the opposite side of the room sat a large desk and a straight chair. The sheetrock had been newly painted last week, according to Ally, and Christie liked the pale chocolate color of the walls.

Christie turned as she heard footsteps and voices.

"Do you think Christie will like that?" Garrett asked as he and Hannah walked out of a small room. The bathroom.

As Christie's eyes met Garrett's she blinked slowly, trying to breathe carefully as heat enveloped her. Surely, she didn't have to feel like a teenage girl with a crush. She tore her gaze from Garrett and stared instead at Hannah, who had begun an excited inventory of the room.

"— and Daddy even bought one of those shell-things that makes the bathroom smell nice. We plugged it in, didn't we Daddy?" Hannah looked at her father for confirmation. At Garrett's nod, Hannah rushed on excitedly, "It's supposed to be a surprise. We got up early and cleaned everything."

"I'm touched by the way you both have worked to make this room comfortable." Amazingly, Hannah had turned into a chatterbox, and Christie wondered if it was because she was now out of the house. Perhaps she saw her as more of a threat to her father's attention than Christie had realized.

"Thank you." She found she could smile at him now that the heat had subsided from her face. She was an adult, surely a few kisses wouldn't rock her world off kilter?

"It doesn't look too bad now that it's cleaned up." Garrett nodded with satisfaction, but she wondered what thoughts went on in his head. Christie turned away and surveyed the remainder of the room. Even the small kitchenette had been cleaned. Opening the cupboards, she found pots, dishes and silverware in the drawers.

"I'm sure Ruth can probably find curtains that will fit the windows."

"You've thought of everything." A lump of gratitude tightened her throat. "You've gone to a lot of trouble. It doesn't look like there's much more for me to do."

"There's a couple boxes that have to go in storage. When I get time I'll go through them and get them out of your way. I've packed them in the closet for now."

Christie looked at the closet door. "My stuff doesn't take up much space."

"I've noticed. I have a rug in the attic that I'll bring over. On some mornings it's cool, so you'll need that on the floor. Also, there's a small heater in the wall. I'll show you how to work that."

When Garrett and Hannah finally left Christie walked over to the floor-to-ceiling windows overlooking the yard below. She could see Garrett and Hannah walk toward the house together. Sliding the window open, Christie heard Hannah's delighted giggles as Garrett swung her onto his broad shoulders. Hannah put her cheek against the top of his head. Christie smiled at their loving relationship, and recalled the silky softness of Garrett's hair, the roughness of his whiskered cheek against her own.

"She's leaving soon, isn't she, Daddy?" Hannah's voice floated back to her from below. "Then it will be just you and me. And Uncle Randy."

"That's right." Garrett's voice sounded almost resigned, and that made Christie wonder if she was hearing what she wanted to hear. What if Garrett didn't want her to leave and was too proud to ask her? Would she stay if he asked? Could she stay with a man who was once her sister's husband?

Both she and Garrett were young and healthy, mutual attraction wasn't unusual, except that Garrett still held feelings for Judith. Christie feared she might be grasping at something that wasn't there, something Garrett couldn't give her. Emptiness filled Christie. No one should have to fight a ghost.

With determination, she stepped back and surveyed the large, airy room. Her eyes fell on the bed frame. Carefully, she maneuvered the frame across the floor and set it before the window. Next, she dragged the mattress over and after pulling the plastic off, set it on the metal box spring.

She made up the bed with the soft blue floral sheets, the cotton thermal blanket, and the homespun quilt with bright red and white quilted strips. Stepping back, Christie felt pleased. Each morning she woke up, each night she fell asleep, she would see the hills in the distance, the barns dotting the landscape and Garrett's house. Until it was time to leave.

A short while later she heard footsteps coming up the stairs. She walked out to the small landing and saw Garrett coming up the stairs with a rolled-up rug. Christie stared at the bundle in wonder and stepped back into the room out of his way.

"This rug should cover the middle of the room," he observed, letting one end drop to the floor.

Together, they unrolled it. The fibers had been dyed in several shades of blue and soft rose. "It's gorgeous," she finally managed. "How very generous of you."

Garrett walked toward the door. "There's more," he said over his shoulder. "I had Buddy carry over a rocker."

Garrett walked back out the door and Christie heard a scuffling noise, then he reentered the room carrying a honey-colored wooden rocking chair. The arms were curved like teardrops while the seat and back were woven cane.

Staring at the rocker, Christie was totally overcome. Before she thought about it, Christie blurted, "Was this Judith's?"

Giving her a surprised look, Garrett said, "No. Judith liked more modern furniture."

"Oh." Embarrassed, she turned away.

Garrett's hand was at her elbow, gently turning her back to him. She stared into his light gray eyes.

"You're being so generous." She swallowed hard, blinking to keep back the tears that threatened. "I feel like all I'm doing is taking."

"What's troubling you?" he demanded in a low

voice.

"What you've done here for me means so much."

"Are you sure you're not upset because of the other night when I kissed you? I want to promise it won't happen again but I can't."

"It's not about that."

His grimace said he didn't believe her.

"I'm touched by what you've done. It's so special." Very definitely, Christie added, "And as far as the other night, I feel like it's my fault." She looked up at the ceiling. "Boy, this is awkward. I know you still have feelings for Judith. I'm the one who should have backed off."

Garrett put his hand up to stop her words, his face grim. "We need to talk and get some things straight between us." His light colored eyes met hers, the sincerity in their depths unchanged from the first day she had met him. Garrett pulled the rocking chair around and indicated she should sit. Christie did so, sitting with her hands pressing into her thighs, tension gripping her.

He pulled out the desk chair and straddled it. The action pulled his jeans tight against his thighs. Christie quickly looked up at his face.

"Judith died almost nineteen months ago. Hannah was only six and a half." Garrett met her gaze directly. "Judith was leaving me the day she died. She drove too fast and was killed in the accident. Somehow, Hannah survived."

Christie was stunned. "My sister was leaving?"

"Our marriage had been over for awhile. We lived in the same house, but there was nothing there. I guess I let it go on so long because I didn't want to admit to failure." The regret in his voice touched her. "And maybe I was too busy."

He looked down at his hands. "In looking back, I know we should never have married. We were so wild, neither of us ready for the commitment that marriage brings. Judith loved to travel. She hated being tied down. I accused her of thinking responsibility was a dirty word.

"Back then all the money I had was tied up in the horses. I knew once my two-year olds started making a name for themselves on the track things could snowball.

"After she left, it got a lot worse before I pulled myself together. When I started the farm, all I had were six broken down mares with great bloodlines and one unproven stallion. I took a chance and bought the mares at a bankruptcy auction. They were passed over by other bidders, but good bloodlines don't disappear just because of age.

"I was certain I had a winning combination. I just needed to convince the racing world and the way to do that was by winning. Along the way I took some gambles. One gamble I went too far and lost a lot of our money and almost lost my farm. About that time Judith got tired of waiting for the dream to come true. She was very unhappy. I found out later she was ... seeing other men."

"Oh, Garrett." Compassion filled Christie. That must be the most painful betrayal. "I know what it must cost you to tell me that."

He gave a stiff nod. "After she died, I had a recurring dream or maybe you'd call it a nightmare. In it, I knew that if I'd stopped her that last day, she'd still be alive. I'm the one that found her in the crumpled mess of the car. It still churns my guts into knots."

Compassionately, Christie moved to kneel before him. She cradled one of his hands with her own, the sting of tears in her eyes. "Oh, Garrett, I'm so sorry."

"That's how your sister died."

"We're each responsible for our own actions. Judith chose her course, she left. I have to believe she found something better here with you. But in the end, something was still driving her. It wasn't your fault."

Garrett clenched his jaw. "Hannah still suffers flashbacks from that accident. She rarely talks about it. For weeks afterwards the doctors weren't sure she'd talk at all."

"That poor kid, to have gone through something like that."

"You know I'm not Hannah's biological father, but when Judith and I first married I insisted on adopting her."

Christie's throat tightened with sympathy. "I understand how very much you love Hannah. I'm growing to love her also."

Gently, his fingers threaded through the hair at the base of her skull as he watched her intently. "What about you, Christie?"

"What do you mean?" she asked, wary now as she sat back on her heels.

"I understand you wanted to find Judith, but what made you leave everything behind and take to the road? What secrets are you hiding?" The questions were direct. Garrett had revealed his hurt to her, how could she not reciprocate? Suddenly, there was nowhere else to hide.

∞ Chapter Eight ∞

Secrets. That word alone made knots form in Christie's gut. All her life she had harbored secrets of one kind or another. She had never let them all out at once. A little at a time, but never all at once so any one person knew all of the secrets she grew up with. Except Ellen. Maybe Judith.

Christie looked at Garrett, read the honest inquiry on his face. "You may think you want to know, but no one really wants to be burdened with another person's secrets. Not even you."

She was too aware of Garrett's closeness. She wanted to be cradled in the shelter of his arms, but she kept her hands still in her lap. "You're a good man, Garrett. You wouldn't understand the stark reality of my life."

"Christie, tell me why you're all alone."

Christie considered his words, holding her breath. What harm would it do to tell Garrett? She would be gone in a few weeks anyway. Maybe she could tell him some of the secrets. She stood up and moved across the room, rubbing her arms against a sudden shiver.

"Almost a year ago my sister Ellen found out she was sick." Christie remembered the day in detail, how murky it had been outside. "No words can convey the horror and disbelief I felt when the doctors diagnosed Ellen with leukemia." She fell silent, giving herself a moment. "Ellen was optimistic. I was terrified. I'd cry at the drop of a hat. One minute I'd be okay, the next it would come over me. I'd hide them from her. . .in the bathroom, my bedroom, until it passed. It seemed like it happened all the time in the beginning. Ellen and I have always been together. We had each other to lean on while growing up. From that day in the doctor's office I knew our lives would never be the same."

"What about your parents?"

She looked at him. "We weren't close to my parents," she said carefully. "My aunt Rose raised us until I was ten, then she died."

"Why not your parents?"

Christie rubbed the tense muscles in her neck. "My parents had problems and the State decided my aunt provided a more stable living environment. When aunt Rose died we went back to live with my parents until I turned sixteen."

"They resolved their problems?"

"The State thought so." Christie shrugged. "It was mostly just Ellen and me. Of course later on there was Ellen's husband. Near the end he left her."

"He walked out on your sister?" Garrett's jaw

was tight.

Christie paced the floor, needing movement to expel the nervous energy surging through her. "Yes," she said in a low voice. "He walked out about six months before she died. I hated him for abandoning Ellen." Christie felt again the tide of anger, the hopelessness. All her life, Ellen had been abandoned by one person or another. "I think I still hate him," she admitted starkly. "It colors every thought I have about him. As bad as it sounds, every time I speak to him I don't let him forget what he did." She couldn't help the way she felt. "I hate when I say the words that will hurt him, but I can't seem to stop."

She lifted her chin. "I kept working and for a while, Ellen seemed to be okay. We prayed it had gone into remission. Then one day, everything toppled around us. I got a call at work. Ellen had been rushed to the hospital with a high temperature. From there, it was all downhill."

"Did she come out of the hospital?"

"She insisted on coming home. I had nurses during the day but she grew progressively weaker. About that time Darrell, her husband, left. He couldn't handle seeing her fade a little more each day." Those had been his words before he'd left for good. Ellen had accepted his leaving, and Christie had never understood her total forgiveness. "Darrell and I never really got along, but that sealed it for me."

"So you put your life on hold?"

Christie frowned at him. "I was going to school and working. I had to quit. Ellen needed me."

"So you left after she died and ended up on the

road?"

Tears filmed her eyes. They clung there and did not fall. Garrett's face wavered before her.

"Ellen wanted me to find Judith. She said as a family we should reconnect. It was really important to her. I left two months after my sister died, the day after I lost custody of Eric, her son. I knew he and Darrell needed time together and everywhere in my apartment were reminders of my sister. The books she liked to read, the puzzles she worked on near the end. I had promised Ellen we would beat this. I promised I would take care of her son, and it was all a lie. I failed at everything I promised. I couldn't do any of it."

"You couldn't keep your sister from dying," he said urgently.

"In my head, I know that." Her heart didn't listen to her head.

"So Eric is with his father?"

Christie nodded, clenching her fists and taking several deep breaths. "Yes, it's better for him that way."

Garrett moved closer. She felt the heat emanating from his body. She wanted to feel his strength.

"On the surface that sounds like a natural conclusion. Does his father let you see him?"

"He said I could. But I left. I ran." She swung around. "I gathered the money I had left and packed a bag. I found myself at the bus station. I hopped the first bus leaving the station. Later, somewhere in Michigan, I guess, I looked at the bus schedule. I saw Kentucky listed as one of the destinations. I remembered the promise I'd made to find Judith. I suddenly knew what I had to do for my sister. I bought a ticket."

"And here you are." Slowly, he put his arms around her and gathered her close. Christie closed her eyes, wanting to forget herself in his hard, comforting arms. Garrett's chin rested lightly on the top of her head.

"You said you lived with your parents for a few years. Did another family member take you in after that?"

Christie tensed and pulled away. "The past again." She shook her head. "I got a job when I was sixteen. Ellen and I moved into a tiny studio apartment."

She could see the questions forming in his eyes.

"You supported your sister and yourself?"

Christie nodded, her mouth completely dry. "Ellen was sick a lot as a kid, and she had trouble keeping jobs." She knew the next questions would be the hardest to answer.

"Did you quit school?"

"No. I worked at night in a dance club." She went on before she lost her nerve. "I danced for tips at a strip club."

Garrett's eyes still met hers, but she couldn't read his expression.

She gave him a level glance. "I did what I had to do. I'll never apologize for surviving."

"Your parents?" She could see a white line around his mouth.

She shrugged. "With us gone, there were two less mouths to feed. We were glad to be out of there and they didn't miss us."

Garrett cursed and turned away.

Christie watched him warily, noting the clenched fists and the way he kept his shoulders rigid.

She had done what she could to feed her and Ellen.

"If I'd been around I would have horsewhipped your parents," he said fiercely, his voice deep with anger. "For the way they failed all three of you."

All three of them.

Christie blinked in surprise, but then chided herself. Why be surprised that his anger was for her, Ellen and Judith? Garrett would never let his children fend for themselves. Right now he was raising another woman's child.

"What are you going to do now?" he asked briskly.

Christie cleared her throat, deeply affected by his anger on her behalf. "I need to find a final resting place for my sister."

Garrett's brow furrowed. "What do you mean?"

She looked at him warily. "Ellen made arrangements to be cremated. I was given her ashes and I have them in a keepsake urn, it's a beautiful wooden book with running horses inlaid on the cover. It was her last wish that together Judith and I find the right place to scatter them. I've been looking since I arrived in Kentucky." Christie saw the guarded look on his face. If he thought she was crazy, now was the time to find out. "Darrell thinks I'm crazy," she said flatly.

"That's why you were so upset that first day when you couldn't find your duffel bag?"

"Yes. I thought I'd come all this way and then to lose the ashes. . .." She drew in a deep, quivering breath.

"What a task you've set yourself."

Had she expected him to tell her it was a crazy idea as Darrell had suggested?

"There's nothing else I can do." Christie felt exhausted.

"Even though you and Ellen weren't close to your parents, don't you think they should be contacted and share some of the responsibility?"

"No!" Christie shook her head vehemently. She pushed back the emotion that clouded her when she thought of her parents. "No," she said more quietly. "This is something I'll do on my own. I owe it to my sister. I wanted Darrell to be a part of this final goodbye, at least for Eric's sake, but he thinks I'm on a fool's errand. He's furious I even considered doing something like this."

"I can understand how much you want to honor her memory, but all I'm saying is let someone else share the burden."

Christie paced the floor. "There's no one else, only me. That's how it's always been. I won't let her down," she added fiercely.

Again.

The word was inside her head but she had never said it out loud. She had let her sister down and this was a small way toward making amends. That was a secret she couldn't tell anyone, not even Garrett. How could she admit to letting down the one person who had truly loved her?

"I appreciate you letting me vent all this, Garrett,

but I know what I have to do. I promise it won't interfere with my work here. Physical labor is a big change from what I'm used to but I love being around the horses. Maybe that's what I need, not to worry about the rest of the garbage in my life."

"What kind of work did you do?" he asked quietly.

"I worked as a freelance stenographer for the courts." She worked for the same court system that her mother repeatedly violated, but that wasn't something she wanted to admit to Garrett. Christie chewed her lip. Secrets, so many secrets.

"Listen, Christie, if I can help, I will. Take the truck whenever you need it."

"I appreciate that."

"You asked me before where Judith was buried. I can take you there."

She drew a deep breath. "Thank you. I've thought about it, but I'm just not ready."

Footsteps sounded on the stairs leading to her apartment. Hannah suddenly appeared in the door.

"Hi Hannah," Christie said.

Hannah just stood there watching them, and Christie could almost see the wheels turning in the child's head. Did she think Christie was trying to steal her father away?

Hannah shifted her weight onto one foot and stood with a hand on her hip. "Ruth was looking for you, Daddy."

Garrett glanced over at his daughter. "Is it urgent?"

Hannah seemed to debate that a moment, her gaze shooting over to Christie. Vigorously, she shook her head. "Yeah. She needs you right away."

"I'll be along in a minute, Hannah." He walked across the apartment. "You'll still come for meals at the house?" he asked Christie.

Christie saw Hannah's mouth turn down.

"Yes, Garrett, thank you. Thanks for everything. You too, Hannah," she added. Hannah's eyes widened in surprise.

"You're welcome," Hannah muttered. "Do you really like it?" she added, a tad of uncertainty creeping into her voice.

"I do, and I know your Dad couldn't have done all this without your help." She smiled at Hannah. "I bet he realizes just how lucky he is to have a young lady like you to help him out."

Hannah frowned a bit, clearly uncertain as to how to respond.

"Let's get out of Christie's way," Garrett said. "See you later." With his hands on Hannah's shoulders, he ushered her through the door.

When he would have closed the door, Christie said, "You can leave the door open."

"You'll have more privacy and quiet with it closed," he said.

Christie shook her head. She didn't explain it was a strange quirk of hers. As he and Hannah left, she turned toward the window. How could she expect anyone to understand her need not to feel closed in, the need to see to her sister's ashes, the need to move on with her life. . ..

She did want to move on, but with a deep sigh, she realized she was getting more and more entrenched in life at Winding Creek Farms. Maybe the only thing Garrett felt for her was physical attraction, but for Christie it went deeper. He knew how to treat people right and he hadn't seemed disgusted with the decisions she'd made. There had been a sense of understanding between them.

Christie ran her fingertips over the smooth wood of the rocking chair. The use of such a treasure meant a lot to her. Perhaps too much. Christie wondered what kind of heartache she was letting herself in for. Why did she care about a child who wanted her gone and a man who was determined to remain alone?

¤¤

Hannah held onto Garrett's hand as they left Christie's apartment. As they crossed the yard Garrett lifted a hand to Ally, who was busy with one of the yearlings in the round training pen beside the barn.

"Do you know why Ruth wanted to see me?"

Hannah suddenly released his hand and hung back. "Um, she probably doesn't need you anymore. You were up there a long time. I'm going to play on my swings, Daddy." Hannah turned to dash off.

Before she could Garrett caught her arm and gently turned her to face him. "Hannah."

She remained silent, not quite meeting his eyes. Garrett went down on his haunches, concerned by the stiff resistance of Hannah's body. "Ruth wasn't looking for me, was she?" he asked quietly.

After a slight hesitation, Hannah shook her head no.

"But you wanted me to leave Christie's apartment, didn't you?"

She looked down at her red boots. "Yes."

"Why?"

She lifted her head and he saw the film of moisture in her eyes. "We fixed up the place for her, Daddy. Now she can be over there and not in our house. You're supposed to be in our house with me."

Garrett tried to search for the right words of assurance for his daughter, not certain what they might be. "Hannah, I know we've had a lot of changes in the last year or so and sometimes change can be pretty scary. It's like a hard bump you have to climb up over. It's okay to be scared."

"You don't get scared," she scoffed.

"Of course I do, honey, but I also realize change can be okay. If somebody needs help, I'll give them a hand. It won't take any of my attention away from you. You're my daughter, my first concern, but sometimes others hit that hard bump in the road and need me. Do you understand?"

"I guess. Can I go play?"

Garrett let out a deep, resigned sigh, uncertain if he'd gotten through to his daughter. "Go ahead. I'll be in my tool shed."

Hannah ran away from him toward her swing set. Garrett followed, then walked past her to the tool shed behind the house.

He needed some mental stimulation right now. Maybe if he fooled around with his dirt bike it would take his mind off everything else. As he pulled his tools out of the shed where he kept the bike, he kept thinking of what Christie had revealed about her earlier life. He kicked some rags aside, still furious over her parents' obvious neglect. How does anyone abandon a child? Christie and Ellen had had no one but each other and they had been children. What about Judith?

When he'd met her she'd been full of neurosis and barely veiled insecurities. Did he want to go that route again, care about someone who came with a busload of unresolved baggage? Judith's sister. In the end, Judith hadn't been able to overcome her past, and it had helped to tear them apart. Christie was cut from the same cloth . . . same background.

What kind of desperation did it take to leave home one day and head out to unfamiliar territory so you could keep a promise? Garrett sensed there was more that Christie wasn't telling him. What would it take for her to trust him with the full truth?

Garrett adjusted a brake cable, then pulled himself up abruptly. Why was he worrying about Christie? She planned on leaving when the month was up. So what if she had problems. Everyone had them. There was no sense getting worried about her plans. He had his own agenda. Garrett looked at Hannah playing on the swings. He needed to keep her safe and secure. She was coming along so well, he wouldn't chance a setback by changing anything at the farm. . .especially not taking a lover when Hannah still felt the loss of her mother so keenly.

Christie's voice was in his head. *I did what I had to do to survive.*

He felt humbled. He'd never been so desperate. Even when he'd almost drowned in debt, he'd known he would survive, even if meant working somewhere for minimum wage. From the time he was sixteen he'd had a part time job for spending money. His parents had provided for him. He hadn't worried about rent or if he had enough money for a gallon of milk.

Garrett started the bike and revved it up a few times. When he cut the motor, he heard a vehicle drive into the yard. Randy drove by in a dark blue pickup and gave him a salute, then parked by the exercise ring where Ally still worked with the horse.

"Hi Ally!" Randy called out. "How's my favorite redhead today?"

With amusement Garrett caught the "yeah right" expression Ally tossed Randy's way.

"You're distracting my help," Garrett said mildly, wiping grease from his hands. "Cut it out unless you're serious."

Randy made his way over to him. "Serious as a heart attack. What's up? You look like you've got a load of trouble on your back." Bo Peep came rushing over to Randy and he bent down to pat the dog, then squinted at the bike. "Need some help with the bike?"

"No." Garrett dropped a wrench back in his toolbox and looked at his brother with a raised brow. "You're becoming quite a regular around here. Two, three times in one week. I feel honored." He grinned.

"Am I supposed to call first?" Randy drawled, his smile crooked. "I wanted to show you my new truck."

Together they walked over to the truck to check out all its features. "It's a beauty," Garrett said, running his hand along the pickup bed fender. "Quite an improvement on the last one."

"Yeah, I decided I needed more reliable transportation."

"You're getting quite responsible these days," Garrett said dryly.

"Sometimes you've got to shake things up a little," Randy stared across the yard to where Ally worked the horse. He turned his attention back to Garrett. "I also wanted to tell you about Les. I've been nosing around. He's not working and no one really seems to know what he's up to during the day."

Garrett swiped a sleeve over his forehead. "Come on over into the shade."

Under the shade of a big Maple tree behind the house Garrett dropped down into a lawn chair and indicated to Randy the hammock he'd hung from the tree that morning. Bo Peep settled beside him and watched him with her big brown eyes. He fondled her silky ears and glanced over at Hannah still playing on her swing.

Randy sprawled in the mesh hammock, booted feet crossed. Tipping his hat back he regarded him intently. "So what's going on that you're keeping track of Les?"

"He stopped here one day for Kim's check. He'd started drinking and was acting pretty belligerent. I've been keeping in touch with Kim to make sure she's all right."

"I'll have the guys swing by their place on a regular basis."

"Thanks. I knew I could count on you."

"So, what else is going on?" Randy asked.

Garrett plucked a blade of grass and chewed on

it. Thoughtfully, he regarded his brother. "It's business as usual."

Randy's glance was skeptical. "What's up with Christie?"

"What do you mean?"

"Ruth mentioned she moved into the apartment over the barn."

"Now you're tapping Ruth for information? Next thing you'll be telling me Sam joined the local square dancer's club. Since when did Ruth become such a fountain of information?" Garrett asked with resignation.

"Since there's someone here at the farm who might be able to loosen you up, big brother. Hannah called me this morning and couldn't wait to spill the news — I sense she's a bit relieved that Christie's over in the barn."

"Yeah, there's a bit of a problem with Hannah. Nothing I can't handle. As to the other, I don't need loosening up. I'd appreciate it if you stopped grilling everyone about my business."

"Do I detect a touch of evasiveness?" Garrett couldn't miss the smile in his brother's voice. But he could damn well ignore it.

"Hannah's not happy anytime someone new comes in. I suppose with Christie staying in the house she was even more possessive of me." He shrugged. "Anyway, Christie is leaving in a few weeks."

"Have you told Hannah Christie is her aunt?"

"No."

"Don't you think it's about time?"

His jaw firmed. "I will when I'm ready."

Randy squinted his eyes and looked over toward Ally. "Ally likes Christie and Buddy swears Christie is the next best thing to an angel. She's been helping him with some kind of school paper. Legal stuff." Randy threw him an intent stare. "What do you think?"

"I think you ask too many questions and you're damned nosy."

"Is that so? Well if you're not interested, maybe Christie would like to go out with the fun loving brother."

"Do you know one?"

Randy just smiled.

The idea of Christie and Randy together put Garrett in a bad mood. "I think you ought to narrow your concentration to one woman."

Randy blew on his fingernails and pretended to polish them on his T-shirt front, but Garrett suspected some of it was mere bravado.

"Nothing wrong with playing the field," Randy said. "Speaking of which, how about a double date this weekend?"

"No."

"It'd be fun," Randy said patiently.

"Wouldn't that ruin your plan to use the Harley's seductive powers?"

"I can use it another time. What do you say? Do you want to go out Saturday? Remember how we used to —" Randy stopped mid-sentence, as if suddenly realizing he'd let his mouth run away.

Deliberately, Garrett finished the sentence for him. "How we used to double date, you and your girlfriend, me and Judith? How could I forget?" It seemed like a hundred years ago. "Thanks for the invite, but no thanks. I'm not into reliving the past."

"Garrett." Randy sat forward. "You can't use Judith as a measure for every woman."

Garrett gave his brother a narrow-eyed glance. "That'd be a pretty damned short measure. Anyway, it's past history."

"Judith was selfish and not meant for the long run. Cut yourself some slack and have fun."

"What — with her sister? Leave it alone."

Just then Garrett noticed Christie exit the barn and walk over to join Ally at the corral.

Randy glanced at the girls. "You could ask her to stay longer. How's she doing in the barn?"

"Fine."

"No complications from the accident?"

"None that she admits to."

"I'll ask her if she wants to do a double date," Randy said blithely, uncrossing his boots.

Garrett shot him a narrow-eyed glance. "I'm past the age where I need my brother to get me a date."

"Your choice," Randy murmured. "I'm going to start some fun. That Ally needs some excitement in her life."

"Why don't you tell her that. . .I'm sure she'll appreciate it."

Undaunted, Randy rose to his feet. "Maybe I will." He sauntered toward Ally and Christie.

As Garrett watched his brother picked up a section of the water hose Ally was using on the horse. He kinked it so the flow of water almost stopped. Ally saw him and voiced a protest. Randy released the hose and the force of the water caught

Ally across the legs, soaking her pants and boots.

"Randy McIntyre!" she yelled, "if I didn't have hold of this horse, I-I'd give it to you good."

Randy wagged a finger at her. "Promises, promises."

Garrett followed in his brother's wake. Knowing all hell would likely break loose with Ally's temper when it came to Randy, he ducked around behind Christie and relieved Ally of the horse's lead line. "I'll take Houdini out of harm's way while you take care of my brother," he said. Garrett led the horse into the barn, laughing when Randy yelled as Ally turned the hose on him.

Garrett settled the horse in his stall. He could hear female squeals and his brother's protests. It sounded like even the dog had joined in with continuous barking.

When Garrett walked back outside the trio was still at it. Randy had hooked up a second hose and stood on one side with Christie and Ally squared off against him. They were all soaked to the skin. Bo Peep stood halfway between the house and barn, hopping back and forth and barking excitedly.

"What is this, kindergarten?" Garrett asked.

Garrett had only a moment to notice Christie's white T-shirt plastered to her body before a blast of water hit him square in the face. Spluttering with disbelief and the shock of the icy well water, he looked furiously at the culprit.

Christie held the hose. She froze, watching him with wide eyes. Garrett put his hands up to his eyes and swiped at the water dripping down his face.

"I'm going to get you for that," he promised,

giving her a menacing scowl.

With a squeal, Christie jerked the hose up and sprayed him again. Quickly, she ducked to the side, dragging the hose with her.

"Garrett!" Randy indicated the bucket on the ground.

Garrett moved across the now muddy ground as Christie kept the water spray trained on his back and shoulders. By now he was so wet the spray didn't matter. In fact it felt good. He picked up the rubber bucket beside Randy and looked down into it. It was two-thirds full of water and had a skim of horsehair along the top.

Garrett advanced on her, grinning no doubt like a fool.

"Put down the hose," he said softly, turning his head quickly to avoid another blast of water.

"Not a chance." She shook her head in vehement refusal, her wet hair whipping around her face. She continued to walk backwards but finally came to the end of the hose length. Garrett knew he had her.

"Give it up," he said, threatening her with the water in the bucket. Bo Peep barked at his heels, adding to the confusion.

"Never!" Christie shouted, spraying him in the chest.

Garrett lifted the bucket and poured the water over her.

Christie spluttered and squawked, squeezing her eyes tightly closed but still keeping her fingers clenched on the water nozzle.

At that same moment Randy lobbed a handful of mud and hit Ally in the chest.

"What a foul trick!" Ally yelled. "This means war."

Garrett laughed so hard he dropped the bucket. Randy wasn't any better. He kept laughing as he and Ally wrestled with the hose until he let her pry it from his hand. Ally and Christie now had complete control of the water. Garrett and Randy stood there and howled with laughter as they were squirted from both sides.

Finally, when his sides hurt from laughing so hard, Garrett looked at Randy and gasped, "What do you think, should we do the old McIntyre rush?"

"Great idea," Randy said, shoving the hair out of his eyes. He was a muddy sight. Looking down at his own clothes Garrett realized he was the same.

"Now!" Garrett said. He rushed Christie and Randy rushed Ally. In the ensuing wrestle to take back the water hose, Garrett and Christie slid on the muddy ground and began to fall. Garrett twisted so he didn't crush Christie. With a whoomph sound, Garrett landed with his back in the mud, Christie sprawled on top of him, her laughing face near his.

He stared at the wet, bedraggled woman plastered to him and all laughter stilled. Every part of her body was making itself known to him as slender curves intimately pressed against him. His body had felt tired earlier but now he felt most definitely full of energy.

Looking at the sparkle in Christie's eyes, Garrett felt in that moment as if the world narrowed down to soft brown eyes, milky skin with a faint scatter of freckles and full, red lips. He couldn't resist. He didn't think. He lifted his head out of the mud and kissed those red lips. Realizing what he'd done, he let his head drop back to the ground. Christie's eyes widened and a flush touched her now serious face.

"Well, hell," Garrett muttered, his glance fixed on her mouth. He had a notion to kiss her again and lifted his head to do just that.

∞ Chapter Nine ∞

"Hell indeed, Garrett McIntyre! What is all the noise about? My Lord, I thought I needed to call emergency services."

Garrett shifted his focus. Ruth stood on the outskirts of the muddy mess they'd made, a stern expression on her face. Sam, beside her, was struggling to keep a straight face.

Just then Bo Peep appeared beside Ruth and started her excited barking again. Christie looked at the dog and said, "Hush!"

Garrett said, "Bo Peep, that's enough." With a small whine, the dog lay down and stared at him, chin resting on her paws.

Garrett groaned. He would never live down playing in the mud. Christie scrambled to get up, her knee inadvertently catching him in the groin. Garrett groaned again.

"Sorry," she muttered, low enough so only he

could hear. She got to her feet, almost falling again as her foot slipped in the slick mud.

Garrett got to his feet and helped her right herself. He looked around. "Where's Ally and Randy?" They'd disappeared.

Ruth crossed her arms. "All I see are you two playing in the mud."

"I think they made off for the creek behind the barn," Sam muttered.

Garrett kept a straight face. "Well, it's time I got cleaned up. It's been a long day and I think I need a shower." He looked at Christie with mild inquiry, as if they weren't covered from hair to toe with drying mud. "What about you?"

"I'm going to do the same," she said, struggling to keep a straight face.

Garrett flicked mud from his shirt collar.

Ruth marched away, but not before Garrett had seen the glint of laughter in her eyes.

Sam merely shook his head as he headed in the direction of the barn.

A bit more soberly, Garrett began to rewind the hose. That's when he noticed several of his employees standing at the edge of the yard and in the barn entryway.

Garrett threw Christie a quick glance, but she was busy rewinding the other hose. Knowing the damage had been done to his serious, hard-assed image, Garrett gave the hose in his hand a few experimental squirts. "Anybody else?" he challenged the onlookers. There were a few laughs, but no takers. After some good-natured ribbing everyone wandered off to their cars.

He might have made a fool of himself in front of his employees, but he discovered he didn't care. It had been worth it to see the laughter on Christie's face. For once, Garrett wished he had Randy's easy manner with women. He might have persuaded Christie to go down to the creek as Randy had done with Ally. Who knows what might have developed from there.

Ruefully, he looked at the brown streaks of mud on his clothes, then pulled his shirttails out of his pants and yanked the material off his shoulders.

"You've got mud on your neck," Christie said.

Garrett twisted around to find her behind him. She reached out a slim hand and rubbed at a spot just above his collarbone. The touch of her fingers against his skin was disturbing, warm. After a moment he grabbed her fingers and held them still against his chest. "It's okay, I'm going to take a shower." He cleared his throat, feeling as if her fingers were burning a hole in his chest. Her fingers moved beneath his, gently stroking the hair on his chest. Garrett was very conscious of the rise and fall of her breasts, the faint sound of her breathing. He stared into her eyes and took a step closer.

Before he let rational thought intrude, he bent down and lightly touched his tongue to her lips. Christie closed her eyes, rested her other hand on his shoulder and he swore she stopped breathing.

In the next instant she stepped back. He saw her gaze shift and she stared behind him, then lifted her startled gaze to his. "I have to get cleaned up." She turned and hurried toward the barn.

Garrett knocked some of the caked mud from his

jeans. Reaching down, he gently caressed the dog's golden head, aware of the way his nerves jumped over the kiss he'd shared with Christie. "Come on, Bo Peep."

When he turned toward the house, he saw his daughter standing there. "Hey kiddo."

Hannah frowned at him and crossed her arms. "I saw you and Christie." Garrett read the mixed emotions on her face: Anger, sulkiness, perhaps fear. "You're full of mud."

Garrett grinned, ignoring the first part of her statement. "Yeah, I know. I can't believe I forgot how much fun it is to play in the mud."

Her eyes grew very wide. "But — but Daddy's don't play in mud."

Slowly, his heart rate came back down to normal.

"Christie's leaving soon, isn't she, Daddy? I think she should go back to her own place."

Garrett surmised now that out of the house wasn't far enough for Hannah. He lifted a brow as the storm signals deepened in Hannah's blue eyes and the tight, straight line of her mouth. "Christie's leaving when Kim is ready to come back to work."

"She should leave now." Hannah clenched her fists.

Garrett motioned Hannah over to the chair he had earlier vacated in the back yard. "Hannah, come and sit down with me a minute. We really need to talk."

Stubbornly, she shook her head and crossed her arms tightly over her chest.

"Hannah," he said sternly, pointing to the chair.

Reluctantly, she thumped her bottom down and

slouched in the chair.

Garrett pulled a chair close to hers and watched her intently, but she didn't lift her head. "Why don't you like Christie?"

Hannah shrugged and started playing with the webbing on the chair.

Garrett waited, feeling the mud soak through his jeans and drip down into his boots. He shifted his feet and stared at the water now puddling beneath him.

"Daddy, I'm hungry and Ruth made my most favorite special dinner tonight." Hannah's voice bordered on a whine and she jutted her lower lip.

"Then you'd better give my question some thought and answer it." She looked at him in surprise and the corners of her mouth quivered, but Garrett knew he couldn't give in. "Ruth made cheesecake with strawberry sauce, too," he added. "So tell me, has Christie been mean to you?"

"No."

"Did she make you eat that terrible jelly roll she baked last week?" Garrett put his face down by her soft pink cheek. "I know . . . when you sleep she goes in your room and plays with your favorite dolls."

Hannah looked up, startled. She began to laugh. "Daddy!"

"Well, I'm just trying to figure out why you don't like her."

"I don't want her to be my mommy!" she blurted, all laughter wiped from her face. She hunched her shoulders again.

The breath stopped in his lungs. Shit! Garrett put his hand on her shoulder but she twisted sideways and clenched her small fists.

Garrett took several deep breaths, trying to figure out the fears in Hannah's head. Finally, he rubbed the back of his neck. "No one will replace your mom," he said bluntly, "and as sad as it makes us, it was time for her to go to heaven."

"No!" She shook her head. "It wasn't her time." Her voice went real low. "It wasn't. It was all my fault." The tears suddenly fell on her cheeks. "Daddy . . . I made the car crash. It's my fault Mommy died!"

Garrett felt such shock as he stared at the torment on his daughter's face. The dark look in her eyes would haunt him a long time. "No honey."

"I cried and cried because I didn't want to leave you and Mommy said she'd take me back home, but the car crashed."

Garrett swallowed hard. "It wasn't your fault. Sometimes adults make mistakes." He spoke gently but firmly, even though his guts were twisting up inside. "Why didn't you tell me this before? We could have talked about it."

"I've been real bad and I always get into trouble, but not on purpose, Daddy. I thought if you knew, you wouldn't want me anymore. I'm not really your little girl."

Garrett knelt at his daughter's feet. "Let's get this straight. You are my girl and you always will be. I will love you forever and ever, no matter what." Gently, he tilted her chin. "No matter what," he added fiercely. "Do you understand?"

Watching him intently, she slowly nodded. Garrett touched a teardrop hanging on the end of her nose.

"As far as you not liking Christie," he said firmly, "it really has nothing to do with being disloyal to your mom's memory. Someday I may decide to get married, but it won't change how I love you." Garrett placed his palm over his heart. "I swear, this old heart of mine is big enough for you and a few others. Do you think I love Grandma and Randy?" he asked.

Wide-eyed, Hannah nodded.

"Well, I love Grandma and Randy and you. That's three people I have room to love."

"What about Ruth and Sam and Bo Peep?" she demanded breathlessly.

Garrett began to smile. "Ruth and Sam and Bo Peep, too."

"And all your horses, Daddy. You love them too."

He squeezed her fingers gently. "That's right. I've got a pretty big heart. Even though I love all those people and all the animals, I still love you."

Hannah squeezed his fingers fiercely. "I love you too, Daddy, forever and ever and always."

"There's one more thing you should know, sweetheart." Garrett knew it was now or never. "The reason Christie came here was to find your mom. You see, she's not here to try and take your mama's place. Christie is your mom's little sister. She's your aunt."

Hannah took a moment to think that over. "Are you sure, Daddy? They don't look at all alike."

He nodded. "I'm sure. She wanted to stay and get to know you. You see, she never knew about you until she came here."

"Just like we didn't know about her." The wonderment in his daughter's voice tightened

Garrett's throat.

"That's right. So I guess it's kind of like a gift, finding out you have an aunt."

"You're pretty smart, Daddy."

Garrett laughed, not having expected that. "Let's get going or Ruth will have our hides."

"I never had an aunt before, huh, Daddy?"

"No, you haven't."

Hannah jumped to her feet and then ran up the back steps to the kitchen. At the door, she did a little dance and then planted her feet. The warning look she threw him was very adult. "Are you going to take your boots off?"

"I guess I'd better."

"You got mud on my pink shirt too, Daddy. Do you think Ruth will yell at you?" she added with barely suppressed glee. "This time you're the one in trouble, not me."

"I might as well go inside and get it over with."

Hannah held the screen door partially open. As if they were co-conspirators, she peeked out at him and said in a stage whisper, "Hurry, Daddy. Ruth's not in the kitchen."

"Says who, little missy?" demanded his housekeeper from somewhere beyond the kitchen.

Garrett looked at Hannah, hiding his grin. "Busted," he said, not minding at all. For the first time, he actually felt like he'd made some headway with his daughter.

¤ ¤

"Randy, I don't know why I let you talk me into coming down here!" Ally stepped back from the narrow creek and dabbed at her mud-crusted clothes. "It's no use. I'm a mess."

Randy grinned. "You came because you find me irresistible."

"This shirt is ruined and I don't know how I'll get these jeans clean." She was determined to ignore the sizzle burning her stomach. She'd been crazy to come down here with him. Crazy, but oh so tempted.

"I'll buy you another one."

Distractedly, Ally looked around the sun-dappled woods. "I'd better get back. Everyone will wonder where we are."

"Who cares?" Randy lazily played with the strands of fiery red hair resting on her shoulder. "Last time I knew we were both single."

Ally pushed wet hair off her forehead. "I care," she muttered. The twinkle in Randy's appealing blue eyes was hard to ignore. "Damn you anyway. You really think you are irresistible." It wasn't fair that one man could be so attractive. "I won't be labeled one of Randy McIntyre's women," she added tartly.

Randy clutched his chest dramatically. "Ouch. You really lay it on the line. I thought you cared about me."

"I do care about you, but Randy, you're the type who'll be a major heartache in any girl's life. I had enough of that with my ex-husband. My next birthday I'll be thirty three, seven years older than you. I'm not looking for just a date anymore." She rolled her eyes in good-natured exasperation at his puzzled frown. "Randy, we're nothing alike. I'm not into the party scene."

His eyes grew serious and intent and Ally found it hard to look at him and not want him.

"I haven't been into it for a while either. Give me a chance, Ally. You might find we'll have a great time."

Ally swallowed the dryness in her throat, her resolve weakening. She'd never seen him so serious. The Randy she was used to always had a joke and a ready smile. "Randy, you're a nice guy — but you collect women like trophies." Darn! Her argument sounded like it was getting weaker.

"Not anymore."

"I'd have to think about." Was she crazy? Give him an inch he'd take a mile. . ..

Randy leaned close and dropped a kiss on her mouth.

Ally stared at his face so close, his expression very, very serious. Almost against her will she leaned forward for another kiss. As she touched his mouth Ally found she liked it too much. She was suddenly full of heat and wanting. Ally pulled back. With despair, she watched the flecks in Randy's eyes deepen and the funny, squirmy feeling in her stomach intensified.

"I'm not into casual," she said. "Everything about you is casual." Resisting the urge to touch her burning lips, she took several steps back the way they'd come.

"I can change," he said.

Ally sent him a doubtful look over her shoulder. "I'm interested in someone who'll be around for the long haul. I plan on having kids and my own small farm." She stared at him with a jaded eye. "You've never struck me as a nine-to-five guy. Kind of like putting a round peg in a square hole." On the up side, she found him sexy and so much fun, but that she kept to herself.

"Sounds like you want boring." His mouth turned down.

"Look at your brother. He's steady but no woman would ever say he's boring."

"Maybe you need my brother."

"Garrett and I are friends."

"I know." A cleft came and went in his cheek. "But I couldn't resist teasing you."

Ally rolled her eyes and started laughing. With a small amount of despair, she wondered what drew her to this man.

At the base of a steep incline, Randy held out his hand. She looked at it, square, the fingers blunt and strong. Ally slipped hers into it and felt an unfamiliar sense of inevitability and comfort . . . excitement and coming home. Crazy.

"My mother always said men and cats don't change their stripes."

"Maybe you should ignore your mother's bit of wisdom this time around."

She moved closer and tilted her head back to Randy. Tentatively, she touched his cheek with her palm. "Sometimes temptation is hard to ignore." Despite all wisdom to the contrary, Ally wanted something more than her dull, safe life. So when Randy lowered his head slowly to her, she met him half way, knowing he would provide just what she needed in that moment. As for the future, she had no idea.

¤¤

When Christie walked outside the barn early the

next morning she saw Hannah sitting in her tire swing slowly swinging back and forth. When Hannah spotted her she left the swing and came toward her.

Christie braced herself. She'd seen Hannah's face the other night when Garrett had kissed her. The child had not been happy. She put down the rubber water buckets she'd carried outside and began to scrub them with a brush.

Aware that Hannah stopped just behind her, Christie turned sideways and directed a glance at the child, with a small smile. "Hi. You're up early."

"Daddy said I got up before the birds this morning." Hannah pushed back the powder blue hood of her jacket. "We had breakfast together. I saved you a donut." She pulled a slightly crumbled doughnut in a plastic bag from her jacket pocket.

Surprised, Christie stopped scrubbing. "How did you know chocolate is my favorite?"

"You always eat chocolate."

"That's nice of you to save me one. I'll eat it when I finish my chores." Christie bit her lip indecisively, wondering if she dared extend the hand of friendship one step further. "You'll never guess who's been visiting my place."

Hannah looked inquisitive. Interestingly, Christie didn't sense any of the earlier hostility. "Your cat Albert."

"But how did he get in?" Hannah asked with delight.

Christie thought about dodging that question, then decided against it. She squatted down on her heels. "It's a long story, but I leave my door open. I think Albert caught the scent of a snack I was cooking and he came to visit. He's been stopping by all week. He's quite made himself at home."

Hannah played with the zipper on her jacket. "Maybe I could see him sometime," she said.

"Sure." Feeling elated at Hannah's apparent turnaround, Christie continued to scrub the buckets. "I bet he'd like that."

After a long silence, Hannah asked hesitantly, "Why do you leave your door open?"

Christie's hands stilled. She looked into inquisitive eyes. "Do you have a night light in your room?" she asked.

"It's an old one. I used to be afraid of the dark."

"Well, leaving my door open is like a night light for me. It's my security. If I want to leave, I can walk out that door anytime." Christie looked around, but they were alone. "I'm afraid of being stuck inside," she admitted in a low voice. "When I was small I used to hide in a closet with my sister Ellen."

"Weren't you afraid?"

"Yes. But I was more frightened of what was outside the closet." She stood up, needing to move around.

"Were you afraid of monsters?"

Christie hedged around the truth. "Yes, I was afraid of monsters. Now that I'm older I know there are no monsters, but I still like to have the door open."

"I used to be afraid, but Daddy made the monsters go away."

She smiled at Hannah. "That's what the best dads do."

"Did your dad make the monsters go away?"

Christie couldn't tell her that he was the monster they hid from in the closet. "All good dads chase them off."

"Daddy says he doesn't know much about girls."

"He knows how to love you. My parents didn't know how to care about each other, or about my sister and me. Your dad's way ahead of the game."

"My mom said if you depend on yourself, you'll never be disappointed."

Christie thought how sad that sounded. "Sometimes it's okay to let others help you."

Hannah tilted her head to the side. "Daddy said Mommy was your sister."

It took Christie a moment to realize what she'd said. Her heart beat loudly in her chest. "Yes. I was younger than you when your mom left home. I never really knew her."

"But that's so sad," Hannah said. "That you never knew Mommy and she was your sister."

The tightness in Christie's chest wanted to break loose. She picked up the buckets and moved back into the barn. "Now I have to get back to work."

"I'm going to read a book," Hannah said, falling into step behind her. She detoured into the office as Christie entered each stall and snapped the buckets back in place.

When Christie walked by with a new collection of buckets, she saw Hannah rifling through several books in Garrett's desk by the tack room door. Another facet of Garrett revealed. He kept books on hand for his daughter.

Christie stopped in the doorway. "Won't your

dad be wondering where you are?"

"The rule is I can be in the barn or by the house, so Daddy will know where I am. I'm going to read in my favorite place." Hannah looked at her with bright eyes. "Come on, I'll show you." Hesitantly, she reached out her hand toward Christie. Christie put down her buckets and grasped the small hand. They walked down the barn aisle to an open doorway on the left. She kept waiting for the bubble to burst, but Hannah kept reaching out to her.

Christie flicked the light switch and looked inside the room at the bales of golden straw. "I love the way this room smells. This is a perfect place to read!" she declared, bringing a smile to Hannah's face. The child settled on a broken bale of straw. With her blond hair all wispy around her face, she looked adorable and so young.

"You can read with me," Hannah said quietly. "If you want to."

Christie felt an actual pain, recalling the times she'd curled up on the couch with Eric and read his favorite book.

"Well," Christie said cautiously, "only for a few minutes. I have a few chores to finish."

Christie sat beside Hannah. Wriggling around a bit, she extracted a piece of straw from where it had worked its way under her shirt.

Hannah became engrossed in the story, and Christie enjoyed just spending time with her. At one point she looked up to find Garrett standing in the doorway. She snuck a look at her watch upon seeing the stern expression on his face.

"Hannah, I've been looking for you," he said

quietly, his sharp glance seeming to see everything. "I've been calling." Self-consciously, Christie straightened her legs. Unbidden, thoughts of their last, brief kiss came to mind. A rush of emotion flared, causing butterflies to flit through her stomach. When she stared at Garrett and saw the hint of color on his cheekbones, her stomach started a wild fluttering. She wondered if he was remembering too.

"I didn't hear you, Daddy. Me and Christie were reading. You said I could read while I waited for you."

"I thought you meant in the house." Garrett turned his head toward Christie. "Good morning, Christie," His mouth curved. "You've got straw in your hair."

"Oh." Christie ran her fingers through her hair. She allowed her glance to linger on him, a melting deep in her chest. He looked so big standing in the doorway. Hannah left her side and moved to her father's side. Garrett stood with a hand on his daughter's shoulder as Hannah showed him the books they were reading. Garrett was good with kids, he was the type of man who should have several more.

He wore a lightweight camel-colored corduroy jacket, a deep green shirt with thin black stripes and black jeans. Droplets of water spotted his cowboy hat and shoulders.

He was an attractive man, a cowgirl's dream. And a city girl's dream, a wicked voice whispered to Christie. "It's raining!" Christie blurted, stating the obvious.

Garrett casually ruffled his daughter's hair. "It just began. The weather forecast says it's only supposed to shower this morning. Would you like to ride to town? I can show you around. I can show you where Judith is buried, if you like."

"Sure," she said, caught by surprise. "I would like that."

He gave her a measured look. "If you'd like my help, maybe together we can find a place for your sister's ashes."

Garrett removed his hat and shook the water droplets from it. "I know this area like the back of my hand. I'm sure we can find somewhere suitable for what you're looking for."

"Then I accept your offer. Thank you," she added softly. The rational part of her brain pointed out he might be anxious to see the last of her. The romantic part of her said he just might want to spend time with her.

Christie brushed loose bits of straw from her jeans. "I can leave when Ally gets in to work. I told her I'd fill in for an hour."

He smiled. "She's at the house getting some coffee. I think she had a late night. She's kind of out of sorts today."

"Okay, then I guess we can leave any time." Christie walked toward Garrett and Hannah, then went down on one knee to brush the straw from Hannah's jeans.

"There's straw in your hair," Hannah said with a giggle, pointing a finger up at her.

¤¤

Garrett watched Christie bend over and shake

her hair out, then finger comb the dark strands. Her hair flowed forward, exposing the nape of her neck and the wispy, baby fine hairs. Garrett wondered when he had ever been so tempted to take something he wanted. This gentle woman with the sad dark eyes. He found himself intrigued by her. He wasn't anxious for her to leave, yet he knew it was inevitable.

"Is that better?" came her muffled voice.

Garrett stepped closer, his boots sinking into the pale straw. He cleared his throat. "Let me help." He plucked out several more bits, unable to keep his fingers from lingering in the silky strands.

Christie straightened slowly. Garrett watched her dark eyes move up his legs and over his jeans, then up his chest. It felt like an intimate caress and his body responded embarrassingly fast.

"That must be it," she said quickly. "I don't feel any more."

"A couple more," he murmured, torturing himself with her closeness. He plucked the last of the straw, lightly fluffed the hair and then smoothed a hand over it before stepping back. "That's it." His voice sounded hoarse to his ears. Garrett wondered if he was the only one feeling the sizzle of attraction. He reined in his thoughts. He had told her acting on the attraction wasn't a good idea. He had to at least try to keep to his word.

"Christie, you need a jacket," Hannah observed.

"I'm fine," Christie said.

They all walked down the barn aisle toward the outer barn door. Christie stood in front of Garrett, Hannah at his side. As the teeming rain blew in through the open door, Garrett noticed the shiver that shook Christie's slender frame.

"You can't go out like that," he said. "You'll be soaked." He pulled his jacket off and slid it over her shoulders. For the briefest moment, she leaned back, her shoulder touching his chest. Garrett clamped his jaw as desire bit at him hard and fast. He wanted to do more than touch her shoulders.

Christie turned quickly, her fingers catching the lightweight jacket before it could slide to the ground. "I can't take your jacket," she protested.

"Wear it." He closed his fingers around hers when she would have taken it off. "I have another one in my truck. Wait here and I'll bring the truck closer."

Garrett darted out into the rain and climbed in his truck which he'd had the foresight to park close to the barn. He drove next to the open door where Christie and his daughter waited and placed the truck in park. Leaning across the seat, he pushed open the passenger door.

Garrett watched Christie put her arms in the sleeves of his jacket and bury her nose in the flannel lining. Garrett clenched his jaw, thinking he'd like to be inside that damned jacket where her nose was buried.

∞ Chapter Ten ∞

CHRISTIE WAS GLAD WHEN the rain tapered off and the sun began to shine through the clouds. As they drove down the highway she felt an incredible sense of happiness.

"Look at the rainbow," she said as they crested a hill. "What an awesome sight."

A ribbon of translucent color spread out before them. Farmland, fields and sky, the colors stretched as far as the eye could see with an occasional purple thunderhead serving as a backdrop. Christie had never witnessed anything so spectacular.

"I suppose you see this all the time," she said with wonder.

"It's nice to see it through someone else's eyes," he assured her gravely, turning his glance from her back to the highway.

She looked down at Hannah who sat between them and realized she'd fallen asleep.

"She was up really early this morning," Garrett said.

Christie pressed the child against her shoulder as her head bobbed forward. "I used to wish I'd find the gold at the end of the rainbow," she mused.

He smiled. "A leprechaun's pot of gold?"

"My aunt Rose would say if you let your heart follow your dreams you'd find the gold."

"Your aunt Rose is a wise woman."

"Yes," she agreed with a lift of her chin. "She was. As I mentioned, she died when I was ten. Ellen was thirteen. It was an awful time in our lives. The blanket of security that Aunt Rose provided was yanked out from beneath us."

"Another loss."

"That was a long time ago," she said quickly. She looked out her side window. "I don't think I've ever seen so many fences. Everywhere you look there's a fence, and those stones, what type of stone is that?"

"Limestone, they're native to the area."

Garrett slowed the truck and pulled to the side of the road. He half turned in his seat toward her. Christie splayed her fingers on her thighs as she stared at his face, taking in the faint shadow of beard along his jaw and the sharp inquiry in his eyes.

He tapped the steering wheel. "Christie, if you don't want to talk about your past I'll respect your right to privacy, but you can trust me if there's something you need to say."

"Strangely enough, I've probably told you more than I have anyone else in the last six years."

"Trust me," he said.

Those two words were like stones dropped in a

still pond. Christie managed a short laugh. "You say that now, but I know from past experience —"

"Christie, we don't have any past experience."

"Garrett, I learned years ago to keep my emotions in check. It's safer. Old habits are hard to break." She pressed her fingers together nervously as he shifted the truck into gear and pulled back on to the road.

Desperately, she battled the doubt twisting within herself. How much to reveal? Damn. Damn. Her past wouldn't let her be anything but cautious. She cleared her throat. "You know things about me. I think we should talk about you, Garrett."

"I'm just a guy trying to make a living."

"Tell me what it was like growing up in a place like this. Everything is so green and alive. I can't help thinking it would have been a great childhood."

Garrett shrugged. "There's not much to tell. I grew up on the very land where the farm sits now. It's been in our family four generations. My dad owned a grocery store in town but he should have been a farmer. He raised some tobacco on the side but his big love was animals. Ducks, geese, a few cows and horses. I bought the farm off him when he and my mom moved to town after he retired."

"Have you always had a passion for horses?"

"When I was younger I used to rodeo during the summer. The only way my parents would let me go was if Randy tagged along. I guess my mom figured we'd look out for each other. Randy pursued other activities while I entered rodeo events."

Christie smiled, thinking of Garrett's fun loving brother. "No doubt Randy had a lady in each town."

"You know my brother. Randy and I followed one rodeo after the other." He shook his head. "Those were crazy times. Two kids on the loose."

Christie was intrigued. "I've seen rodeos on television, but never in person."

He crooked a brow. "Maybe we can remedy that while you're here."

Christie clasped her hands together. "That sounds like wonderful fun."

"During the school year I went to college and finally graduated with a degree in financial management. What I've always wanted was to start my own thoroughbred farm."

"Your degree must come in handy," she mused.

"Of course. My main focus has always been my horses, improving their bloodlines, keeping up with technology. I've had some lucky breaks in the business."

"You've built a solid reputation. I understand that. In my career as a stenographer, I built the reputation for reliability. Over the years I worked an incredible amount of overtime to turn in accurate transcripts." There had been no lucky breaks for her, though, on the road to proving her worth. "Why did you give up rodeo?" she asked curiously.

Garrett scratched the back of his head. "Well, that's another story. It wasn't just Randy and me, there was a bunch of us. Judith traveled with us on and off a few seasons. She joined our group after she met Randy. She and I dated steadily all one summer and then I talked her into marrying me. I had some money saved from my wins and was anxious to get started on building my ranch."

"So it was you, Judith and Hannah?"

He glanced at her. "Hannah was living with a friend of Judith's. She came to live with us when we settled at the ranch."

"Did you and Hannah hit it off right away?"

Garrett looked down at the little girl between them. "From the first moment I set eyes on her it was like she was mine."

"You two look like you're related, blond hair, blue eyes, though your eyes are more gray."

His face turned somber. "I didn't know right away that Judith had a daughter. She kept it a secret."

Christie looked at him incredulously.

"She said she figured if I knew I wouldn't marry her."

"Would you have married her?"

"Truthfully, I don't know. I found out by accident. I'm afraid it wasn't pretty, the scene that followed. Judith and I together were like two wrecking balls." Garrett shrugged. "Maybe she was afraid for Hannah. I don't know. In the end, Judith realized I wasn't giving in and Hannah came to live at the ranch."

"And now you'd never give her up," she said softly. "Did Judith share your love of horses?" She shook her head. "It's strange for me to be asking you about my own sister."

"She liked the excitement of rodeos, but she didn't ride. She thought she'd like running a horse farm. I guess she envisioned parties and a lot more socializing. Once we settled at the farm it was pretty quiet. I was away at auctions, working with trainers.

I'm not making excuses. It's what I had to do to succeed but I know I should have been around more for her."

"You tried to make all the ends work together." She recognized the loneliness in him, the remembered sense of failure. She'd struggled with the same emotions a good part of her adult life. Christie wanted to reach out and touch him but remained on her own side of the seat. He was an adult, a man used to handling his emotions and dealing with life. It's what they all had to do.

"In hindsight I realize Judith and I were just too different. But when you really care about someone, you're more willing to ignore the differences."

"Judith was older than you."

He smiled. "Only in years."

Christie swallowed with difficulty, but felt pressed to ask the next question. "Did she have a drinking problem?"

Garrett glanced at her somberly. "I've never admitted that to anyone, but near the end it became more apparent that she was in trouble. I tried to get her help, but she refused to even admit there was a problem. Does it run in your family?"

Christie froze upon hearing those words.

"Daddy, are we almost there?" Hannah asked sleepily, lifting her head from Christie's shoulder to look around with interest.

"Almost," her father promised, brushing the back of his hand against her rosy cheeks.

Christie began to breathe again. Right now she couldn't answer his question. She marveled at the love Garrett displayed so easily. Such simple gestures had come naturally to her as a child while living with her aunt Rose. But in later years, living with their parents . . . the only signs of caring had been between her and Ellen.

All her life she had struggled to overcome her family's deficiencies, never daring to step a foot wrong. Seeing the interaction between Garrett and his daughter, Christie wondered if it was possible to mend the jagged edges that represented her life.

Hannah stretched, trying to touch the interior roof with her fingers. "Daddy, can we go to see Mommy?" she asked.

Christie froze. She felt Garrett's searing glance, even though she wasn't looking at him.

"We can swing by the cemetery on the way home," he said quietly. "That's what I planned."

Christie stared out the window, not sure if she was ready for this moment. She finally looked over at Garrett. She nodded. Perhaps it was time for her to stop being afraid. She had to face the truth.

¤ ¤

When they reached Lexington Garrett proceeded to give Christie the grand tour. Along the way he pointed out many areas of interest while she and Hannah counted horse farms. Christie had passed some of the same farms by bus when she arrived in Kentucky, but seeing it with Garrett and Hannah felt different and special. Garrett gave her a running history of the area and its landmarks and she knew it was a day she would never forget.

They spent a good part of the afternoon at the Kentucky Horse Park. Christie stared in awe at the bronze horse statues and was delighted with the hayride Garrett suggested they take.

However, about late afternoon, true to his word Garrett suggested they visit the cemetery where Judith was buried.

"It's a small private cemetery," he said as he drove the truck through the cemetery's ornate black iron gates. "Green Hills Rest."

Tensely, Christie stared ahead at the cemetery's narrow paved roadway. There was a small red wood-sided office to their left and then the road wound leisurely up a small hill.

Christie realized she was digging her nails into her legs as they drove to the top of a rise. Garrett pulled into a parking area and turned off the ignition. "This is it."

He opened his door and climbed out. Hannah slid across the truck seat and was right behind him. Without a word the little girl walked away from them, following a narrow footpath between some dark, aged stones.

Garrett came around the truck to Christie's side. She opened her door and stepped out of the truck on shaky legs. Not far from them Hannah paused beside a rose colored stone. Taking a deep breath, Christie followed the path Hannah had taken.

Christie was vaguely aware of Garrett behind her as she reached Hannah, but she was glad he remained quiet. Judith's stone was square and had roses engraved along the sides and above her name and date of death. Beside the stone someone had placed a small white angel in the grass. On the base of the stone was a small bunch of dried up flowers.

Hannah caressed the top of the stone angel's

head. "I brought Mommy this angel."

Christie cleared her throat. "It's a beautiful angel Hannah. What a thoughtful idea."

Christie knelt, letting her fingers trace the scroll of flowers in the rose colored stone. She felt strangely out of sync, as if something was broke inside her.

"Daddy, I'm going to pick Mommy new flowers."

"I'll come with you," he said quietly.

Christie could hear Hannah speaking to her father as they moved away, but she was glad of the moment to be alone. Her vision blurred at she stared fixedly at the stone. It felt so incredibly sad, finally finding her sister and knowing it was too late.

"I wish I could have known you, Judith." Christie remained kneeling. She felt puzzled. Her eyes remained dry yet her throat hurt from suppressing the emotion inside. She couldn't cry. She didn't know if that was good or bad.

Christie came once more to her feet when her legs began to cramp. She looked around and saw Garrett and Hannah coming back toward her. Hannah ran toward her with a big bunch of daisies. Solemnly, she shared some of the flowers with Christie.

"You can put them on Mommy's stone," Hannah said. "I did it last time. Now it's your turn."

"Thank you."

Christie placed them on the stone base. Standing once more, she felt engulfed by sadness.

A breeze picked up and the sun disappeared behind dark clouds.

"If you're ready, we'll go," Garrett said, glancing

at the sky. "I'm afraid it's going to rain."

"I already felt some raindrops, Daddy." Hannah turned and hurried back to the truck.

Christie shivered. She'd left his jacket in the truck and now realized how much she missed its warmth. Surprising her, Garrett pulled her to his side in a natural, friendly gesture as they turned back to the parking area. She savored his warmth, the momentary support he gave unselfishly.

"Thank you for today," she said. Leaning into him, she placed a quick kiss on his chin. The sandpaper rasp of his whiskers against her lips was nice. "And for bringing me here."

His arm wound loosely around her waist and they walked in companionable silence.

Christies had a sudden thought. Was she falling in love with Garrett? Could life get any more complicated . . . or wonderful?

¤ ¤

Christie woke from a heavy restless sleep. Groggily, she rolled over and groaned when she saw her alarm clock. Five-thirty a.m. After her day out with Garrett and Hannah, it had been almost midnight before she fell asleep. There had been so much on her mind, so many questions about her and Garrett's relationship. She hugged her arms around herself. Surely it had been an aberration on her part; she didn't love Garrett. Love had never come to her so easily. More than likely it was infatuation or just sexual attraction. It would fizzle and she would leave.

She lay perfectly still, drinking in the absolute quiet, hoping to drift back to sleep. The sun had not even come up yet. *Bang. Bang.*

Christie sat up in bed, her heart pounding in fright. The banging noise came again. It sounded like it came from the barn below. The horses. She switched on the bedside lamp, pulled on jeans over her nightshirt and hurriedly stepped into her boots. Christie descended the narrow stairs into the barn as quickly as she dared in the semi-dark. Once in the barn she flicked on several overhead lights. Out of the corner of her eye she thought she saw movement, but when she turned on another light, there was nothing there. Methodically, she checked each of the stalls.

When she looked inside the last stall she quickly assessed the situation. It appeared the young horse had laid down too close to the wall and rolled over. He couldn't maneuver to get his legs under him. Each time he tried to rise, his hooves banged against the wall and he fell back down.

Christie opened the sliding door and knelt at the horse's head. As she spoke soothingly to him, the stall door slid closed.

The young horse seemed to watch her warily, the whites of his eyes distended. She wondered how long he'd been down. Studying his position carefully, she decided the best thing to do was grab his front legs and pull him away from the wall. No mean feat, considering he probably weighed about three hundred pounds.

Christie wondered if she'd be able to pull him far enough away without getting kicked. If she went for help it could waste precious minutes and he might injure himself. Christie knelt down and grasped each front fetlock above the hooves. She pulled. His weight was distributed just enough toward her that with her pulling he rolled over away from the wall. She jumped back quickly as he gained his feet and shook himself head-to-toe.

"Are you okay?" she asked tenderly, running her hand down his soft muzzle. "Now I can go get someone to check you out."

Christie backed toward the door and pulled the handle but the door did not move. She pulled harder, refusing to believe she was locked in the stall.

Was it stuck? Christie gripped the metal bars on the upper portion of the door and angled her head so she could see the latch on the outside of the door. It looked like it was partially caught. She tried jiggling the door but it held fast.

Christie told herself to remain calm but her heart rate increased and an old familiar heaviness settled in her chest. As she paced, she reminded herself not to scare the colt. She chewed her lips, standing near the door and peering out into the aisle. Someone would come very soon. She thought of the sing-song verse she and Ellen had recited as children when hiding from their father. *You can't come in and I won't go out. You can't come in because I locked you out.*

"Hello, anybody out there! Garrett, Ally, anybody." Christie put her back against the stall wall. How could she have let the door close like that? She didn't ever remember that happening before. Being slightly claustrophobic didn't help either, but she could handle this. Christie ran her hand soothingly down the colt's neck. "Now I feel like a real dolt, locking myself in here with you." She thought she heard someone and moved once more over to the chest high metal grill. "Garrett?"

Footsteps. "Christie? Are you down here already?" Garrett's voice.

Christie took a deep breath. "Yes, it's me. I'm uh, stuck in this stall."

Garrett stopped outside the stall, then reached forward to lift the latch. "How the hell did you manage to lock yourself in there?"

She stepped out of the stall and smiled shakily. "I feel kind of foolish saying I don't really know." She must have looked a bit shaken, because Garrett's warm hands touched her shoulders.

"It's okay," he said. Christie noticed now that his hair was disheveled and his shirt hung open, liked he'd jumped quickly out of bed. Following her relief, Christie became aware of new senses kicking in. She felt the heat of his body so close to her own, his warm musky scent in her nostrils. "I have a slight case of claustrophobia," she confessed, staring over his shoulder.

"It's a good thing I saw the lights on. Why were you in there?"

Christie tried to focus, but she couldn't help but think how rough and sexy he looked, a dark shadow along his unshaven jaw. "The door closed and somehow the latch fell into place."

He rubbed her arms. "The stalls are on rollers and will glide closed, but the latches don't lock by themselves."

"I couldn't get out."

He looked at her with concern. "Your face is white. I thought I heard something outside this morning, that's why I got up so early."

He led her out of the stall and into the barn aisle. Christie looked back at the door latch. "I heard a banging noise and came downstairs. The colt was laying half on his back with his feet against the wall. He couldn't get up. I was afraid he'd hurt himself so I pulled him over. I didn't realize until too late what had happened with the door."

"He was cast," Garrett muttered, his eyes never leaving her face.

"Cast?"

"When a horse gets down too close to a wall and can't get up." She saw his glance slip over her, stopping at her untied boots. Self-conscious now, she pulled up her nightshirt's sagging neckline, stuffed the tails into her jeans and pushed the tangle of hair away from her face.

"I rushed down here when I heard the noise," she mumbled.

Garrett looked at the horse in the stall. "Do you know who this little guy is?" he asked.

"Ally calls him Houdini. She said when he was a weanling he managed to get out of any fence you put him in."

Garrett's mouth curved upwards. "That's his nickname. His registered name is Aspiration. He's one of my most promising colts for next year's season. Who knows, maybe even the Derby."

Christie looked at the horse, the sturdy legs, muscled chest and wide, intelligent forehead. "He's a beauty." She rubbed her palms over her face. "The

Derby, huh? That must be why you have sign-in sheets and I've even seen surveillance cameras outside."

"You have to be careful in this business."

Christie looked down at her boots uncertainly then hooked her arm around a saddletree built into the wall. "With all this security, I'm kind of surprised that you hired me."

"Gut instinct," Garrett said with a lopsided grin. "I wouldn't let you in here if I thought you were a threat. I appreciate what you did for Houdini, but next time come and get me or Sam."

Christie lifted her shoulders in a careless shrug. "I was afraid he'd be hurt worse if I left him."

"You might have been kicked or he could have fallen on you. Don't take a chance like that again." His voice bordered on a reprimand.

Christie bent to tie her shoelaces. "It seemed the right thing to do," she said defensively, tying her other bootlace. She felt a draft of air across her chest. Looking down, she realized her nightshirt had gaped forward, exposing her breasts.

She looked up. Garrett's glance lifted from her chest and the impact of those light colored eyes made Christie feel incredibly warm. How easy, she thought, to claim this was love. Love didn't make your heart pound and your lungs hurt for lack of air. It was merely infatuation.

His hands, hard on her arms, pulled her up. The heat of his mouth seared her, engulfing her, his tongue slipping inside as long arms pulled her into him. Infatuation or not Christie admitted she wanted this, to be close to Garrett. She went without a thought for the consequences. Some moments were not meant to be questioned, they were just to be lived.

∞ Chapter Eleven ∞

CHRISTIE BURNED WHERE GARRETT touched her. She was hot inside and out, her stomach muscles contracting. She craved this closeness and wound her arms around his neck, enjoying the strength of his body pressed to hers. Each time they kissed felt more shattering. Thoughts jumped crazily in her head. She did not want to stop Garrett. Her emotions were riding high, making the secrets of her past seem surmountable.

Garrett's big hands framed her face, held her as he pressed against her. There was no doubt in Christie's mind as to the extent of his desire, not with the evidence between them.

"This is crazy," he muttered, burying his face against her neck and holding her to him.

She pressed her lips to his skin with greedy insistence, inhaling the earthy essence of the man. The tendrils of hair at the back of his head were damp under her fingers and he smelled fresh as if he had come from a shower. Again and again Christie wound her fingers through those light colored strands, his murmur of appreciation making the wanting inside curl tighter with tension.

She moved her fingers over his back, aware of the strength and bulk of him, yet the gentleness with which he held her. She placed her mouth over his, taking his lips as if it was her right. She didn't want to think. She needed to feel, experience and lose herself in the moment and the man. She didn't mind burning, if it was with Garrett. "I've never known anyone like you, Garrett." She heard her own words, and she was reminded of her past, the memories that were never far away. She had been engaged, but her feelings then, by comparison, were nothing compared to this.

Garrett eased away from her and her body felt cold where moments before his heat had burned it. She ached with the withdrawal and tried to hold her body stiffly but in truth she felt shaky.

Curiously, she looked at her hand as it lay against his chest, the matt of hair visible beneath the open buttons. She curled her fingers into the fine hair, then flattened her palm against the bulge of muscle there. It felt like an experiment, touching him, watching his reaction, the contracting of his muscles beneath her fingers. Christie noted the faint flush on his cheeks, his eyes hard and searching, telling her without words he was not a man to be trifled with.

She stroked his chest with a fingertip. Garrett gave an audible groan. To Christie, it was a beautiful sound but she knew she was dancing closer to that emotional quagmire.

"Christie, stop."

She pressed two fingers against his beautiful mouth. "I know you're going to say this isn't right but please don't. I can't deny the way I feel. I know you were my sister's husband and maybe this isn't right. Somehow, at moments like this, it doesn't seem to matter."

She stepped back, knowing she probably looked a mess, but she didn't care. She gathered her hair into her hands and pushed it off her shoulders.

"Neither one of us is thinking straight about this," he said in a clipped voice. "Soon, you'll go back to your own life. From what you've told me, Christie, you're used to more than this two-bit town. Like Judith, you wouldn't be satisfied staying in a place like this."

He sounded like he knew what she wanted and her own uncertainty made her feel shortchanged. "And what is it that you want Garrett?" she cried softly, unable to keep the words from spilling out.

The intensity of his focus speared through her. "What any man wants. To be successful."

"You are," she whispered.

"To share my life with someone special. I used to think that wasn't a big order. The older you get, the more you realize everything you don't know."

Christie bowed her head and knew deep inside she wanted to be that someone special. She wanted to believe in forever and ever, but it wasn't something she had ever seen. She and Judith shared the same background, and Judith had bailed out in the end.

"I wish I knew if a forever kind of happiness really exists. I do have faith you'll find who you're looking for, Garrett. This thing between us is easily explained away as mutual attraction." She smiled sadly. "Maybe even in some small way I remind you of Judith. Maybe you're trying to finish where you and she left off."

Garrett watched her grimly. "That's ludicrous. Judith and I finished anything that was between us. Believe me, by the time she left, there was only Hannah between us."

His words disturbed her greatly. Even though she had never really known her sister, she still felt hurt by the words.

"How sad and confused Judith must have felt." She turned and walked quickly down the barn aisle, her chest heaving, her hair in a wild tumble down her back.

"Dammit, Christie!" He sounded angry, but he didn't follow her.

She was crazy to think about wanting this man. Crazy to hope she could have him and be happy. She cared about him as a man; as Hannah's father, the caring adult he'd shown himself to be.

She had never felt more gloriously alive, yet the feeling was tempered with sadness. How could she think of being involved with anyone? Her life was in a state of upheaval. She had virtually abandoned her life to take on a mission that Darrell had called crazy. She clenched her fists. It was terrible what guilt could drive a person to do.

Christie gulped, a cold wave engulfing her. Each

time she got close to Garrett she was blindsided, letting herself lose sight of why she was really here. Did this man have the power to make her forget everything? Was it possible he could help her forget the past?

Christie shook her head. She was living in a fool's paradise if she thought there was a man alive who could do that. She needed to stand on her own feet, not depend on someone else.

¤ ¤

Garrett watched Christie leave, admiring the swing of slim hips, recalling the angry flash of her eyes. Ruefully, he acknowledged she made him want to go up in a blaze. She'd saved one of his most valuable horses from harm, and he'd just about given her hell. Didn't she understand he didn't want her to get hurt? Dammit, he cared about her! He didn't want to, but whatever was there between them felt too damned strong to ignore.

He stared at Christie's slim back, the long legs. With sudden decision, he took a step after her. Hadn't her actions indicated she wanted him as much as he wanted her? Maybe he should say the hell with it and follow her up to her apartment. They could spend all day together in bed and then maybe the night as well. . ..

"Hey, Boss." Ally's voice stopped Garrett cold as she pushed the barn door open behind him. "What's going on?"

Biting back an expletive, Garrett buttoned his shirt while Ally grinned at him. "One of the colts had some trouble but Christie and I got it straightened out." He looked at his watch, then took a closer look at Ally. Something looked out of place but he couldn't put his finger on it. "Everything okay with you? You're here early this morning."

Ally entered the barn.

"Me? Right as rain," she said breezily. "On the other hand, you and Christie . . .." He ignored her sly grin. "Maybe I should have waited a while to come inside. That's probably why Sam was loitering outside, acting like he was busy." She flipped her hand and indicated the door. "I can go right back out again, you know."

Garrett gave Ally a narrowed eyed glance without answering. He began to fill the grain buckets for the morning feeding. Did everyone know he had feelings for Christie? He stopped what he was doing for a moment. Did it matter?

He ran a quick hand through his hair, then resumed filling the buckets with grain. After a moment Ally joined him at the grain bin and began to measure out grain and supplements.

"By the way," she said casually, "I saw Randy at Myrt's coffee shop earlier. He said he might swing by today."

"This morning? I thought he was doing undercover work all week?"

"He's trying out the nine-to-five shift. Can you imagine Randy in a nine-to-five job?" Ally's amusement seemed at odds with the seriousness in her eyes.

"Maybe, but who knows?" Garrett lifted a brow. "Maybe he's ready to settle into a regular routine."

Ally hefted a bucket of grain and tossed him a look of disbelief. "Yeah, and pink rabbits fly. See you later, Boss."

Garrett smiled, and finally realized what was different about Ally. Her flannel shirt had been mis-buttoned, and the entire shirt was two holes off. No big deal, he thought, unless you were the neat and precise Ally with never a button out of place. Interesting.

Garrett gave the stairs to Christie's apartment one last look and wondered if it would have been such a big mistake to have followed Christie up there. Luckily or not, the moment had passed. Sanity was once more firmly in place.

¤¤

Later that evening Christie heard footsteps on the stairs leading to her apartment. She looked up from the T-shirts she was folding. Albert, lapping up a small bowl of water, scooted outside just as Randy came to stand in her open doorway. Wearing a big grin, he knocked on the wood trim. "Hey, Christie, are you busy?"

"Hi, Randy." With a smile, she indicated the pile of clean clothes. "Nothing important. What's going on?"

"I stopped to pick up Hannah — we're going to a movie tonight. I brought some homemade ice cream. Have you ever had it? It's nothing like what you buy in the store."

Christie was intrigued by the idea. "Never tried it, but I'd love to."

He stepped back. "Come on down, I put it in Garrett's freezer."

"Oh, okay. Is your brother around?" She asked casually. She hadn't seen him since early that morning. She'd done her best to detour him all day, hoping to let some of the heat settle down between.

"He's at the house. I told him I was inviting you. By the way, you haven't seen Ally, have you?"

"Not since she left at five." Christie smiled at him. "I think she likes you."

Behind Randy's smile lurked a tinge of anxiety. "Sometimes it's hard to tell."

Christie pressed her lips together, then moved forward to stand in front of Randy. "She does, but she's been hurt bad."

He looked surprised. "What do you know about it?"

Christie shrugged. "Not much, really. Just that the guy she was married to had an eye for the ladies."

Randy leaned back against the doorframe and rested his head against the wood. "I'm still trying to convince her I'm not him."

Christie just looked at him sympathetically.

He straightened. "I won't deny I like women, but deep down I'm just like any other guy. I want to settle with one woman."

"You don't have to convince me," she said gently.

"Right. Listen, I have to run but maybe I'll see you later."

"I appreciate you thinking of me. I'll be down as soon as I finish folding. Have fun at the movies!" she called out as he hurried down the stairs.

Christie put her folded laundry away ten minutes later and as she left the barn she wondered if Garrett minded Randy inviting her for ice cream.

The kitchen light was on in the house. Opening

the door, she came face to face with Garrett. His hair was dark and slicked back and the fresh scent of soap clung to him. Christie's cheeks heated as she remembered their earlier encounter and the sexual energy that had snapped between them. "Hi Garrett."

"I was just coming to see if Randy invited you over. I can't eat all that ice cream by myself," he joked, touching his midsection. Christie's glance was drawn to his flat stomach and lingered there. "I have to be careful. I have a tendency to go crazy on sweets."

Relaxing, amused, Christie said, "Welcome to the club."

He held the door open and she ducked under his arm. "Nothing going on tonight?" he asked.

She smiled slightly. "Nope. Right now my social life is quiet, though Ally and Buddy have promised me a night on the town this weekend. I'm kind of looking forward to it."

"Buddy's taken a liking to you."

"He's a nice guy. I've been helping him with a research paper."

"You're a jack of all trades, aren't you?"

She shrugged. "I have a lot of interests. One thing I wanted to mention is I feel like I'm making some headway with Hannah."

"I agree."

She lifted a brow, studying him closely. "You look worried. I'd never hurt her." Her heart pounded urgently.

"Not intentionally. But I think you're a woman who's had some tough breaks."

"Who hasn't? You know Judith did, and you've had your problems." Knowing this could get too serious, she said jokingly, "What's your solution?"

"Maybe you need something to make you forget what's haunting you."

A tight lump formed in her throat. "An affair?"

"Sorry, that was damned personal," he said awkwardly.

Christie met his eyes directly. "I admire honesty, so don't apologize. But you did catch me by surprise."

"Not everyone appreciates plain speaking," he said gruffly, pulling open cabinet doors. "Since we're on the subject of plain speaking, I've been wondering if you can stay longer than we planned. The doctor's reassessed the break to Kim's ankle. Looks like the cast won't be off for an additional three weeks."

Christie ran her tongue over dry lips. "I've already been here almost two weeks."

"Think about it." He opened the chest freezer and lifted out a large brown container. "It'll take me a few minutes to get this ice cream out. If you want, go relax in the living room and put on some music. There's a bunch of CD's on the shelves."

"Sounds like a good idea." Christie left Garrett in the kitchen. She needed the breathing space. He'd asked her to stay longer.

As she crossed the living room her interest was caught by the pictures lining the fireplace mantle. In one picture Garrett straddled a dirt bike, his hair disheveled as if he'd just lifted the helmet from his head. His wide daredevil grin hinted at a different man than the one she knew. Another picture showed an older man with his arm around a slim, blond-haired woman. The man and Garrett shared a striking resemblance, the same lean cheeks and deep, piercing eyes. It had to be his father so perhaps the woman was his mother.

Christie saw various photographs of Hannah with family members, but Christie didn't see any of Garrett and another woman, her sister.

Christie looked through Garrett's extensive collection of CDs. Not familiar with country music, she randomly chose several CDs and put them on the changer.

Opening the French doors, she stepped onto the terrace. The setting was romantic; warm breeze, muted light, a soft rustling in the brush. Sinking into a comfortable wicker rocker, she stifled a sigh, admitting she didn't know much about romance. Her experience had been limited to a brief engagement six years ago. She'd been young and Allen, her fiancé, had been shallow. An up and coming lawyer, he lived and breathed his work in the district attorney's office, so much so that her background had ultimately gotten in the way of their future as he saw it. His ambition wouldn't let him have anyone in his life who was less than perfect. Whose family was still far from perfect.

The past. . .vaguely, Christie heard the slight creak, back and forth, of her chair. For the moment, she felt incredibly content. . ..

"Christie." Garrett's voice sounded close to her ear.

Christie turned her head and looked directly into

Garrett's blue eyes, his aftershave a pleasant, spicy scent. The man was too good looking for a woman's peace of mind. Just being near him gave rise to fantasies galore.

"Ice cream?"

Blankly, she looked at the bowl he held out, then took it. It was filled with dark chocolate ice cream. "That looks delicious," she said quickly, sitting up straight. Lifting her spoon, she licked off a large dollop of chocolate, her breath stopping for an instant as she noticed him watching her eat. "Delicious," she confirmed, licking the corner of her mouth where the creamy ice cream had dripped.

Garrett touched his fingertip to her lips, then slowly brought that finger to his mouth and licked off the chocolate she'd missed.

Christie quickly swallowed a spoonful of ice cream, stifling a groan as it went right to her head. Immediately, she put her hand to her forehead. "Brain freeze," she moaned, laughing.

"Listen," he said. The music drifted from the living room, a slow, sad song about a woman crazy in love with a man. There was a sensual feel to the music, wrapping Christie up in the words and the tone of the song.

"We have to dance to this." Garrett's voice sounded almost reverent. "Patsy Cline is singing 'Crazy'."

The words were sad, evocative, touching something elemental inside Christie. Garrett held his hand out to her, palm up. Without thinking twice, Christie put her bowl on a small table and placed her palm in his, feeling the calloused texture of his skin, his large hand engulfing hers. Garrett coaxed her closer and he dipped his head toward her.

Snapping out of her trance-like state, Christie pulled back. "I don't dance anymore and I've never danced to country music."

"It's only the two of us," he admonished. "I know you can dance."

"It's not that I can't —" she admitted.

Garrett's laugh was soft, mocking. "Follow me."

His feet moved into a two-step as he guided her other hand to his shoulder. "Your feet are moving, Christie. Don't hold back."

Don't hold back. She tilted her head back, craving his closeness and the way he made her feel special. Her feet fell into step with his, and she rested her head against his shoulder.

"Just feel it," he whispered.

She followed his lead as they danced slowly, the music winding around them, the night quiet and the flagstone smooth under their feet. Christie felt as if she had danced this intimately with Garrett before.

When the music ended, the spell still hovered. Christie breathed deeply of the night fragrances, staring at Garrett.

"I wonder how I've lived my entire life without knowing you. Just being here at the farm makes me realize another side of life. It's been an incredible adventure." A new tightness grew in her chest. "How can I leave you and Hannah?" She almost felt dependent upon them, as if they'd become vital to her. She had thought in the last months she was too frozen up inside, too numb from loss to care again, but now she thinking about staying longer. When the flame between them burned out she would have no choice but to leave. She didn't want to hang around until Garrett got tired of her.

"Maybe you don't have to leave." Garrett slowly released her, let his fingers slip down her wrist, trail gently to her elbow. With a sensual shiver, Christie lowered her hand to her side and stepped back. She dropped her other hand from his shoulder and rubbed her elbow where it still tingled.

"Thanks . . . thank you for the dance." The words spilled from her too fast. She felt incredibly shaky and uncertain. How did one reach this stage in life, twenty-six years of age, without knowing the proper protocol to end a dance...to end an awkward, sexually charged moment? They had shared an intimate dance, and she wanted to curl around him and let him absorb her soul. She'd never wanted to give herself into someone else's keeping, the very thought had always terrified her. Yet, when she looked at Garrett, she wanted him to do things to her she couldn't even fathom.

Christie looked around the terrace, her brain somewhat fuzzy. "Well, goodnight, Garrett." Feeling elated and let down at the same time, Christie backed away.

"I'll walk you to the barn," he said, his voice steady, unruffled. Resentment filled Christie. Was she the only one suffering uncertainty?

"I'll find my way!" she declared, hating the emptiness inside. Blindly, she stepped off the terrace. "I know the barn is around the corner of the house and to the right."

"I have a flashlight." Garrett caught up with her

easily, catching her wrist. He shone the light on the ground at their feet. "I always keep one on the terrace."

"You're practical," Christie said, needing to speak, wanting to push back the intimacy that still held her in its grip. "Not me. Sometimes I'm as scatterbrained as they come." She gave a soft laugh. "Even Hannah's more organized than I am. Her dolls are all in order, lined up by height and hair color." She let her voice trail off, knowing she was talking too much. "I like her," she added. "At times I'm not sure the feeling is returned."

"She's beginning to like you," he said, "though I'll admit I don't always understand an eight-year-old. Sometimes her moods swing between amazing clarity and then petulance."

Christie's heart went out to him. "Keep showing her you love her." The gravel of the driveway crunched under their feet as they reached the barn entrance. "That's all she really wants. See you tomorrow." She didn't want the evening to end. She wanted soft words and intimate caresses. Moonlight whisperings and musky-scented sheets.

Christie pulled her hand free of Garrett's and scooted around him, but he put his hand against the door, preventing her from slipping inside. Christie's heart pounded so hard he surely must hear it.

Swallowing hard, she stared up at his silhouette. "What do you want, Garrett?" With the aid of the overhead security lights she could see him looking down at her.

"More than I should," he admitted in a low voice, his hand feathering along her cheek. "Probably more than I deserve." Christie turned her face into his caress, craving his touch.

His head lowered, his mouth touched hers, hot, hard, everything she wanted in that moment. Christie gave herself totally up to the sensation of Garrett's mouth on hers. Garrett's chest pressed against her breasts and his hips were against hers, creating an ache Christie couldn't deny. She wrapped her arms around his waist, running her hands down his back, feeling the ripple of muscle.

Christie dipped her forehead against his shoulder, gulping in huge drafts of night air, feeling like she'd run for miles. Her entire body ached. Slowly, Garrett pulled away. Christie leaned back against the door and wrapped her arms around herself.

"If I stay longer, things will get complicated," he said harshly. He appeared as affected by the kiss as she was.

"You're right. We don't want complications!" she snapped. Christie slipped inside, frustration and hurt driving her up the stairs to her apartment. Why had he kissed her, make her want him and then walked away? She felt twisted up inside, honest enough to admit she'd wanted the night to end differently. She had wanted to forget who she was and take a risk. The risk of loving Garrett McIntyre, a man so different from everything she was used to. She was inviting only heartache. She had this deep down feeling that a part of him still belonged to Judith.

∞ Chapter Twelve ∞

CHRISTIE HEARD A ROAR from far off as she and Hannah lay on their towels beside the small pond. The last several days had seen a continuation of the searing heat. When Ruth suggested they go swimming, Christie realized it was the perfect way to relax on her day off. Hannah was excited when she asked her to come along and it had been a good opportunity for them to get to know each other a little better. Of course, she'd also had plenty of time to wonder why Garrett had been making himself scarce in the last two days.

The swimming hole was located in a bit of a hollow a fair distance behind the house, shaded by trees on one side. She and Hannah had spent an idyllic afternoon taking dips in the small pond. The manmade pond was fed by a stream that wound its way across the fields. When Sam had dropped them off here earlier, she had fallen in love with its quaintness.

Christie could hear the sound coming closer. It sounded like a motorcycle. "Hannah, let's get everything packed together."

Hannah lay curled up on her towel like a lazy kitten. "I want to swim some more."

Christie gently tugged one of Hannah's ponytails. "Two minutes ago you looked ready to fall asleep. Time to go home," she said firmly. "Sam will be here soon to give us a ride."

The roar grew louder, more menacing. Christie stood, a strange prickling zinging up her spine. "What's that noise?"

Hannah sat up and they both looked toward the top of the hill that led to the house. A rider on a bike was approaching down the narrow dirt track they'd used to get here. "That's Daddy!" Hannah exclaimed, jumping to her feet. "Daddy has his dirt bike out."

The rider approached at a fast pace. From this distance Christie wasn't sure it was Garrett. "Maybe it's Randy," she murmured.

"No, that's Daddy's red helmet."

Fascinated, Christie watched as man and bike seemed to fly over a small hill. She held her breath until the bike landed safely on the ground, then closed the space between them quickly.

With a slide and the hiss of tires on gravel, the bike came to a halt about fifteen yards away from them. The rider, dressed entirely in black, put out long, jean clad legs to straddle the machine, the helmets black-visor hiding his face. Excitement gripped Christie. She wanted to confirm for herself that beneath the dark visor was Garrett, but a

Garrett she had only suspected existed.

¤¤

Garrett allowed his gaze to sweep Christie's slim legs. Cut off shorts, slightly tanned belly and creamy breasts overflowed a skimpy bikini top. Garrett swallowed hard, fumbling with the chinstrap of his helmet.

Balancing his bike, he cut the engine and lifted the helmet from his head. Pushing his fingers through his hair, he hung the helmet on the handlebar by the chin strap.

"Garrett!" Christie's voice vibrated through him. He looked over to see the awareness of him in her eyes. Sensual tension snapped between them.

"Daddy!" Hannah said excitedly. "You told me you don't ride anymore."

Garrett threw his leg over the bike, knocked the kickstand in place and moved toward them. He lifted Hannah in the air. "I do today, sweetheart." He placed her back on the ground.

"That was some entrance."

Garrett turned to Christie. Her glance measured him from head to toe and Garrett felt as if she'd touched him. Mouth dry, he thought of the places he'd like her to touch.

"Daddy, I want a ride," Hannah said.

"You're a brave kid," Christie said to Hannah. "After seeing your dad ride in here, I don't know if I'd want to ride with him."

Garrett gave Christie a smile that matched his wicked mood. "We'd have one heck of a ride, Christie."

Her eyes widened at his challenge. She moved

closer to the bike. "I didn't know you could ride these on the grass like that."

Garrett stood on the opposite side of the bike. "It's a dirt bike, built for this type of riding. It's not street legal." He patted the bike's handle grip, the gesture affectionate. "At one point my father just about disowned me. When I was younger I was in constant trouble for spooking our neighbor's cows with one of these."

Christie regarded him laughingly. "You've piqued my interest. You were in trouble with the law?" He read the skepticism on her face.

"Is that so hard to believe?"

"Maybe not," she said with a small grin.

Garrett looked away, certain every muscle in his body had come to attention. He was dirty from tinkering with the bike and his fingers still bore traces of grease, but here he was with his mind stuck on Christie and how he'd like to put her on the back of the bike and take her somewhere for some long, hot kisses. . .

"Daddy, I want a ride."

Jerked back into the present, Garrett took note of Hannah's slightly flushed cheeks. "Not tonight. You look like you've had a full day. I wouldn't be surprised if you fall asleep at the dinner table."

"Sam's coming for us." Christie rolled up the wet towels and pulled on a shirt and shorts over her bathing suit. Slipping her feet into her sneakers, she leaned down to tie them.

Garrett looked back along the road as a cloud of dust rose. "Here he is now."

"Hannah, you're tired and should ride back with

Sam. I'm going back a different way so I'll see you later," Christie said.

"Are you going to pick those flowers we saw? I can help." Hannah opened her mouth on a big yawn.

Christie laughed and hugged Hannah, surprising Garrett with the easy camaraderie that had developed between them. Knowing his daughter's swing in emotions, he wondered if it would last.

When Sam arrived in Garrett's pickup truck they walked over to meet him. If he was surprised to see Garrett he didn't say so, but helped them gather the girls' small picnic basket and blankets. "Ruth said to tell you dinner will be on in about an hour. She said don't be late."

"Thanks, Sam. Will you be joining us tonight?" Garrett asked, waiting for Hannah to climb into the truck seat.

"Yeah. I guess I've been invited." Sam smiled. "You know Ruth, she made up her mind we all have to try that new gazpacho or some such thing she made."

"She's got us all spoiled with her cooking."

Christie stowed her towel in the back of the truck, then looked up at the sky. "I'm going on a short hike, Sam, so I'll be walking back."

"There's wild dogs in the area," Garrett said. "It isn't a good idea for you to roam on your own."

Sam nodded quickly.

"Randy shot one at Clarey's farm down the road just the other day," Garrett said. "It was sick and looked rabid. I could give you a ride."

The thought of her legs straddling the seat behind him, her arms tight around his waist. . ..

She looked at his bike. "I don't know — the way you drove in here —"

"I'd never put you in jeopardy. It would be a short ride."

She hesitated, then said, "Okay."

Garrett turned to Sam. "Go ahead and take Hannah to the house." He looked at his daughter. "Make sure you tell Ruth you're back."

"Okay, Daddy." She looked disappointed, but surprisingly made no argument. Sam wore a grin as he got into the truck and with a wave drove away.

Garrett straddled the bike and turned the key, revving the engine. Un-strapping the other helmet he held it out to her. "Get on."

From the moment she climbed on the seat behind him his backside was branded by the feel of her sun-warm bare legs. Looking down he saw her sneakers and slim ankles behind his own jean clad legs and steel toe boots.

He revved the motor. "Sneakers aren't the best idea on a dirt bike!" he yelled above the motor. "Keep your legs away from that exhaust pipe." He reached down to slide his hand down her leg, repositioning it away from the pipe. He liked its slim smoothness. "Ready?" he said. She tightened her legs until he felt the clench of her thigh muscles against him.

Shit.

Garrett stared straight ahead, giving himself a minute to get used to the feel of her pressed up against him, then realized it would take a lot longer than a minute. "Ready?" he asked again, hoarsely.

She nodded her head vigorously, her face framed

by the black helmet, her eyes sparkling and excited.

Garrett moved the bike across the gravel and onto the uneven ground of the pasture.

Christie's arms hugged him, her palms flat against his stomach as her breasts pressed into his back. She wriggled to get comfortable and when he thought he couldn't stand any more, she finally stopped moving. Garrett felt as if she was wound all around him.

Gritting his teeth, he concentrated on the terrain before them.

They hadn't gone far when Christie nudged him. He stopped the bike and her hold loosened, then she climbed off the bike.

She looked back at him and then flung her arms out in uninhibited joy. "Garrett, this field is gorgeous. I can't believe it's been under my nose all this time."

Bemused, he watched her run over to a bright patch of flowers and start picking blossoms. Christie ran back toward him and stuck the makeshift bouquet in his face. "Smell these." Cautiously, he looked for bees. She laughed at him. "Come on, it won't hurt."

"It will if a bee stings my nose," he grumbled, but he couldn't hold back a smile. She looked so happy. When he was certain there weren't any bees, he smelled the flowers. "I never paid much attention to flowers. They smell nice."

"I love flowers. They have such a unique color and scent. Ellen adored them, she said they made her feel better. I used to fill her room whenever I could." Her mood turned somber and he noticed tears hanging on her lashes. "There was a florist around the corner from our apartment. He used to send over the flowers that were beginning to get old."

Garrett felt like a fist closed around his throat. "Give it time," he said awkwardly.

Christie looked at her bouquet, the stems crushed and the flowers hanging limply. Without a word she dropped the mangled bunch and climbed back on the bike.

"Christie —"

She shook her head. "It's okay." She put the helmet back on and pressed against his back. Garrett started the bike and headed them in the direction of home. He didn't know what to say to her.

Once more at the house, he left Christie at the barn and she gave him a subdued smile. He had an unsettled feeling in his gut as he walked into the house. In the kitchen he found Ruth bent over the stove as she lifted a loaf of bread from the oven.

"Smells great," he said. "How long before dinner?"

"About thirty minutes."

"I'll be right back," he said. On his way back out the door he pulled a section of yesterday's newspaper from the recycled pile.

Climbing on his bike, Garrett rode back to the field. He looked at all the flowers, then bent down and picked a yellow one. The petals were small and fragile against his rough hands. He'd never thought much about flowers, their structure or the beauty that made each one different. Garrett thought Christie was like a flower. Intricate and complex. He was curious what was below the surface. If he peeled the layers, what would he find? Would she break if he pushed too hard? The more he got to know her, the less she seemed like Judith. Fragile, tempestuous Judith.

He picked another flower, a large yellow one with a deep brown center. He picked more until he had a big handful of different colors and sizes. He hoped this would make up for the flowers that had been ruined.

He pulled the paper out of his back pocket and placed the flowers in the center, then wrapped the paper around it for the ride back. He smelled the flowers, not even thinking about looking for bees this time. They smelled pretty good.

Garrett had formed a picture in his mind of Christie's early life. Deep loneliness, and except for her sister, there hadn't been an abundance of love, something that would take time to overcome. If that was Christie's early life, then it must have been Judith's also.

Garrett parked his bike in the shed behind the house and crossed the yard to the back door. Looking up he saw Christie waiting for him on the steps.

"Hi." She grimaced. "Sorry for being a wet blanket. I wanted to apologize before we went in for dinner."

If she was a wet blanket, she could wrap herself around him anytime. "Don't worry about it. I do understand." Garrett held the newspaper-wrapped flowers out to her. "These are for you. Hope you like them."

Christie took the paper with both hands. Darting him a glance, she opened it and let out a small cry. She stepped forward and the warmth of her body was momentarily against him, her cheek resting on his.

"Thank you," she said. "You're the most thoughtful guy I know."

Garrett cleared his throat. "Glad you like them."

He followed Christie into the house, liking the happiness in her face, the way her dark hair slid along her cheek. Why hadn't someone snapped her up? She was strong and special, but there was also something so vulnerable in her joy that it scared him. Again he wondered, did he want to risk becoming involved and thereby embrace everything that came along with Christie?

∞ Chapter Thirteen ∞

THE DREAM HIT CHRISTIE with terrifying force. Smoke swirled around her head and the air was choking with it. She heard horses whinny in distress, hooves kick the walls and the splintering of wood.

Christie coughed, opening her eyes. The dream was real. She felt disoriented. The clock seemed to swirl, then cleared. One a.m. The smoke was suffocating. Muffled sounds reached her from below and the fear escalated into terror. Something was very wrong. She had to get out. Where were Garrett and Hannah? She thought a moment. She'd left the house only three hours ago.

She rolled out of bed, landing hard on the floor. Drawing a gasping breath, she tried to separate herself from the terror of waking in a smoke-filled room. She had to get her bearings. The doorway should be straight ahead.

Crawling on her knees she found the opening but the smoke was worse when she tried to go down the stairs. Christie leaned against the still cool walls, unable to see anything. If she attempted the stairs she might walk into an inferno.

She crawled back across the room and managed to find the staircase that led down to the inside arena. With a clutch of panic she realized the horse barn below her apartment must be on fire. She thought achingly of the horses.

Without giving herself further time to think, she plunged down the stairs. She half-slid, half-bumped her way down the last two steps. Christie landed near the bottom on her back, her nightshirt riding up her thighs. Her legs felt scraped and a warm stickiness covered the toes of one foot. She bit back the pain and clamped her lips on the moan that wanted to escape.

Dazed, she stumbled into the arena and pulled in gasping breaths of clean fresh air. Half a dozen horses ran around in the enclosure, nostrils flared and their tails straight out. Christie felt the same fear they were exhibiting. All she could think about was she had to get into the barn and make sure the rest of the horses reached safety. She was hardly aware of the soft dirt beneath her bare feet as she dodged the scared horses. She counted in her head, fifteen horses in the barn. She turned toward a small side door and entered the main barn over which her apartment sat.

Choking smoke hit her face. She held her shirtsleeve over her nose, her eyes immediately gritty and burning, terror making her steps falter.

She felt her way down the barn, finding the first stall open. She went down the line, thankful to find all the stalls appeared to be empty. A horse brushed against her and she fell to the ground.

Christie didn't see any flames or feel the heat of fire, just an overwhelming, thick smoke. She leaned against a wall. She couldn't remember if she was at the end of the barn or closer to the middle. Panic began to set in.

She had to move, but she couldn't catch her breath. She felt her way as she crawled on her knees.

"Christie! Where are you? Answer me!" From far off she heard Garrett. She kept her head down but turned toward the sound of his voice.

"Garrett!" Her voice came out in a pitiful croak, the taste of smoke acrid on her tongue. Christie pushed her sleeve into her mouth but the taste wouldn't go away. She closed her eyes, feeling the scrape of grit behind her lids.

¤¤

Garrett told the others to stand back away from the smoke billowing from the barn opening, but then he thought he saw something inside.

"Sam, somebody's in there." He put a wet rag over his mouth, a burning pain in his chest. Fear clawed up into his throat and joined the smoke to choke him. Christie. Where was she? He had to find her.

He tripped over something and fell to his knees on the hard barn floor. Reaching forward, he felt a bare leg. Dread knotted his stomach muscles. "Christie!" He pulled her toward him and then he lifted her on his shoulder and lunged to his feet. She lay too still.

Terror lent him extra strength. Garrett turned and ran as hard as he could from the barn, Christie bouncing like a lifeless doll on his shoulder. Once outside and away from the blinding smoke, he lay her on the ground and checked for a pulse. Sam was instantly at his side, his voice saying something, but Garrett didn't hear. He pushed the wild tangle of hair away from her face, pain and fear clawing at him. She didn't seem to be breathing.

He ignored the stinging in his eyes. He shook her shoulder, but her head lolled to the side. Black soot outlined her mouth and nose. "Christie!" She lay unresponsive. Tilting her head back he put his mouth over hers and breathed.

Pulling back, he tasted deepening anguish through every pore of his body.

No response.

He lowered his head once more.

Christie suddenly lifted her head and shoulders and coughed. Garrett let out a hoarse cry, barely aware of his own relief as he supported her head and neck.

"Okay . . . I'm okay," she croaked, her eyes opening, dark, tear-studded eyes in her soot-blackened face.

"Christie." Was that hoarse voice his? Sitting back on his heels, Garrett lifted her from the ground and cradled her limp body in his arms. He couldn't do anything else. He held her close to reaffirm that she hadn't died. He held her without words, conscious of the tremble of his arms. He had almost lost her.

"The horses, what about the horses?" she asked, jerking forward, looking back and forth. "We've got to get them out."

Garrett laid a gentling hand on her cheek, aware of the terrible shake in his hands and arms as she clawed at him and tried to rise. "Easy, Christie. Sam got everybody out."

"The road?"

"The main gate is closed, they can't get out on the road."

She looked at the barn with the smoke still pouring out the windows.

Garrett felt her shudder. He wanted to absorb her fear, take it away, but there was nothing he could do, especially when the remnants of his own fear were gripping him so tightly.

"Boy, that was close," she said weakly, going limp against him. Garrett clenched his teeth in an agony of reaction. She didn't know how desperately close it had been.

"While Sam was pulling the horses out I tried to find you." He cleared his throat, overcome with the memory of not knowing where she was. He had raced up the stairs and been pushed back by the smoke. "The smoke had gotten so bad, I couldn't see anything. I tried to get into the stairway on the arena side, but it was locked. I ran up the front stairs but I had to double back." Garrett never wanted to experience that fear again. For a ten-minute period, she had been lost to him. It had felt like hours.

"I was hoping you got outside. When I came back down the horses were all out." Garrett blanked from his mind the sick terror that had gripped him. "In the chaos Sam couldn't find you."

"I'm okay, Garrett." Her voice had become reassuring, as if she would soothe him.

Her nightshirt was stained and streaked with dirt. "I thought you were dead," he muttered starkly, staring into her eyes, seeing the evidence of life for himself. He tightened his arms.

"Garrett, I went down the stairs into the arena because of the smoke. I knew we had to get the horses to safety. You carried me out here?" she asked shakily, burrowing into him.

Garrett nodded his head jerkily. "You lay so still." The adrenaline still had him in its grip. He couldn't shut up. "Come on," he said, "you're coming to the house."

Garrett helped Christie to her feet. When she swayed he muttered a curse and lifted her into his arms.

"Boss — Christie — I've got the medical personnel coming to take a look. Christie, are you okay?"

She nodded.

Christie let the paramedics do a cursory examination, but pushed them away firmly when they wanted her to go in the ambulance. "I'm fine."

Garrett moved away and lowered his voice. "Sam, did you see anything?"

"Looks like the fire might have started by the office," Sam said grimly.

"The painters were in there today."

Sam nodded. "Yeah and I told them there was no smoking in the barn and made one of them put out a cigarette. It looks like some rags they'd bundled into a trash bag might've been smoldering for awhile, that's why there's so much smoke. There's a wall gone but it's not a supporting wall. Luckily everything was cleared out of there before they started."

"Do me a favor," Garrett said slowly. "Call and see if my brother's on duty tonight. I'll have him get those guys together and get to the bottom of this."

"The fire company is on its way, too," Ruth said.

Garrett looked at her as she came up behind Sam. Her head was covered with a cap and she wore a man's black robe. She clutched the neckline and pulled it up to her neck as if she were cold.

"Christie, are okay?" Ruth asked.

Garrett turned to find Christie behind him. "I'm okay, thanks to Garrett."

"You're going to the hospital." He put an arm around her shoulders and felt her stiffen.

"No hospital."

Garrett swore. "You need to be checked out."

She crossed her arms over her chest and shook her head. "I won't go." Her gaze met his squarely. "It'll take more than you to get me there."

"Stubborn woman. We'll talk about it inside." Garrett glanced quickly at Sam. "When the fire chief arrives let me know. I'll be at the house."

"Sure, boss, but I saw Marcus from the sheriff's office around here somewhere so I'm guessing he's been in contact with Randy. I'll double check." Sam looked at Christie. "Are you sure you're okay?"

"Fine."

Garrett reached out and lifted her off the ground and into his arms. She squirmed to pull her nightshirt down where it had ridden up over her knees. "Put me down, Garrett, I'm okay."

Garrett turned and strode with her to the house.

"Do you think it was deliberately set?" she asked, her voice shaky. "I still feel kind of confused. When I blacked out in the barn I don't remember anything until I saw you looking down at me."

"It could have been catastrophic." Garrett felt sick thinking of the losses to human and animal life. "Every animal in the barn could have been wiped out." He tightened his arms when he felt a shudder shake her. Losing all of his animals didn't bear thinking about, but he couldn't deal with the thought of losing Christie. "God, Christie, you could have died."

"But I didn't," she said firmly. "I'm okay."

Garrett let out a long breath. "I had an uneasy feeling and couldn't sleep, so I checked the grounds. By the time I got to the barn, smoke was already beginning to pour out. I phoned Sam as I got into the barn but within seconds the smoke engulfed everything."

He shouldered his way through the kitchen door. Christie's arms had crept around his neck and he needed them there. He didn't want to put her down, but he knew he would have to. He tightened his arms on her slim frame, the remembered fear skittering down his back.

"You can put me down now," she said. He continued through the house. "Garrett, really, I'm okay. The smoke was just so choking in there I got disoriented. Nothing happened."

Garrett entered his bedroom and stood just

inside the threshold with her in his arms. Watching her look around the simply furnished room, Garrett was reluctant to put her down. "Sorry, the room's a mess."

His arms tightened involuntarily as he thought of her sharing his queen size bed with him. When her attention settled on the rumpled bed Christie turned dark eyes to him. "Um, why don't you put me down?"

He walked past the bed to the opposite side of the room. He decided it wasn't a good idea; he and Christie in close proximity to a bed.

"I'd feel better taking you to the hospital," he said in a low voice.

"Let's not argue about it. I won't go, and you're needed here. If I start to feel sick, I'll let you know. I just need to get cleaned up."

"You can take a shower in here. I'm re-grouting the shower in the guest room." Garrett opened the door to his bathroom and flicked the light switch. "I've got to talk to the fire inspector. Randy will be here too, no doubt. The room is all yours. Take a shower and go to sleep. You look exhausted."

Christie's hand came up and touched his cheek. "So do you," she said softly, trailing her fingers across his skin.

Garrett clenched his jaw. He could see their reflection in the mirrors lining one wall. "We both look like hell."

"But we're alive," she said.

He knew how close they had come to a different ending tonight. Just thinking about it made him want to keep her in his arms.

Christie stared at him intently, then she too turned to the bathroom mirror. She groaned aloud. "Oh my God, is that me?" Their eyes met in the mirror and she deliberately ran a glance over his soot-streaked cheeks and neck. Gently, she reached her fingers out once more to touch his jaw. "You saved my life Garrett. I guess that means my life is yours, huh?" The small smile playing at her lips looked sad. "You can have it if you want it, Garrett."

He jerked his head back from contact with her fingertips, unable to stop his immediate reaction. He wanted her to touch him, but not in gratitude. A cold, heavy lump settled in his chest. As if she picked up on his doubt Christie dropped her arms and wriggled to be set free.

"Take a bath, a shower, stay in here as long as you like," he said shortly. "I'll dig up something for you to wear."

Slowly, Garrett loosened his hold and let her step back. He watched her eyes, saw the awareness flicker deep in their depths, the same awareness he felt. Why did he tease himself with something he wouldn't allow himself to have?

Garrett stood stiffly.. He had thought she was dead, and he had felt dead inside. It was a feeling he couldn't shake, some of that bone-deep despair still clung to him. Again he thought, what if she hadn't started breathing on her own?

Needing a moment, he turned his back on her and leaned over the sink. He stared at the new bar of soap Ruth had placed there. Slowly, he gripped it and lathered his arms and hands. Grimly, he ripped his T-shirt off and flung it in the wastebasket. Right now the burnt odor clinging to him was just too much. Grimly, he met Christie's gaze in the mirror. She stood slightly behind him, staring at him. She blinked and looked away, but not before he had seen the desire in her eyes.

Knowing he had to leave if he wasn't going to blow his good intentions to hell, he quickly dried himself. "I have to go." Garrett backed out of the room. Christie stood still; dirty, disheveled . . . lost. He stopped. "Are you okay?"

She laughed just a little bit, as if he had said something funny. "I'm fine. I'm a survivor, Garrett. You should understand that about me by now."

He was very aware of the sweep of her glance across his chest. He stiffened his resolve not to touch her. "You may be a survivor, but that almost changed tonight." Desperately, he turned toward the door and gripped the casing. "I'll leave you to get cleaned up."

"Daddy?" Hannah's whimper reached his ears. She stood on the threshold of his room. Garrett quickly crossed the room and squatted beside her as she rubbed her eyes.

"Sweetheart, why are you awake?" he asked with concern.

"There's too much noise," she said plaintively. "You smell like smoke," she added, wrinkling her nose.

Garrett pulled Hannah close in a quick hug. "Let's get you back to bed. Everything's okay."

Garrett moved to his dresser and pulled out a T-shirt. He turned to Christie as she stood in the bathroom doorway, looking ready to fall asleep on her feet. Slowly, she began to unbutton her nightshirt.

Seeing a span of creamy shoulder, Garrett clutched his shirt in his hand and left in a hurry. There was nothing else he could do. It would be too easy to lose himself in Christie.

Garrett looked at his daughter, who stared at Christie, a frown between her brows. Before she could say anything he urged her from the room, closing the door behind him. Getting involved with Christie would put an end to this torment . . . and create a whole new load of problems. He was already in way over his head.

¤ ¤

Garrett reentered the house several hours later. He and Sam had talked to the fire police and the investigators. Everyone had finally left, including Randy, who would be contacting the painters. There would be an investigation but it seemed likely the fire had started from a carelessly discarded cigarette butt. It had smoldered for hours before catching paint rags on fire, even though the rags had been bundled into a trash bag for disposal. Considering the damage could have been catastrophic in loss of life, both equine and human, they had been lucky.

Garrett walked into his bedroom. Christie lay curled up in his bed, her dark hair splayed across his pillow, slim shoulders barely covered by the sheets. She had washed away the black soot from the smoke, but again Garrett saw her in his mind's eye, again he felt the terrible fear that he had lost her. He resented the deep ache, the fear he experienced. He wanted to remain untouched by her, but he wasn't.

He had an overwhelming urge to crawl into his bed beside her and touch her, wake her to make sure she was still breathing and alive. He wanted her awake and responsive to life; to him.

He carefully reached out and pulled the sheet and blanket over her shoulders. He made sure not to touch her skin, afraid the slightest contact would undo his resolve to remain detached. Despite his care, she stirred. Quickly, he stepped back. He needed a shower to finally rid himself of the smell of smoke. Maybe it would free him from the weight sitting on his chest, but deep down he knew he was kidding himself. That weight involved more than tonight's fire.

Garrett entered the bathroom and closed the door softly. He turned the shower on full blast, welcoming the hot, stinging spray. When had he begun to care for Christie more than he should?

Garrett ducked his head under the water, letting the hot spray wash over his face and neck. The soot and grime from the last several hours washed away, swirling around his feet and down the drain.

He put his head back, wishing he could ease himself out of this restlessness that gripped him. He had asked Christie to stay on longer but she hadn't committed herself. Right at this moment he couldn't envision letting her go, but he honestly didn't know how she could stay either.

¤ ¤

Christie stretched and turned over, feeling the sheets warm and soft twisting around her body. She'd been so tired after her quick shower she had dropped into Garrett's bed naked. The soft sheets were scented with Garrett, a faint memory of his aftershave clinging to them. Recall of the horrible fear of the night before began to trickle in.

Christie looked at the digital bedside clock. It had only been four hours ago.

She saw again Garrett's face when she opened her eyes as she lay on the hard ground. The first time she had seen him, when she'd pulled Hannah out from in front of that truck, she'd seen the same panic on his face. Garrett had looked like he'd been brought to his knees. No one wanted someone dying on their property! No wonder he looked so ill, his face ashen. She wished it was because he loved her and thought he'd lost her, but she knew that was far from the truth. He desired her and probably cared about her, but love, well, that was something a man like Garrett might keep to himself.

Raw emotion coursed through her. In the aftermath of what had occurred, her emotions were close to the surface, burning inside her, wanting to be released. She wanted to rejoice in her feelings for Garrett, yet the hard lump inside urged her to push those feelings aside.

Garrett. He shouldered responsibility without asking, he was a good father and an honest man. Anyone who came under his care knew they were special, including her. He had offered her a job and a place to stay when she had reached an all time low. In his way he had looked after her like she was part of his family. That's the kind of man Garrett was. How could she help but love him?

She had never known anyone like him. She loved him with a growing passion. . .but apparently that wasn't enough. She had given him enough opportunity to come to her and he had turned her down. Another man might have taken what she offered and then went on. Not Garrett.

With her background and one broken engagement behind her, Christie didn't fool herself into thinking love was so easy or that she knew much about it.

Resting on an elbow, she traced patterns on the pillow beside her. She had no future at Winding Creek Farms if Garrett didn't love her. Christie cocked her head, suddenly aware of the sound of the shower running. Garrett. She could picture him in her head. His hair dark from the water, slicked back, the water running down his chest, over a flat stomach and... .

Restlessly, she left the bed, her gaze on the closed bathroom door. They could have both died tonight. Smoke inhalation could kill you before flames ever reached you. Right now Christie knew life was too precious to waste. *Go for it, Christie...*

Christie heard the words in her head. Encouragement from her sister. She envisioned Ellen's face before she became so ill, the laughter in her eyes, the sheer love of life her sister had never tried to hide. Could her sister have known she had a limited time on this earth? Christie swallowed back the tears. Why had Ellen been the one to die? She had loved life and it had hurt her time and again.

Desperation seized Christie, confusing her with its depth of anguish. Nothing terrible had happened tonight, no lives had been lost, why then did she feel so awful? Tears welled behind her eyes. Angrily, she rubbed the heel of her palm across her face. It's over, she told herself, don't go into a tailspin now. Reaching forward, she picked up the clean shirt Garrett had left out for her. With trembling hands Christie settled the shirt around her shoulders. She pulled the front of the material up to her nose and inhaled deeply. The want inside deepened to an all-consuming ache. Biting her lip, Christie stared at the bathroom door. Did she dare show Garrett how much she cared? Was she prepared to take that step? There would be no going back.

∞ Chapter Fourteen ∞

IN THE SHOWER, GARRETT shook his head under the hot spray, hoping it would wash away the last of the fear. Everything should be okay, but he still felt unsettled, on edge.

The shower door slid open.

Stunned, Garrett looked into Christie's dark, turbulent eyes. She wore one of his flannel shirts. Dark blue, it contrasted sharply with her light skin. Reaching mid-thigh, the old, soft fabric had slid off one shoulder as the flannel molded her breasts. If she had come in here naked, she couldn't have looked more alluring. Garrett had no control over his body's response. There was no room left for denial. She looked deeply into his eyes, then her glance dropped lower.

He could have resisted, he really could have, if she hadn't reached out a hand and trailed her fingers down his chest, and then further, tracing his ribs, his waist. How could she look so vulnerable, yet so wanton? Passion and want, or was he seeing what he wanted to see? A woman who desired him and one he had fought against desiring in return . . . or at least he'd fought against acting upon that desire.

After what had happened, almost losing her, Garrett couldn't hold out against what he so badly wanted. When he'd thought her dead, he had felt a deep empty hole in his chest. He needed her warmth to know she was really alive. He had been brutally reminded tonight how fragile life could be.

"I want you, Christie." Living, breathing, giving, Christie Jenkins. He reached forward, his wet fingers undoing one button, two, leaving a wet spot where they brushed her breast. He pushed the material aside, watched the shirt pool at her feet. She stood before him, naked in body and heart, and he felt humbled. He wanted to give her back what she was giving him. In that moment Garrett wanted to give her everything he was.

Without words he pulled Christie toward him until she too stood under the hot spray. He watched the water run down her cheeks and across her lips. Tenderly, he pushed the hair back from her face, the thick, silky strands clinging and capturing his fingers.

Christie leaned into him, her breasts now against his chest. Garrett closed his eyes, his breath hard and fast, feeling as if he'd run far to get to this point. How many times had he thought of Christie like this?

Garrett couldn't turn her away, not when he wanted her this much, not after the night they'd had.

Christie was special, he knew that, and vulnerable. That thought made him pause, but in that moment she cupped his jaw and urged his mouth down to hers. Her lips were warm, wet, touching his softly, then more deeply, as if she were thirsty and she wanted to drink him.

Garrett loved the feel of her flesh, soft and warm, alive beneath his questing hands. She stood on tiptoe against him. He pulled her into the shower fully, dropping his mouth to hers, pushing her gently against the shower stall.

The gentle, life-affirming caress of her mouth breached his final barrier. Reaching behind him, Garrett pushed down the shower nozzle, and the spray ceased. He stepped from the shower into the steam-clouded bathroom. Christie's hand entwined with his and she brought his hand to her heart.

Grabbing a large towel, Garrett began to dry her skin, his lips following the path of the towel, watching her eyes, reading the desire burning there.

She wound her arms around him.

"You're so beautiful, Christie," he said softly. "I've wanted you for a long while. I tried to keep my distance."

Her eyes were clear and direct. He couldn't mistake the desire there. She ran her tongue over her lips and he groaned, trying to slow the rampaging of his heart.

Tenderly, she brushed the hair from his eyes. Garrett dropped the towel over her shoulders and behind her neck, using it to pull her to him. He saw the change in her when their flesh contacted again, hers warm and slightly damp, his still dripping. She squeezed her eyes tightly closed and her hands gripped his arms with a new tension.

"My turn," she whispered, gently tugging at the towel. He felt the trembling of her hands as she slowly, caressingly, wiped the droplets from his back, then moved to stand in front of him. When Christie touched the towel to his stomach he pulled her with him into the bedroom.

Slowly, he lowered her to the bed and rolled until she lay on top of him. Spikes of her hair lay across her shoulders. He caught her hair and gathered it in one hand and slowly rubbed the towel over it. He separated the strands and ran his fingers over her scalp. Her face peered at him from the depths of the towel. Deep brown eyes, slim straight nose and full red lips.

He abandoned the towel when she pressed her lips into his neck, a shock of heat spiraling to the core of him. Christie's movements against his body increased the heat and urgency he felt. Garrett needed to complete the unbelievable closeness he now felt. He needed Christie.

¤ ¤

Christie felt every hard, muscled part of Garrett. The man was built so tough. She stretched sensuously beneath him, loving the feel of his body along hers. She ran her toes up the back of his hair-roughened legs, her hands slowly tracing the contour of his back, remembering and cherishing each shudder she felt in him. This man reacted to her.

Christie felt so strange, so heated, a terrible want building inside her. She wanted to love Garrett.

There was no doubt, no question. She needed to experience all of him. It felt right. Nothing else was as important as the two of them right now.

Garrett's tongue traced erotic patterns over her lips and Christie's body reacted immediately, muscles clenching as his hand moved down her back, her hip, then lower to cup the rounded softness.

His mouth moved to her breasts, his lips teasing the tender flesh.

Reaching over to the bedside table, Garrett pulled a foil packet from the drawer. There was still a question on his face. If she wanted to stop, he would, she could see the message in his eyes. Tenderly, she pulled him closer, offering him everything she was.

"I want you Garrett." She pushed against him, and he groaned aloud, his hand pressing into her hip to hold her still. She could see the powerful effect she had on him as an expression curiously like possessiveness hardened his face.

Emotion coiled deeply inside Christie, waiting to burst forth. She wanted to push him over the edge, follow him down and then save them both. She splayed her fingers and moved up his chest, her lips feather-soft on his jaw. She insinuated her leg between his.

Garrett's lips and teeth skimmed her shoulder, making Christie shudder. She thrust her breasts against him and this big man began to shake. Christie arched her neck, bombarded by pleasurable sensations, her overloaded senses wanting even more.

When Garrett sought her warmth she welcomed him. It felt so right, his body with hers, giving and taking, one hard, one soft.

"Christie." The hushed whisper rasped across her jaw, up her neck, hungry mouths met as Garrett thrust forward.

Christie gave a soft cry, unable to believe the heightened sensation, like an explosion in her brain. Consumed with the rupture of emotions let loose, she squeezed her eyes and shook, hardly aware her nails dug into his skin, unwilling, unable to let go as sensation reached to the very tips of her toes. Surely the energy of their coming together flew around the room, skimming the walls until slowly it dissipated. Christie felt free of all the pain and loneliness in her life. In this glorious moment of forgetfulness the past meant nothing. It held no power over her and in a flash of fire, she felt totally free.

In the aftermath she lay as still as Garrett. She didn't open her eyes in case it was a dream and it all vanished. "I love you," she whispered inside. The words came directly from her heart and could not be contained. Once said, they could never be withdrawn.

¤¤

Garrett jerked awake, his breathing hard and painful, waiting . . . willing the bad dream to fade away. He stared at the ceiling, then at the woman beside him, her skin smooth and supple. He ignored the damp chill on one side of his chest, the side that wasn't touching the smooth skin of Christie's back. His arm was still around her as she lay curled against him, having finally fallen into an exhausted sleep. He didn't want to let her go.

With the sheet twisted about his hips and one of his legs touching hers, Garrett thought about the intimacy they'd shared. They had made love, there was no getting around it. It felt as close to love as he had come in this life.

Judith had never touched the spot in him that Christie had. That thought scared the hell out of him.

Christie stirred against him, turning into him even before she woke, her fingers splayed across his stomach, moving to his chest, gently tugging the hair. She sat up, leaned over him, a tangled length of dark hair like rich silk against his chest. He reached out to twine his fingers through it.

¤¤

Christie woke with incredible joy and a feeling of release singing inside. She turned her head to find the source of her joy. Garrett. He melted her heart, just looking at him. This strong, tender man. Honest. Her smile faltered at the seriousness of his expression. Be strong, she told herself. Don't stumble now.

Christie looked around, saw the shirt she'd worn half draped on the end of the bed, one sleeve trailing the floor. She reached for it, trying to bide herself time.

"Hey, come here." Garrett said softly, his calloused yet tender palms sliding across her bare skin.

Christie slid to the edge of the bed, wanting to fall back to the bed, let him touch her. She pulled the shirt over her shoulders, staring at him as she buttoned the shirt.

"Garrett, there's something we have to talk about," she said slowly. She hated that a hint of wariness entered his expression.

"What's that?" He put his arms behind his head, causing the triceps to flex and bulge.

Christie looked away. "There's something you should know. When I got that letter from Judith two years ago, she asked me for something." Christie swallowed, pain a constriction in her chest.

"I'm listening."

Christie bit her lips nervously and then rushed on, "She told me she had gotten involved with someone — and she needed to get out. She needed money to leave."

"And?"

"I sent her money. I had a thousand dollars saved up. I sent it." She looked at him. "I'm sorry," she whispered. "She had never asked for anything, I didn't even know her, but I knew she needed help. She was my sister," she ended on a whisper, knowing her voice was pleading. His frozen expression broke her heart. Christie put out her hand but he ignored it.

"And you're telling me this now? Why?"

"I- I wanted to be honest with you. I care about you Garrett. And I care about Hannah. I can't go on with this secret between us."

Garrett reached for his boxer shorts, jerked them up his legs and settled them on his hips. Christie stared at the dusting of hair on his chest and the hard ridge of muscle beneath. She pressed her fist to her own chest, fighting a heavy, sinking feeling.

"So you helped my wife leave me." His jaw

bunched and a vein throbbed along his neck.

"Yes." Christie pressed her balled fist to her mouth. No, she railed, her moment of joy couldn't turn so sour. She wanted to cry. She had followed her heart and made a mess of it! "I'm sorry, I should have told you earlier. I was afraid."

Christie turned to watch him pull on a pair of jeans.

Flat stomach, wide, muscled chest dusted with hair. She recalled each place on his body she had kissed. Each spot she shamelessly wanted to taste and explore again.

Garrett thrust his arms into a shirt, not bothering to snap it. "Afraid that I'd be angry?" His voice came out harsh and she threw her head back.

"There's nothing else I can say. You needed to know." Her emotions were slipping past her control. "I didn't ask her any questions. I didn't know about you or Hannah." She took a deep breath. "There's no reason you should be angry, you know."

"Christie, this is a lob out of left field." He shook his head and came to stand next to her, his hand cupping her cheek for just a moment, but then he stepped back. "I have to go check on the buildings."

Christie watched him go, her shoulders slumping. She looked around the room, remembered how safe she'd felt here a few short hours ago. She didn't feel like the same person. Their lovemaking had changed her forever. Perhaps even now she didn't know how much.

A deep, dark emptiness engulfed her. It had only taken one night to reach the grandest heights and then surely the depths of misery. Right now her soft heart felt like it had shattered into a million pieces.

It was no consolation that Garrett had to be feeling the same emptiness.

∞ Chapter Fifteen ∞

GARRETT REACHED FORWARD AND lined up another block of wood. His wide-bladed axe sliced the air, splitting through the wood, sending pieces flying in opposite directions. He had energy to spare today. He couldn't seem to expend it.

Hannah sat a safe distance away in the grass by her swing set, watching him act like the crazy, work-demented fool he'd turned into the last several days since the fire. Even Bo Peep seemed to be watching him with a wary expression in her soft brown eyes.

"Daddy, why do you work so hard?" Hannah asked now, lying with her chin propped in her hand.

Garrett reached for the steel thermos Hannah had brought him. Unscrewing the cap, he lifted it and took a deep gulp of water. Wiping his mouth with the back of his hand, he reached for another block of wood and threw his daughter a glance. "It's got to be done. I might as well do it now."

"Is Christie the lady you're going to marry someday, Daddy?" Hannah asked, reaching out as a butterfly flew past her face.

Garrett missed his mark and swore, then dropped the axe when it glanced off the side of his boot. Hannah was right. Why was he working so hard? Pulling off his leather gloves, he walked over to his daughter and dropped to the grass beside her.

"Why would you say something like that?"

"Well, because she's living with us again."

Garrett replied carefully, "Christie will be leaving soon. Her stay with us is just like a vacation of sorts, then she goes home to her own place. I'm glad you two are getting along better."

"At first I didn't like her. I know why she had to come here, though. She was sad and wanted to see Mommy. It's not her fault Mommy wasn't here."

"Hannah, I'm glad you're okay with Christie being here. I didn't know how you would feel about her," he finished truthfully.

Hannah gave him a thoughtful look. "Christie is okay. She really cares about us." Her answer was off-hand and Garrett couldn't get a handle on her expression. He looked up at the clouds skittering across the sky. Rain, he thought distractedly. The sky was clouding over for rain.

"If Mommy and Christie are sisters, how come they didn't grow up together?"

Garrett took a deep breath. "Sometimes there are reasons families fall apart. I think that's what happened in Christie and Mommy's family."

"Did you love Mommy?" Hannah asked in a small voice.

Garrett stared at her, perplexed. How do you tell a child that even with the best intentions, love doesn't always mean forever?

"You mom will always hold a special place inside my heart, Hannah."

Hannah screwed her face up in a frown. "Why do you marry a lady?"

Garrett reached out an arm and pulled his daughter close. "A man and woman get married because they respect and care about each other. They want to spend the rest of their lives together and raise a family." Garrett felt his heart stop for a moment. The explanation had come so simply from his lips. He did respect and care about Christie, but he felt like he'd been deceived again by a woman he'd come to care about.

"Why can't you marry Christie? Then she could be my mommy, couldn't she, Daddy? We could have babies too."

Garrett clenched his jaw, then relaxed it, determined to make it through these questions. "I know you miss Mommy," he said quietly. "That's the way it is when you love someone and lose them, but we don't just invite someone else to be a mommy, just because you like them."

Hannah shrugged her small shoulders and her voice dropped. "Nah, I guess not." She lifted a hand to touch his cheek. "If you got married Christie could stay."

Garrett gave a silent groan. His daughter was like a dog with a bone once she got something in her head. He stood and lifted Hannah into the air. He knew he was taking the easy way out, distracting her so she screamed with delight, but he felt bruised and didn't think he could handle anymore mommy questions right now.

Since the smoke damage to the barn Christie had been staying at the house. He had insisted and was surprised when she yielded. Luckily, most of the damage had been minor, though who had started it still remained a mystery. All logic pointed to the fire beginning as they'd thought, but the painters swore up and down they hadn't smoked in the barn after that one warning. Les Doyle had come to mind, but Garrett knew he was being unfair. Les might not be able to hold his drink, but he'd never done anything as serious as arson.

As for Christie, Garrett knew she spent time with Hannah, but he hadn't seen much of her.

Christie had taken to staying out in the barns until late in the evening. Garrett didn't like to see her working so hard but from all accounts she seemed to enjoy spending time with the horses.

Garrett rubbed the back of his neck. Even when he'd had the sole care of Hannah and struggled to brink the farm into the black financially, he hadn't felt this disoriented or lost. His concentration was off, and he didn't like it one bit.

If Christie decided to leave there was nothing he could do to keep her here and he wasn't even sure if he wanted her to stay. Despite his initial anger at her disclosure, a part of his also felt like he was being unfair. He'd wanted her each day and night since that one incredible night, but he had erected barriers and this time he was determined to keep them in place.

Hannah climbed onto her swing seat. Garrett stood behind her and pulled the swing back. Over by the barn he could see Christie talking with Buddy. He clenched his jaw when Buddy grabbed her arm and leaned down to her. Christie laughed at whatever Buddy said and patted him on the back.

"Daddy, you can let go," his daughter said.

"Hang on tight." Watching Christie, he gave the swing a push.

Christie leaned down by the water spigot to get a drink. She laughed as Buddy playfully pushed her face into the water. Squatting down, she cupped her palms and splashed the water on her face and neck so that the water ran down her T-shirt. Garrett watched a smile of enjoyment spread across her face. He could almost hear her murmur of appreciation, a small sound she made deep in her throat. He remembered it from their night together. There was a lot he recalled from that night.

He rubbed a hand over his face, feeling the dryness of his mouth. As he watched, Christie sat down on a bale of straw and Buddy walked away into the barn.

He couldn't seem to tear his gaze from her. She looked up once and seemed to look right into his eyes across the distance, but then she looked away as if she'd never seen him.

"She's a good girl, that one." Ruth said from behind him, startling him.

He turned to Ruth. "Are you looking for me?"

His housekeeper raised her brows in surprise.

"Why no, Garrett. I've come outside to get a breather is all. I've been canning dilly beans all day and the kitchen is like a furnace. We might have to eat out on the terrace tonight. It's like a breath of fresh air out here in comparison." Ruth fanned herself with one hand. Her gaze strayed toward the barn. "Buddy's taken a fancy to our Christie," she added casually, "don't you think? I heard him asking her if she'd consider moving into town when her month here is up."

"Our Christie?" Garrett looked at his housekeeper with a raised brow, wondering if he'd ever really known her. "When did you become an advocate for Christie?"

"Well, you have to admit she fits here. Seems like she's been here longer than the short time she has, doesn't it?"

"She's been here less than a month," he said, giving Hannah another push on the swing.

"Christie is my aunt," Hannah said matter of factly, clinging to the swing chains.

Ruth looked at Garrett with raised brows.

"Judith's sister," he admitted in a low voice. "I wanted it kept quiet until it was confirmed."

"I suppose you played it safe and had Randy check her out."

"Of course. I can't take any chances."

"I admit at first I wasn't too sure about a city gal — but Christie's all right," Ruth said with a definite nod. "She pulls her own weight. She's even won Hannah over."

"You're happy because she knows how to do her own laundry," Garrett said dryly.

With a stern look Ruth slapped his arm. "Garrett McIntyre, you know Christie is a good girl. Do you know she took out that old typewriter that was stored in the hallway closet and typed up my medical forms for me? I hate dealing with those insurance companies and their hard-to-read forms. It's all changed since I left the business. I get all mixed up. I'm not butting in but you just make sure you treat her right."

"Thanks for not butting in," he said dryly. She would skin him alive if she knew how he wanted to treat Christie. How he had already treated her. "She's leaving in two weeks," he said.

"Do you want her to stay?" Ruth asked in her direct manner. *Yes.*

Ruth lifted a brow and chuckled. "That's what I thought."

Had he said that out loud? "Some things aren't that simple," he muttered. "She's got her own life back in New York and I'm sure it's a far cry from anything we've got down here. She might not like it after six months or a year."

Ruth shook her head in what looked like despair. "Garrett, haven't you learned anything in your thirty-one years?"

"Thirty," he corrected irritably.

She waved a hand. "Whatever. Women need to feel wanted. Some of us need the words. Sometimes you have to take a chance and go out on that limb. God knows there's no guarantee in this life."

Abruptly, Ruth turned and walked back to the house, and he could hear her muttering about thick-skulled men.

Garrett watched her go with a frown.

"Daddy, you stopped pushing." Hannah's voice

brought him back from his thoughts. Hannah hopped off the swing and reached her arms around him and squeezed tight. "That's okay, Daddy. I was through anyway." Garrett looked down into his daughter's happy face and dropped a kiss on her soft cheek. For Hannah, it was so simple. Why couldn't it be as simple for adults?

¤¤

Having finished her chores Christie sat on a bale of straw beside the barn. Her thoughts felt scattered. She had tried, unsuccessfully, to block that glorious night with Garrett from her mind. She didn't think she'd ever forget how he'd made her feel. Cherished and special. He had opened her eyes to more than one experience. She had to let it go, but how do you wipe love from your heart?

She had come to a decision about where to scatter Ellen's ashes. In the end it had been so simple and obvious. The meadow on Garrett's property was the perfect spot. She had known it the first time she'd seen it. Then, it had become doubly important to her when Garrett had gathered a bouquet of flowers from that meadow. She knew Ellen would have loved it too. Since this used to be Judith's home, in Christie's mind it pulled them all together.

Once she scattered the ashes, there was nothing to keep her at Winding Creek Farms. She and Garrett weren't exactly talking at the moment which made the situation awkward and strained. Christie chewed on the corner of her thumbnail.

Everything had changed. He looked like he'd been carved from stone. She couldn't talk to anyone in the barn without giving herself away, not even Ally, whom she'd become friends with. They'd shared some confidences, but this felt too close to home and Ally was herself in the throes of a new relationship with Randy. Christie knew she was on her own.

"Christie, so are you going with us tonight?" Buddy asked, exiting the barn with Ally following close on his heels.

"A night out on the town sounds good, doesn't it?" Ally said with a grin. "No work tomorrow, so we can hang out and have a good time."

"What time are you leaving?" Christie lifted the weight of her hair off her shoulders.

"Around six." Ally looked at her watch. "About two and a half hours. We'll take two cars. You can ride in with Buddy and I'll meet you guys over to O'Malley's."

"Sounds like fun." Tossing Ally a deliberately lighthearted smile, Christie said, "This might be the last time we can get together before I leave." There wasn't anything to keep her here tonight. Garrett certainly hadn't sought out her company. The weight of Christie's emotions threatened to depress her, but she defiantly tossed back her hair. She wouldn't chase a man who'd made it clear there was no place for her in his life. She'd done what she felt was right, not only when Judith had contacted her but also in telling Garrett.

"There's Garrett now," Ally said, looking past her. "I'll see if he's free. Maybe he wants to ride into town with us." Ally turned away and Christie felt her heart sink down to her toes. How could she and

Garrett pull this off? Spend a night together, out with others. . .

"Hey, Boss!" Ally called out. "Christie, Buddy and me are going into town for a steak and a few beers. Are you game for a night out?"

Garrett walked over to where they had gathered. Christie looked at him, thinking he looked tired and hot. Just a little while ago she'd watched him split wood. His wide, muscled shoulders under that white T-shirt had brought back memories of how good he looked without a shirt. Tightly muscled arms and the strength of his arched back as he swung the axe over his head had made her feel hot. He worked so hard.

A sudden thought hit Christie and a ray of hope made her sit up straighter. Could he be as miserable as she was?

Garrett gave each of them a nod. Was it her imagination or did his glance linger on her just a bit longer? Christie clasped her hands tightly.

"Thanks, but I'm getting behind on some paperwork so I'll have to pass. Where are you off to?" he asked casually. Again, Christie swore his glance lingered on her. She gave him a tentative smile, then called herself a fool for caring.

"We're going to introduce Christie to some of the nightlife. She's riding in with Buddy and I'm going to meet up with them later."

Garrett's glance at her seemed casual, but she saw the emotion in his eyes for just the briefest moment. He cared. "Maybe I'll make it next time. Have fun."

"We will," Christie said with a bright smile. She

turned to Buddy. "I'll meet you out here later." She threw Garrett a cursory glance, pretending her heart wasn't breaking in two. "See you, Garrett." She hurried away from the barn before the hurt became too unbearable.

¤ ¤

Les chugged another beer back, then wiped his mouth with his hand. From his corner in O'Malley's bar he'd been watching that woman of McIntyre's for the last half hour, but the two she was with kept pretty close tabs on her. He planned to get her alone one more time and warn her off for good this time. Les pulled out his wallet and looked at the meager bills inside. If he didn't run her off he knew Kim would be out of a job big time. McIntyre might not hire his Kim back at all if he took a permanent fancy to that other one.

Les had a notion the doctors were babying Kim, making her stay off the ankle, but she'd told him every day she felt stronger. Christ, he'd just about wanted to puke when she told him she'd gone down to apply for food stamps. He wasn't taking any charity. No way. Les banged his glass on the bar top, but it was just noisy enough the bartender didn't hear him. Les narrowed his eyes in the smoky interior and wondered if maybe the bartender was ignoring him. Everybody in this town seemed to have an attitude about one thing or another. He wondered why he'd stayed around this long.

Les grabbed his change and pocketed it, not bothering to leave a tip.

¤ ¤

Christie took another sip of her soda and glanced around the crowded room. O'Malley's had turned out to be an old bowling alley turned into a bar and pool hall. She'd enjoyed several games of pool that she'd played really badly, but Buddy hadn't seemed to mind and he'd insisted on teaching her to play. Now, having sunk her fourth eight ball and losing the game again, she walked over to their table while Buddy went to the bar for a refill.

Ally had been waylaid and was over by the bar talking with some friends. She and Buddy had shown her a good time. They'd had thick steaks and fries and she'd been introduced to just about everyone in the bar. Being a local hangout, everyone seemed to know each other, a fact which never ceased to surprise her, having lived in an impersonal city her whole life.

Christie lifted her soda and chased the straw around the glass for a moment before catching it and taking several deep swallows. Looking around the crowded room, she suddenly felt as if she were being watched. Casually, she scanned the room, but everyone seemed to be enjoying themselves in their own corner. Shrugging off the feeling, she left the table and walked across the popcorn-strewn floor. As she moved past a narrow corridor besides the ladies room, a hand reached out and roughly latched onto her wrist. Another hand covered her mouth and in the shadowy corridor she was half-pulled, half-dragged backwards. Off balance, she couldn't get her footing. A door opened and she was yanked outside into the night air.

The steel door clanged shut and she managed to

get her feet under her. Sweat and alcohol swirled around her nostrils. Frightened, she bit the fleshy part of the palm covering her mouth, shoving a hand upwards towards the man's face, the heel of her hand hitting his nose a glancing blow. He cursed, his hold slackened and she swung around and lurched away. She stared into Les Doyle's face, her chest heaving with fear as he blocked the doorway. A quick glance over her shoulder showed a fence and a dark alleyway.

He took a step closer, blood streaming from his nose.

"Stay away or I'll scream so loud they'll hear me in Lexington."

"I know what you're doing," he said furiously, holding a bloody handkerchief to his nose. "You took my wife's job. Do you know how much we need that job?"

"We've been over this. I didn't take her job. She's recovering. When she's better she can come back. Garrett said so."

"Don't play with me. She's not coming back if you're there playing up to the boss. I'm not blind, I've seen you and him."

A chill crept up her back and she went deadly calm. "What are you talking about?"

Les smirked. "Never mind. If he's not careful, he'll lose that farm and his shirt, too."

"What do you think will happen when I tell them you forced me out here?"

"Right now my alibi is I'm at home with my wife and kid, so that makes you a liar. You might better keep your mouth shut."

"You're not me."

"You've got a real smart mouth, but I'll make it simple. All you have to do is leave. Everything was fine until you showed up."

"Kim broke her ankle before I came here." She narrowed her eyes at him. "By the way, how did she break her ankle, Les?"

"She hurt it out in the yard," he said, his eyes narrowing. "I take good care of her and little Tommy," he snarled. "I want you out of town fast or next time I won't be so nice."

He moved in closer, but Christie had had enough with his drunken threats. She pushed against him and yanked the door open. She stumbled back inside the hall and frantically searched the room until she saw Buddy and Ally. They must have seen panic in her face, because they both rushed toward her.

Ally reached her first. "Christie, what's wrong?"

"Les Doyle was here. He dragged me outside."

"Where is he?" Buddy asked, looking behind her. "I'll straighten him out."

Christie gripped his arm. "Leave him alone, he's just a troublemaker." She could feel a bad headache coming on. "If you don't mind, I'd like to go home." She shivered with reaction.

Ally put an arm around her shoulders. "I'm calling the police to report this. He can't just drag you somewhere against your will."

"I just want to get out of here," Christie said, rubbing her cold arms. "He went out that door but I'm sure he's gone by now."

"That goes out back and then opens onto the street." Buddy strode down the corridor.

"Geez, I'm sorry this happened, Christie. All we wanted to show you was a good time."

"You have. It was a great time until he showed up."

"I have Randy's cell number, he'll know what to do. This time Les has gone too far. I heard Kim took the baby and left today. Probably best move she's made all year." Ally pulled a cell phone out of her pocketbook and punched in numbers. "Why don't you sit down while I call? If I get his answering service, I'll leave a message."

Christie sat at an empty table behind her, keeping her eyes trained on the corridor from which Les had appeared. In no time Ally rejoined her.

"Do you want a drink or something?" Ally asked, her eyes heavy with concern. She held up her mixed drink. Christie stared at it a moment, then shook her head.

"No, thanks." Christie gripped her fingers together on the tabletop.

"He hurt you!" Ally exclaimed, outraged, as she reached for her hand.

With a frown Christie looked at the red puffiness of her wrist. "It's okay."

Buddy came back inside. "He's gone." Disgusted, he looked around the almost empty barroom. "He must have climbed the short fence out back and left that way because the gate is locked. Just in case I'll ask around to see if anyone's seen him."

Christie waited around with Ally until Randy arrived. When he first walked in the room, if it wasn't for his dark blue uniform she would have mistaken him again for Garrett.

He came right over to her. "Christie, I got Ally's message. Are you okay?"

"I'm okay. I was more scared than anything."

"Look what he did to her wrist, Randy," Ally said with disgust.

Grimly, Randy examined the discolored skin. "I'll put a call out on the radio. Hopefully we can round Les up by morning." He looked at Ally. "Did you see him hanging around?"

"No, but I heard Kim left, so maybe that's what set him off."

Christie shuddered. "He'd been drinking. He accused me of stealing his wife's job. It seems he's been stuck on that since we first met, even though Garrett told him that's not so."

"Let's get you home, Christie," Randy said. "You look pretty shaken up."

"I'll take her," Ally said.

"We'll do the best we can to bring him in," Randy said. "I promise you that."

Christie stopped in her tracks and turned back to Randy. "Wait, there is one more thing that struck me. He made a remark that if Garrett wasn't careful, he'd see he lost the farm, and his shirt too. I know the fire is still under investigation. You don't think Les could be involved, do you?"

Grimly, Randy said, "I've already brought that up to Garrett. We're checking out any lead we can. The best thing for you to do is get back home." He looked at Ally. "You take Christie and I'll follow in my car."

There was nothing more Christie could say. The night had turned sour and she just wanted to get back to the ranch. Right now it seemed the only safe haven.

∞ Chapter Sixteen ∞

GARRETT TIPPED HIS CHAIR back against the wall of the house. Dusk settled around him on the small porch, the night painting the hills in an eerie half-light. Even the night creatures were quiet tonight, as if a storm brewed somewhere.

Hannah had finally fallen asleep and Sam had taken Ruth out to a movie, so he had the house to himself. Garrett had had plenty of time to go over the angry words he'd spoken to Christie. He was honest enough to admit he was missing her like hell. Garrett closed his eyes. What had happened to him? Had he become so afraid of being hurt that his only recourse was to push her away? She'd been honest with him. She could have kept it a secret, the money she'd sent Judith, but she'd elected to tell him the truth. And to hell with the money anyway. Judith would have found another way to leave even if Christie hadn't sent her the money.

What man in his right mind would push a woman like Christie away? Soft, warm, kind, sexy as hell. When they'd danced under the stars to the sad, soulful croon of Patsy Cline she'd felt like she belonged in his arms. It had almost felt like forever, a notion he hadn't entertained in a long time.

As he wrestled with the idea of trying to mend the hurts he had inflicted, Garrett heard the sound of a car in the driveway. Thinking perhaps Christie had returned, he rose quickly and walked across the terrace. He loped around the corner of the house, his heart racing like a teenager's in anticipation of seeing his favorite girl.

A dark car sat idling in his driveway, the headlights cutting a path across the yard. A tall stranger stood on his back step at the screen door.

Garrett halted. "Can I help you?" he called out.

The man turned and walked back down the steps toward him. Garrett sized him up. Early twenties, long black hair on his shoulders, lean face, slim build.

"I thought I'd have to drive back to that last town I went through." Relief showed on the man's face. "I'm Darrell Anderson. I'm looking for Christine Jenkins."

Garrett's head reared back. "Christie?"

The man nodded. "Yeah, Christie. I had a hell of a time tracking her down. All she mentioned was Winding Creek and Kentucky. Luckily, your place is well known."

"Are you Darrell, her brother in law?" he asked crisply.

"Yeah — so she's mentioned me. My son's been

missing her. I had time off so I decided to drive down."

Garrett could now see Darrell was sizing him up.

"Who are you?" Darrell asked.

"Garrett McIntyre. I own this ranch. Christie works for me."

Darrell looked startled. "What . . . she's working down here? She didn't mention that."

Just then the back door of the car opened and a small figure climbed out. A child walked over to the man and clung to his side. Garrett swore his heart stopped. The boy's face was framed by hair as dark as the man's but the eyes, mouth and brows were a miniature replica of Christie's.

¤¤

Christie called goodnight to Ally as she stood by the barn. After Ally drove off, followed by Randy in his cruiser, she studied the moon a moment, enjoying the quiet wash of the night air against her face. Christie pushed her fingers through her hair, rubbing her temples in an effort to dispel the headache that had started earlier. She was glad she'd moved her belongings back into the barn. The smoke odor had dissipated in a surprisingly short amount of time so she had decided to get out from under Garrett's feet.

Surprisingly, the house was still well lit. Usually Garrett only had his office light or the living room light on this late. She held her wrist up to see her watch by the security light overhead. It was almost midnight. Something must be wrong.

Christie moved across the moon-washed yard, glancing quickly to the right and the left, suddenly leery of the shadows near the buildings. She realized she must be more shook up by Les's attack than she'd earlier realized. She had never been fearful of being out here at night, and that she was now made her angry. She wondered about the other times she'd felt like she was being watched and hurried her steps. Could Les have been out there in the shadows watching her at other times?

Her legs felt shaky as she walked up the steps and into the house through the kitchen door. She would check to make sure everything was okay and then go back to her apartment. As she crossed the kitchen she could hear voices. She walked down the hallway and stopped at the living room entrance.

Stunned, she looked at her brother-in-law, Darrell, in Garrett's living room. Darrell and Garrett were both inspecting an old rifle lying across the oak coffee table. A part of Christie's brain noticed the glass door was open to the gun rack behind Garrett's chair. Beyond that, her thoughts felt frozen.

"Darrell!"

Both men stopped talking. She gripped the door handle, staring at Darrell, then darted a glance at Garrett but his face wavered before her. She could see his mouth forming words but she couldn't hear them.

Garrett came over to her and gripped her cold hands. She looked up at him, glad for the strength in him. "Your hands are so warm," she murmured, allowing him to draw her into the room.

"Christie, sit down. You look like you've seen a ghost."

She found herself on the couch. When Garrett

moved back she noticed Eric in Garrett's large chair. She gave a small squeal of excitement, then clapped her hand over her mouth. His body was curled into a tight ball and he was sound asleep.

Hurriedly, Christie looked up at Darrell. "Why are you here?" she demanded.

"I was worried about you."

She gave him a searing glance, unable to contain the anger that always seemed to flare. "Why were you worried? You didn't worry about Ellen or Eric when you left."

"Jesus, Christie." He pushed his hands through his hair and the gesture seemed one of impatience. Darrell had never been one for patience. "How long do I have to pay for that?"

Christie felt like she'd been dashed with cold water, suddenly mortified by what she'd said. Why was she being hateful? She tried to pull the emotion back inside but it was growing. So much anger, so much anguish. She felt incredibly unsettled and looked at Garrett helplessly. "My family seems determined to intrude on your life here."

"It's not an intrusion," he said quietly, his eyes watchful. "I've invited Darrell and Eric to stay at the farm while they're in Kentucky."

"What?" She glared at Darrell.

Darrell looked away from her. "I had planned to find a motel," he said. "Garrett thought maybe you'd like to see Eric and if he was here close by it would be easier. . ." he let his voice trail off.

"Also, Hannah and Eric could meet," Garrett said.

Christie felt frozen and confused. Was Darrell being considerate of her feelings? She stood up. "I'm sorry, Darrell," she said stiffly. "It's just been a shock. I didn't expect to walk in and find you." She turned to look at Eric, loving the angelic face, his features relaxed in sleep. Gently, she touched his arm and then looked up at Darrell, fighting back the tears and emotion; the memories. "I'm so glad you brought Eric. I have missed him."

"Well, we'll be here in the morning and then he'll be able to talk your ear off."

Christie didn't miss the relief in Darrell's voice. What kind of person was she that she had such a blind spot where he was concerned? At least he had come back in the end and taken care of his son. It's more than her father had ever done for any of them.

"It's late," Garrett said. He lifted the rifle from the coffee table and placed it back in the gun cabinet. Closing the door, he locked it and pocketed the key. "The rest of this can wait until tomorrow. Let's get you two settled in the bunkhouse."

Christie looked at Garrett in surprise. "They're staying in the bunkhouse?"

Garrett nodded. "Sure. There's enough room with only Emmet and Joey there now. It's rough but it's clean."

"And I really appreciate it, Garrett," Darrell said. "It's been a long drive and I'll admit I'm bushed."

Christie clenched her hands. She had to make up for her earlier attitude. Was she some kind of monster? Why couldn't she just believe Darrell when he said he had been worried about her?

"Darrell, I'll see you get settled in," she said firmly, looking at Garrett to see if it was okay with him. He nodded.

Darrell watched her with wary surprise. "Okay. I'll get Eric and I'll follow you."

The intensity of Garrett's light colored eyes seemed to bore into her. He probably thought her attitude was horrible; harboring resentment against her sister's husband. Christie wished she knew how to get rid of those feelings but each time she saw Darrell she was reminded of the way he'd abandoned her sister. How could she ever forgive that? Was it even up to her to forgive him?

¤ ¤

Christie led the way on the short walk to the bunkhouse, her mind going in all directions. On the one hand she was glad to see Eric, but on the other hand, Darrell's presence made her tense, wary. She rubbed the back of her neck and shook her head. Darrell was Darrell. He was Eric's father and she had to make the best of the situation.

Christie opened the bunkhouse's wooden door. She had been in here once with Ally, so she knew the basic layout. She flipped the switch and indicated Darrell should precede her into the room.

"Emmet and Joey won't be back until Sunday night, but I'll leave a note on the door letting them know you're here. They're nice kids, you won't have a problem with them."

Christie opened a side door off the main kitchen/living room combination. "The bathroom is through here and the extra bedroom has two beds."

Christie stood in the bedroom doorway as Darrell carefully laid his sleeping son on the mattress. Eric stirred and opened his eyes. He let out a small cry when he saw Christie, one that went straight to her heart. "Aunt Christie!"

She moved to kneel by his side and gently pushed the hair off his forehead. "Hello, Eric." Tears started to her eyes. "I'm so glad to see you, Kiddo."

"I missed you," he murmured, putting his arms tightly around her neck. Christie met Darrell's eyes over Eric's shoulder. They seemed to say, 'I told you so.'

"But now we're together," she said brightly, pulling back. "And you've gotten even more handsome."

Eric gave her his sweet smile and he yawned.

"You need to go back to sleep," Christie said. She stood, intending to pull the blanket back over Eric, but Darrell's hand was there first. Eric closed his eyes and drifted back to sleep.

Christie backed up against the door, surprised by Darrell's care as he covered Eric. When he left the bedroom she stepped back into the main room and pulled the door to the room closed.

"Garrett seems like a real nice guy," Darrell said. "He was kind of protective at first and wouldn't let out much information. Almost made me a little suspicious, wondering what your relationship is with him."

"My relationships aren't your concern," she said sharply. "Why are you here?"

"I told you why." He let out a deep breath and sank into one of the armchairs beside a small fireplace. Pushing a pair of cowboy boots to one side he stretched his legs out. "I know I've given you reason to doubt me in the past," he looked at her with one eye open, "okay, plenty of reason," he amended. "But I'm on the up-and-up. I want what's best for my son." He gave a big sigh. "Christie, let's have this out, we can't avoid it any more. I loved Ellen, but I left, plain and simple. I was scared, I didn't want to deal with her illness, the responsibility of it. I knew you'd be there for her," he ended bitterly.

Christie felt the hair rise on the back of her neck. "Of course I was there. What does that mean?"

"You were always there to pick up the pieces," he said. "If Ellen needed someone, she'd run to you. Hell, she was so dependent on you she sometimes forgot I was her husband. Do you know what that's like? You knew every minute detail of our lives. There was no privacy."

Feeling the couch at the back of her knees Christie sank down onto the cushion. "But I was her sister. We took care of each other. You know our parents weren't there."

"I know. I understand. But I never liked it. Call me shallow, but she needed you more than she ever needed me." He tipped his head back and looked up at the ceiling, then looked sideways at her. "In the beginning it caused a lot of fighting. After a while I accepted it. Do you know why?"

Wordlessly, Christie shook her head.

"Because I loved her. Ellen was a wonderful, vibrant woman, I don't have to tell you. I loved her and I knew she loved you. I knew when I got scared and left you would stay. She wouldn't be alone."

Now Christie looked away, memories slamming her. "I could never leave her."

"You stuck it out no matter how terrible it got.

She always had her Christine Louise."

Christie flinched. Her parent's name for her. "Don't call me that."

"Sorry. I'm bushed."

Christie stood up. "Get some sleep. Garrett said to come to the house in the morning for breakfast. I'll see you and Eric then."

She walked quickly to the door. She needed to get out in the open air. Too many conflicting emotions were pushing at her. Her stomach churned to think she may have come between Ellen and Darrell, perhaps contributed to their breakup. Why had she never seen that?

"Christie?"

She stopped with her hand on the doorknob. "Yes?"

"We can't change the past. It's the future we have to deal with."

Christie closed the door, feeling numb. Had she over-protected her sister, interfering in Ellen's life by loving her too much? Did she put an emotional stranglehold on the people she loved? Her interference had helped Judith flee her husband.

Her emotions churned and tension held her rigid. One thing was clear to her where she and Darrell were concerned. She had to figure out a way to meet on common ground for the sake of her nephew. It's what Ellen would have wanted.

As Christie reentered her apartment moments later her mind searched for answers. A light still burned in Garrett's house, but she couldn't talk to him. Wearily, she wondered if there would ever be a right time to let all the secrets out in the open.

Christie had just brushed her teeth when she heard heavy footsteps on the stairs to her apartment. Quickly, she walked to the door and peered down into the stairway. "Who's there?" she called, her voice echoing back to her high and thin.

"It's Garrett, Christie. I just talked with Randy. Can I come up?"

"Yes."

"He told me what happened." He entered semi-dark room and Christie quickly turned on another lamp. "Are you okay?" he came immediately to her. Gently, he reached for her hands and turned them over, muttering an angry curse as he saw the bruising on her wrist. She read the concern and the fury. He put his arms around her and she let him, savoring his closeness, his caring. She wanted to hang onto him and not let go. Not realistic, but for right now it felt wonderful.

"I was just shook up," she said, "but I'm okay now." She stepped back.

He looked at her doubtfully. "You don't look okay. I want you to stay at the house until they find Les. It's the safest thing to do."

She turned away. "I'll be fine," she assured him.

"That's right, you will be. Come on." He gently urged her toward the door.

She held back, but he wasn't giving up and she was tired. Maybe it wouldn't hurt to let him take charge for one night and not worry about being the strong one.

"Okay. I am worried about Les being out there . . . maybe watching me."

"Randy filled me in, but I want you to tell me

what happened."

As they walked downstairs and back to the house she related everything that had occurred that night. By the time she had finished, Garrett looked even more furious. "The guy's off his rocker, but then, when he gets drinking, he seems to lose all sense of decency."

Christie couldn't help the shiver that crawled across her. "Are his wife and little boy okay? Ally said Kim left with the baby."

"They're fine. Randy spoke to Kim at her mother's house. Randy's going to keep in touch with her."

As they entered the house, Christie couldn't help but look around outside one last time. "I wondered if Les might have had something to do with the fire."

"When they catch up with him he'll be questioned about that too." Garrett glanced at his watch. "It's late, why don't you try and get some rest. You'll be safe here, I promise."

Christie felt the threatening prick of tears and blinked quickly. "Thank you Garrett."

He stared at her intently, and she thought he would say something more, but in the end all he did was nod his head.

"Goodnight." She wanted to stay with him, but she turned and walked down the corridor to the room where she had stayed before, wishing things had been different.

¤¤

Christie continued her work routine in the barns. With Darrell and Eric at the farm the last three days she knew she would be staying at least until they left. The authorities still hadn't been able to locate Les, and that preyed on her mind also.

Christie dumped a wheelbarrow load of sawdust in the next stall and paused to look at Eric. He'd been helping her all afternoon and she could sense something was bothering him, but he'd remained quiet when she'd gently prodded him about what was wrong.

"Aunt Christie, can I smooth that sawdust for you? Ally showed me how to do it."

Christie smiled. "Sure, just keep the pitchfork tines pointed away from you." Christie kept a close watch as he leveled the sawdust. "So what did you and Hannah play this morning?"

"We played games and then she showed me the ponies. They're really neat. They can find carrots in your pocket without even seeing them."

Christie laughed at his obvious amazement. Eric was a city kid, just liked she'd always been a city kid. Although maybe now that was changing, Christie mused. She didn't want to be a city kid anymore.

As Eric finished with the pitchfork she took it from him and led the way from the stall. "We'll make a country boy out of you yet."

"I liked the puppies," he said suddenly, kicking his heel against the ground. "Dad said I couldn't have one, even though Hannah's got lots. He makes me mad."

Christie squatted beside Eric and pushed the hair out of his eyes. "Those kind of dogs grow pretty big and they need room to run. It's tough having a dog that size in the city."

He crossed his arms. "He could stay at our

apartment."

"Eric, I bet your dad would love to have a dog, but he knows a puppy wouldn't be happy in an apartment all day while you're in school and he's working."

He looked thoughtful. "Do you think Daddy always wanted a dog and he could never have one?"

"I think you should ask him," Christie said, seeing Darrell enter the barn with Ally.

"See you later, Aunt Christie." Eric ran to meet his father and Christie could see him talking to Darrell. Darrell looked at her thoughtfully a moment, and then he smiled and took the hand Eric held out to him. Together, they walked from the barn.

"Whew! Are you as hot as I am?" Ally asked, dropping down to sit on a bale of hay. "I can't remember the last time we had a stretch of weather like this in June."

"Might as well be a hundred," Christie muttered, feeling a trickle of sweat slide down her cheek as she too sat on the long bale.

"Got any plans for after work?"

"No."

"Well, it's Garrett's birthday. We've reserved a room in town at one of the restaurants. Everyone's going. There'll be music and dancing. Say you'll come."

Christie felt her heart race, then slow. Garrett's birthday and she hadn't known. She didn't know a lot of things about Garrett. Christie pushed back the ache. "Is it a surprise?"

"Yeah. His mother planned it. And Randy," she

added.

Christie thought Ally's voice sounded too nonchalant. She gave her a coy look. "Oh yes, Randy."

Ally's cheeks turned a delicate pink. With a small laugh she shrugged. "You know Randy, he likes to play both ends so I don't take him seriously."

"Maybe you should," Christie suggested gently.

"Sometimes I think he's the best thing that ever happened to me, the next minute I can imagine him flirting with every woman he comes in contact with." Ally shrugged and looked across the driveway. "I don't want to take that route again. I keep thinking it won't last."

"I can understand the fear."

Ally sighed. "But you think I'm wrong."

"I think you're smart. You'll figure it out."

Ally smiled and draped an arm across Christie's shoulder. "Thanks for the confidence. Now what about tonight? There's a bunch of us riding in my car if you need a ride."

"I don't know, Ally —"

"Come on, Christie, don't tell me you're thinking of staying home. It'll be loads of fun. I invited Darrell and he's planning on going. Anyway," her smile turned teasing, "Garrett would miss you if you didn't show up. Now I'm going to give you a little advice. Don't let the opportunity pass to get to know this guy. I know the boss likes you."

"Seems he likes everyone here," Christie supplied casually. "It's nothing more than that."

Ally raised an eyebrow in obvious disbelief.

"Christie, come on, level with me. I like to think

I've gotten to know you in the time you've been here. I think you and the Boss would be good together. I've never seen him pay attention to anyone else the way he does you. I'd take that as a good sign."

Christie cleared her throat. "Have you known Garrett long?"

"Most of my life. It's a small community and we all know each other at some level."

"Did you know Judith, his wife?"

"I'm sorry to say I did." Ally gave her a straight look. "Look, I don't gossip, but I know for a fact Judith made Garrett miserable. She'd say one thing to his face and sneak around behind his back. Everybody knew it, which of course made it worse. That girl had a bunch of problems." Ally lowered her voice. "I was here the day she took off. I was still working in the barns, finishing up some painting and whatnot. Luckily, it was late, and no one else was around. It was hard not to hear what was going on since Judith was screaming. Some of the things she said, she was downright cruel. The best thing she did was walk out. It was too bad she forced Hannah to go with her. That accident messed that little girl up pretty bad for a while."

"Hannah didn't want to go?" Christie asked quietly, disturbed by what Ally had revealed about Judith.

"Nope. She wanted to stay with Garrett. She'd called him Daddy from day one and it was like she was his second shadow. He was probably the first bit of stability she'd ever had in her life. That poor kid begged to stay with him but Judith made her go, pulled her out to the car by the arm. I don't think Garrett even knew Judith was leaving until her car tore out of here."

Christie felt an ache in her chest for Garrett and Hannah, for the wounds inflicted. "Judith sounds like she was a lost soul. Her leaving really hurt Garrett," she said flatly.

"To give Judith her due, though, she was a good mother to Hannah. She just had a lot of insecurities. But truth to tell, it would've hurt Garrett worse if she'd stayed. Those two were like a pair of Kansas twisters. You can only take so much of that kind of living and then it starts to wear you down."

Christie looked askance at Ally. "Are you kidding? Garrett seems one of the most even-tempered guys I've come across."

"Normally he is, but she brought out the worst in him. . . the worst in each other." Ally leaned closer. "Garrett hasn't been an angel by any means, but there aren't many men who'd raise someone else's child. He's done a good job raising Hannah, too." Ally stood up and dusted the hay off her jeans. "So what do you say, are you with us?"

Pushing aside her misgivings, Christie nodded. "Sure. I'll have to stop somewhere to pick up a gift."

"Not to bother. We're all putting in toward a new bike helmet and jacket, since he's started riding again."

"He hasn't been riding that long?"

"Not that much since I've worked here, about three years now." Ally arched a brow and gave her a slow smile. "He's starting to have a bit of fun like in the old days. I'd venture a guess somebody's a good influence on him. What do you think, Christie?"

Truthfully, Christie didn't know what to think. Her heart was telling her to love the man and take a chance, but her head was saying run like hell and save herself potential heartache.

"I don't want to miss Garrett's party."

¤ ¤

Later that evening Christie sat at the table next to Ally while Darrell and Eric sat across from them in the restaurant's dining room. She'd ridden into town with Darrell and on the way over he'd thanked her for explaining to Eric about big dogs in small apartments. For a moment, Christie had almost felt close to her brother-in-law. It had been the first time they'd spent any time together and hadn't ended up in an argument.

Garrett and Hannah hadn't arrived yet. The restaurant was full of people. Randy stood behind Ally and played with a strand of her hair, then urged Christie out of her seat and introduced her to his mother, Caroline McIntyre. Christie recognized her from the pictures in Garrett's living room. Caroline was an attractive woman dressed in a gorgeous midnight blue dress, flitting from person to person. Christie had felt decidedly underdressed beside her even though the older woman commented with admiration on Christie's soft blue floral slip dress. It was light and cool and packed easily. For some reason Christie had thrown it in her bag before she left New York, never dreaming she would be wearing it. The matching sandals were perfect for the warm evening.

Ally had taken Christie under her wing and

introduced her to several of Garrett's friends and their wives. Christie had sensed their curiosity and friendly interest and she'd wished she would be here long enough to develop lasting friendships. She had never experienced such warmth and a feeling of coming home as she did since staying at Winding Creek Farms. It would be difficult to leave.

Christie was seeing the social side of Garrett's life. She knew he was involved in quite a few community undertakings and she was finding small towns a quaint novelty. Garrett's friends seemed genuinely interested in her and didn't hesitate to ask about her life in New York.

When people began to whisper that Garrett had arrived she was aware of a pounding in her chest. An unreal stillness enveloped her and then she saw Garrett walk through the door and people began to yell surprise and throw paper confetti. Eric of course, had a great time pelting everyone within range from the confetti-filled paper cup he'd been given.

Slowly, Christie turned her head, looked past Darrell's curious and suddenly knowing eyes. All sound fell away as she met Garrett's glance, saw her presence register on his face. He gave her a quick smile then he turned as people greeted him on all sides.

"So you and Garrett are involved," Darrell said beside her.

Christie looked at him.

"He was Judith's husband, for Christ sakes!"

Christie opened her mouth to tell him to mind his own business. Instead, she said, "Don't you think

I know that? I can't forget it."

Darrell frowned but didn't say anything further.

Garrett looked incredibly handsome in a dark blue shirt with an equally dark tie tucked across his flat stomach. Black jeans hugged long legs. A jacket was slung over his shoulder, and he was laughing and talking. Christie kept her glance on him, as if a part of her needed to imprint this moment on her mind. Hannah stood by her father in a long pink, frilly dress, ivory colored bows in her hair. Christie wondered if Ruth had helped her pick the dress and had fixed her hair.

One after another, friends greeted him. Women hugged and kissed him and hung on his arm. Jealousy bit at Christie sharply and she became annoyed with herself but she couldn't bear to think of Garrett with other women. . .making love with other women. She thought of him as making love only to her. She wanted Garrett to be hers alone.

Wondering why she did this to herself, Christie looked around wildly. She caught Ally's glance and the other woman lifted her glass. So Ally knew she and Garrett were involved. It didn't matter. He was an adult, he must have had affairs before now. Christie shook her head, disliking the idea that she might be just another affair. Maybe she and Ally had more in common than she'd realized. Both of them hankering after a McIntyre man who wouldn't or couldn't commit.

"Christie," Randy said, startling her when he appeared at her side. "How's the wrist?"

She moved it this way and that. "No problems." She lowered her voice. "Have you found Les yet?"

He looked disgruntled. "No, it's like he vanished."

"Well, he has to turn up somewhere. Speaking of which," she added lightly, "you've been pretty scarce around the farm all week."

Randy's smile reminded her of Garrett. He was a fun-loving guy, and she could only imagine the trouble the two of them could have found together as boys.

"I've been putting in a lot of overtime and I'm seriously considering buying a small farm on the outskirts of town. It's too good a deal to pass up. There's an attached barn with room for a few horses. The place needs work but I like doing that kind of thing, and Garrett's real good at fixing up places, so I'm going to rope him in on this."

"I had no idea you were looking to buy something. I wish you luck with it."

"By the way," he said, looking past her shoulder. "Have you seen Ally? I've lost her."

Christie wondered if Ally had anything to do with him wanting a place that had room for a few horses. "Yes. She was over by the buffet a few minutes ago. I think she was looking for you also."

Randy flashed her a confident smile. "I'll find her."

"Randy. Christie." She turned instinctively toward Garrett's voice, her body instantly filled by warmth.

Randy shook his brother's hand. "Happy birthday, Garrett. What's it feel like to be an old man of thirty?"

"Same as yesterday," Garrett said with a laugh.

Christie studied him, taking in the carefully

brushed back hair, lean jaw and the smile in his eyes. He was a man who would be at ease and confident in any surroundings.

"Happy birthday," she said, aware of the sizzle of attraction when his attention turned to her. "Many more."

Garrett's intent gaze made her feel as if she was the only woman in the room. Reaching forward, he took her arm and drew her closer to his side. "Don't I get a birthday kiss?" he murmured, turning his back on his brother.

Surprised, Christie raised a brow. "I think you've had your quota of adoring women already. I don't want to be one more in a long line."

"You're in a category all by yourself, Christie," he murmured. He lowered his head, bringing his face close to hers. She could see each whisker on his smooth shaven face and the laugh lines beside his eyes. It had been too long since she was this close to Garrett and every fiber of her wanted to be closer. She wanted the birthday kiss, or any kiss from Garrett for that matter.

When his lips touched hers, warmth sped through her, infusing her with heat and want. The sounds of revelry fell away. Christie felt only Garrett. She brought her hands up to grip his arms and then his arms circled her back. Christie knew she might be asking for more heartache, but she put all her desire for him into the kiss.

He stepped back, but his eyes remained locked with hers for countless seconds. Christie felt too muddled to read what might be there in the deep seriousness. Slowly, the sounds of the crowded room once more impinged on her ears.

Self-consciously, she looked around, but no one seemed to be paying them any special attention. Even Randy had disappeared, no doubt in search of Ally. Christie wanted to ride the feeling of that kiss for another few minutes. Ride it until reality intruded.

"Will you come with me, Christie?" He held his hand out, palm up. "I'd like to introduce you to my friends. Ally mentioned she started the introductions, but I'd like to pick up where she left off."

Telling herself this didn't change anything, yet feeling as if her life was taking another turn, Christie twined her fingers with Garrett's. In that moment, with the memory of his mouth on hers, she might have followed him anywhere.

"We need to talk Christie." As if he couldn't stop himself, Garrett dropped another leisurely kiss on her mouth. Christie could barely breathe, but she knew her eyes had to be saying what her heart felt. There was something different about him.

"Tonight," he promised.

¤¤

Several hours later Christie stared at her flushed face in the restroom's bathroom mirror. Quickly, she wet a paper towel and wiped her hot cheeks with water. What an unbelievably fun party! How had she let Garrett persuade her to dance most of the night?

The band had sounded wonderful and for the first time in a long time Christie had felt the music flow through her. She and Garrett had danced so well together. Fast dances, two steps, line dancing which she knew nothing about but she'd been game to try. Right now the flow of adrenaline still raced through her veins. She hadn't wanted the music to end. Christie recalled the look in Garrett's eyes, the heat and promise he made no effort to hide.

She gripped the edge of the sink, waiting for the accelerated beat of her heart to even out. The excitement inside made her want to sing and shout. She couldn't keep still. "I can't believe I'm doing this. I can't believe I love him."

"Some things are meant to be, you know."

With a muffled cry, Christie swung around.

"Ally!"

Ally grimaced. "Sorry, I didn't mean to startle you. I was in the bathroom stall."

"Er. . .I was just talking to myself, it didn't mean anything," Christie murmured, feeling as if her cheeks were bright red.

Ally lifted a brow, but her eyes were kind. "If you love Garrett, don't let him go. The man you love is worth fighting for."

Christie leaned back against the counter. She put her head back and looked up at the ceiling. "That sounds like an old cliché, but to quote another one, sometimes it's easier said than done."

Ally nodded somberly. "You're right, and I'm a fine one to give advice."

Christie lifted a brow. "You and Randy?"

Ally's eyes flashed with excitement and then she looked miserable. "That man is going to be the death of me yet." She leaned over the sink to wash her hands. "At least with Garrett it's easy to see where you stand. He's so crazy about you. The man never takes his eyes off you."

Christie swallowed her surprise.

"Randy is another story, but I've decided to take him at his word and take the plunge. He says he's serious and he wants to settle down."

Thinking of Randy's plans to buy a small farm, Christie said warmly, "I don't think you'll be sorry. Does this mean marriage?"

Ally laughed, and her eyes had lost their earlier sad look. "Hell no, not yet. I'm talking a long engagement. I can't let go of all my hang-ups at once, you know."

"I wish things were that easy for Garrett and me."

"They are. You're both single, attracted to each other. There's nothing standing in your way."

"I wish that was so." Christie gave Ally a rueful glance. "You'll probably hear it sooner or later. The big thing between us is Judith."

"She's gone, and Garrett's better off without her."

"She was my sister."

Ally looked shocked, then embarrassed. "Damn me and my big mouth. I'm sorry, Christie."

"You were just telling me the truth. I was young when she left, I barely remember her, but it's like she's standing between us."

"Honey, only if you and Garrett let her. He was over her a long time ago. Don't hang onto her ghost at the cost of your happiness." She pressed Christie's shoulder. "Eventually, things will come out right for you and Garrett, you'll see. But in the meantime, I sure as heck wouldn't kick the boss out of my bed."

∞ Chapter Seventeen ∞

G‌ARRETT OFFERED C‌HRISTIE A ride home. When Hannah smiled at her and said "pretty please," Christie was truly lost under the spell of the entire evening. Why refuse when she wanted to be in his company?

"Let me find Darrell," she said. "I got a ride in with him."

"I told him earlier I'd give you a ride if you needed one."

"Oh." Christie wasn't sure how to feel about that. Was Garrett so confident of her that he could make that decision?

"Eric was tired so they left about an hour ago."

She'd been having too good a time to notice Darrell or anyone else leaving.

It was almost midnight and most of the party had broken up. Christie should have been exhausted but she still rode the earlier high of dancing with

Garrett, meeting his friends and being included in his family circle.

On the way home, with Hannah buckled between the two of them and sound asleep, Christie knew she had to speak with Garrett about the decision she'd made. "You know why I came to Kentucky."

He glanced at her then returned his attention to the road. "Yes."

"I've decided the closest I'll be to fulfilling Ellen's last wish is to leave her ashes here."

The atmosphere in the truck changed subtly. Tensely, Christie grips her hands in her lap.

"I'd like to scatter Ellen's ashes on your property."

"The meadow?" he asked quietly.

Christie tried to see his face but the night was dark all around them, not even a streetlight offering any light. Some of the tension eased from her shoulders. "Yes. I guess I'm not surprised you know."

"I've seen how much you love that meadow."

"It's so in tune with what Ellen would have wanted. What do you think?"

He sighed. "Of course, Christie. I know how important it is to you."

Relief filled her. She relaxed fully against the seat, feeling slightly dazed now that it was almost over. She had Garrett's consent, and in the end, it had been so easy. "You have no idea how much this means to me."

"I think I might," he said quietly.

Christie looked up at the sky.

It's time to be at rest, Ellen. Time to let everyone find peace.

"So where do you go from here, Christie?" he asked, his voice low and intent.

She looked at his profile, momentarily highlighted by the headlights of a passing vehicle.

"Are you leaving once you scatter your sister's ashes?" he ground out, as if the words were torn from him. "I want you to stay."

"I can't seem to focus on that until I take care of Ellen's ashes." She fiddled with the door handle. "It seems to be common knowledge that we, uh, have feelings for each other. Of course," she added dryly, "after that kiss tonight, anyone wouldn't have to guess."

Garrett turned onto a two-lane highway. "For the record I never worry about anyone else's opinion. Are you concerned about what others might think if you stay on here?"

"Others . . . meaning who?"

"Darrell."

Christie shot him a surprised glance. "Why should I care what Darrell thinks?"

"He came all this way to see if you were okay. It sounds like there's something really intense between you two."

Christie sat bolt upright. "Believe me, there's nothing between Darrell and I, just some unresolved stuff that involves my sister and of course, my nephew." Christie swallowed hard, deciding to get some of it off her chest. "Most of the time we're barely civil to each other. I can't seem to deal with this anger I have toward him. I'll grant you he seems different than he used to be but I don't know if the change in him is real. He said he's sorry for abandoning my sister and he's a good father to Eric, but there's just something sticking in my throat when I look at him."

Garrett ran a hand through his hair and nodded solemnly. "Sometimes it's nearly impossible to forgive the hurt, but if you hang on to it, after awhile that's all you've got." He heaved a deep breath. "Look at Les. He's not the first man to lose his job, but he lets it eat at him instead of looking for another job. The way he's treated you is proof of him trying to shift the blame for the mess he's made of his life. Now he's hip deep in trouble and I don't know how he'll ever get out."

Christie pondered his words. "You're right. The anger's balled up in a tight wad inside." She lowered her voice. "Sometimes I'm afraid what will happen if I release it. Maybe I'll go off the deep end and snap. The idea of a total loss of control terrifies me. All my life I've always tried to do the right thing, but sometimes I wonder if I've been too rigid, maybe even unfeeling."

He pulled the truck into the farm's driveway and drove up to the front of the barn. Turning off the engine, he turned to face her, his arm along the back of the seat. "Take care of Ellen's ashes in whatever way you're comfortable with. Once your mind is at ease, let's see if there's a way we can meet in the middle. I'll admit right out I want you to stay, Christie. I'm sorry for blaming you for helping her leave. That wasn't right and I'm ashamed of myself.

"My marriage with Judith near the end was

pretty bad, but I made my own share of mistakes. I've seen the other side of the coin, too. I know people can be happy together." He grinned and shook his head. "Hell, look at Ruth and Sam. They're as happy as can be. If you knew Sam before he hooked up with Ruth, you'd wonder how Ruth had the nerve to look twice at such a surly guy."

His hand touched her shoulder. "What I'm saying is, caring about you is important to me, and that caring involves looking out for each other. Are you game?"

For the first time in days, Christie felt a ray of hope. Her thoughts raced wildly. Could it be possible to find such happiness? "I want to stay, but I can't move forward until I resolve the past."

"Fair enough. So let's set about resolving the past."

Christie looked at him in surprise. "You make it sound so simple." She looked out the truck's wide windshield. "There is nothing simple about my past."

Garrett reached a hand behind her head and gently pulled her toward him, careful not to jostle his daughter. Christie liked the way his mouth touched and lingered on hers. His kiss generated heat all the way through her body. She didn't want to let fear and uncertainty in but the thoughts wouldn't stop. Garrett said he wanted her to stay, at least until they figured out if things could work.

Christie had always relied on herself. That way, there was no room for disappointment or hurt. Could she trust Garrett? What if he changed his mind again? Slowly, she sank back into her seat.

"Christie, I know I hurt you," he said, his voice deep with regret. "And saying I'm sorry seems pretty inadequate, but I regret how I acted. Please think about staying."

"I have to tell you," she murmured doubtfully, "I've always taken care of myself. It's been easier than relying on someone else." She searched his face in the dim light. She wanted to hold his words close to her heart, hoping that if they both acted responsibly, they wouldn't hurt each other. Would her past always make her question what he said? When would she learn to trust?

"It's hard to stop a lifetime of fears and worries." When she looked at Garrett she had the crazy notion to throw caution to the wind. Her heart and soul demanded that she let him talk her into staying. How she wanted to believe that he'd never hurt her again. Could anyone live up to such a promise? Sometimes being hurt just went along with the package, but then, so did forgiveness.

"I have something for you." She smiled at him and unzipped the backpack she'd stashed behind the seat. "Ally let me borrow her backpack." Carefully she lifted out a tissue wrapped rectangle and held it out to him. "This is for you."

With his surprise evident, Garret took the package and pulled the tissue wrapping away to reveal the simple framed photograph of Hannah.

"Ally had that developed for me. I thought you'd like that picture of Hannah and the puppies."

He smiled at her. "It's perfect. Thank you." He placed his hand behind her neck and urged her close to him, his mouth sure and wanted on hers. Christie savored the kiss. Heaven.

Hannah signed, then mumbled in her sleep. Garrett gave a soft laugh, opened his door and leaned in to lift his sleeping daughter from the truck. "She's exhausted." Looking at Christie over Hannah's head, he said, "Thanks for coming tonight."

"It was fun. I like your family and your friends."

"I'd like to take you dancing some night. There's a few decent places in town."

"That sounds like fun." She'd love to be close to him as they danced. "I'd like to take you up on that." Reluctantly, she turned away, knowing she had to get up early in the morning. "Goodnight Garrett."

"'Night, Christie."

Before she entered the barn, Christie looked back at Garrett across the shadowy driveway. "Happy birthday." On impulse, she blew him a kiss. He laughed aloud and she told him to hush, he would wake Hannah. Christie slipped inside the door, excitement thrumming in her veins. She couldn't let him go. That knowledge wound around her and became a conviction.

¤ ¤

Late the next day Christie walked her apartment floor, then sat in her rocker and rocked furiously. Standing, she paced once more and stared out her window. Darrell was in the yard below where Hannah and Eric were playing on the tire swing. Christie put her arms around herself, enjoying the sound of Hannah and Eric's laughter on the late afternoon air.

She wiped her damp palms on the back of her jeans. She had asked Darrell to come up to her apartment. She wanted to tell him her decision regarding Ellen's ashes. She hoped he and Eric would be a part of this but she expected an argument. Having come this far, she wouldn't back down, but she was nervous.

Finally, there was a knock on the wall outside her door.

She stood by the window, feeling curiously unsettled. She turned to see Darrell standing in the open doorway.

"You still leave your doors open?"

She shrugged, unwilling to discuss something they both already knew.

Darrell leaned against the doorjamb. "Eric asked me if you're going back with us." He crossed his heels. "Are you?"

"No."

He lifted a brow. "I guess I can wait a couple more days, but I'm due back at work by the end of the week so you have to be ready by then."

Steadily, she said, "Garrett has asked me to stay and I'm seriously thinking about it."

Darrell walked across the room to her, his eyes narrowed. "You're going to take him up on that offer? Christie, I can't believe you!"

"Lower your voice, Darrell. Sound travels and I really don't want —"

"Christie, first you take off without saying where you're going! Now you're thinking of staying here so you can hang out with Judith's husband?"

"It's not like that."

"How long do you think this will last?" Darrell sank down into her rocker and put his hands on his knees. He stared at her like she was a stranger. "When did you get to be so selfish? I've never seen you act this way."

Christie clenched her fingers together. "What way, Darrell? Thinking only of myself? Maybe it's time I started doing that."

"Eric is your nephew, what if he needs you and you're too busy down here having a good time?"

"He's your son, the judge gave you custody. You act like you're mad I'm staying, but it has nothing to do with you!"

"You've said that before, but it does have something to do with me. I feel responsible," he added gruffly, surprising her. "Ellen would have wanted me to look out for you. Do you really want to stay in the middle of nowhere? How can you think about throwing everything away? Your life is in New York. It's where you belong."

"What am I throwing away?" She asked in exasperation, walking away from him. "An empty apartment? A job where I spend all day in family court being reminded of what people do to a child in the name of love?" She lowered her voice. "What's so crazy about being with people who care about me? I love it here. I feel at home in a way I've never felt before. Everything out here is so fresh and green."

"It's new. A novelty!" he snapped, his voice disparaging. "This is a nice place, but it's also the first time in twenty-five years you've been out of the city. Ellen used to say you were city through and through. You'll miss it in no time flat." He looked around the room. "Look at you now, staying in this place over a barn. You don't belong here. You don't belong with him. I've been talking to people who knew Judith. She couldn't hack it, what makes you think you can?"

"How dare you interfere! You had no right asking about my sister. And you're wrong." Christie held back her temper. Why did he think he could tell her what to do? "Where do you think I belong, Darrell?"

"With us in New York." Darrell stood up and walked quickly to her. "You could be there for Eric too."

She shook her head. "I can visit." She took a deep breath. "I am choosing to stay here."

"Hell, Christie, until six months ago you were an A student at one of New York's most prestigious law schools." He narrowed his eyes. "Have you told your cowboy that bit of news? He's got a nice place but it's nothing compared to what you could do."

Christie pressed her palms together tightly. "That's what I wanted six months ago. Maybe I don't want that anymore."

"You're throwing away your scholarship?" he asked incredulously.

"I'm not throwing anything away." Christie paced the floor restlessly, hugging her arms around her waist. "This isn't why I asked you to come by," she said abruptly. "I know you don't like the idea of scattering Ellen's ashes, but I've found a wonderful spot. I would like you to be there tomorrow at four. Maybe once we put this behind us, we can get along together as a family."

Darrell spun away from her, his hands dug deeply into his pockets. "Christ Christie, why did you have to start this again? Why couldn't you just bury her like everyone else does the dead? You just won't let her go."

Christie stiffened her spine. "Because it's what she wanted."

"And you always did what she wanted!" he snapped.

"I cared about her. I tried to make her happy."

He swung toward her. "And I didn't. That's what you're saying. That's what it always comes down to. You're so much better than me."

"I didn't say that."

"I loved her!" he shouted.

Christie felt as if she bled inside. "You walked away."

"I couldn't stand to see her wither away until there was nothing left."

"You cared about yourself more."

"I never stopped loving her."

"You wished she'd die." The words were horrific and fell from her lips in the midst of anger. She stepped back at the torment she saw in his face and suddenly knew he'd never stopped loving her sister, but he'd dealt with it in the only way he knew how. She put her hands up to her mouth, the fear inside escalating as emotion spun out of control. Numbly, she took a step toward him. "I didn't mean it, I'm sorry —"

Without a word Darrell walked past her and out the door. Christie watched him go, she couldn't stop him. The wounding inside was too great. The pain she had laid at his feet the final insult.

A shadow fell across the door. Christie looked up slowly, numbly.

Garrett stood there without saying a word.

Christie hunched her shoulders. Perhaps it was better that he see and understand the real Christie Jenkins. Angry, scared and perhaps with too much baggage to ever lead a normal life. Christie felt the weight of her own anger and knew everything she held dear was crumbling away at her feet. She wondered if this was how Judith felt at the end.

¤ ¤

Darrell raced down the steps and out of the barn. Once out in the yard he looked wildly around for Eric. He finally spotted him playing with Hannah by the house. Darrell hurried over to his son, his mind still churning over what Christie had said.

"Eric, come on, we've got to go."

Eric looked up at him in surprise. "Now Dad? We were going to play another —"

"Right now!" he said sharply. "We're going into town."

Eric stared at him wide-eyed, and Darrell lowered his voice, tried to smooth over the anger and hurt riding him. "We'll come back later or tomorrow." He made himself smile and he swallowed the bile in his throat. "Say goodbye."

Darrell gripped his son's hand and they walked to his car together. Darrell had the strongest urge to drive right through town and all the way back to New York without looking back. Christie had gone too far. She'd always been so smart and now this. When he stopped at a streetlight outside of Emerson, it suddenly hit him that he wanted to run. He didn't want to deal with all this mess she was bringing up. Ellen's ashes, her death, the burial.

Christie basically had said she loved Eric but the implication was Eris was his responsibility, totally. Frightening.

Remembering the way Ellen had been sick, Darrell thought about Eric. His son had seen it all, had seen his mother fade and then die, and he'd made it out whole. He was a good kid, but Darrell felt like his brain was being slammed with all of it and he just wanted to cry.

Darrell pulled over to the side of the road. Looking in the rear view mirror at Eric, he suddenly felt his heart slow down. After several more moments, his thoughts began to clear. He released his death grip on the steering wheel. He wondered if this was the reason Christie left New York, because she couldn't deal with any of this stress. The hurt.

Darrell admitted to himself that it was hurt and the pain of loss bombarding him, ripping him apart. God forgive him, he'd blamed everyone for the mess of his life except the one responsible. Himself. Darrell put the car in park and dropped his forehead to the steering wheel. He had left Ellen when he should have been with her and Eric. And Christie. Christie had been the strong one and that's what ate at him and made him mad.

"Daddy? Will we ever see Aunt Christie again?"

Darrell lifted his head and met his son's eyes. "It's okay, Eric. Everything is okay. We'll see Aunt Christie before we leave again. We're going to stay in town tonight." He got a sudden idea. "We'll get some pizza and see a movie tonight."

Eric clapped his hands and spouted off a string of new movies. Darrell drove back onto the road.

Maybe by tonight he could pull himself together.

¤¤

Later that evening Christie sat on the back steps of Garrett's house. She didn't know how she had ended up there or how long she sat by herself. It seemed extraordinarily quiet in the near dusk.

All afternoon she had relived the moment she had flung those terrible words at Darrell. She had blindly walked past Garrett, wandering around what seemed like hours. Darrell's car was gone. Had she caused such harm that he'd taken Eric and driven out of her life for good? Christie bit back a sob, knowing it was what she deserved after the hateful thing she'd said to him.

The kitchen door creaked open and banged closed, the sound familiar and hollow, the way she felt.

Christie hugged her legs, her chin resting on her knees. She saw a jean-clad leg out of the corner of her eye. Garrett dropped down to the step beside her. He stretched his legs out and one thigh brushed hers. That slight contact burned but tension rode Christie, making her stiff inside and out. Her shoulders ached, her head hurt and the place inside where her heart should be felt like it was bleeding. The intensity of emotion was overwhelming, and any control of her life seemed to have slipped away.

"You missed dinner," he said, conversationally. "I saved you a plate of my famous roast beef."

"I didn't know you could cook," she said, still strangely out of sync with her surroundings.

"I haven't always had Ruth."

Christie ducked her head and traced her finger

over a knot of wood on the step. "There's a lot of things you don't know about me, Garrett," she said.

"There's probably a ton of things you don't know about me either." He put his face close and reached out to gently tilt her chin up. "I know I want to learn more about you, Christie."

"I find that hard to believe after what you must have heard earlier."

Garrett dipped his head and rested his forehead against hers. The gesture was so simple and trusting Christie wanted to cry. His hand moved to her shoulder, pressed a moment and then fell away. Christie missed that brief contact, the implication of intimacy between them.

Christie traced imaginary circles on her up-drawn knees. "He didn't deserve what I said to him. He's left, hasn't he?" She tilted her head back against the wooden post supporting the handrail.

"Darrell decided to spend the night in town. I called a friend who owns a local motel. He and Eric will be back tomorrow."

Suddenly she noticed how the stars hung brightly in the cloudless sky. "He's coming back?" Christie took in a great gulp of air. "Thank God. I've made such a mess of things," she said in a rush. "I snapped that day after the custody case. I threw clothes in a duffel bag like I was a crazy woman. I just knew I had to get out. I must have called work, took a leave of absence. I left my apartment, told the landlord he could have everything in it." Christie looked at him, dry-eyed. "I walked out. At the time it felt like it was the only thing I could do."

Her lungs hurt. Tension gripped her so tightly it

was unbearable, physically and mentally. "All this time I lied to myself. I realized it when I said those terrible things to Darrell. He might have left my sister but at least he said goodbye. I didn't do that. I never abandoned my sister physically, but I did emotionally, before she died. I was so angry and tired."

"Caring for a terminally ill person takes a toll on anyone. There's no need for you to be making excuses."

"I was an honor student in law school. I quit so I could be home at night with Ellen. There was one moment when it all was just too much." When she looked at him she knew the tears hung on her lashes. Every part of her body trembled and she felt so exhausted. "I wished it was over. In my heart I wished she would die. I accused Darrell of wanting her dead. It was me . . . me, Garrett. She died two days later."

Garrett's arm encircled her shoulders, assuring her without words that she wasn't alone. She felt a tremor in her hands as something inside began to crumble. She tried to hold it back but her shoulders started to shake.

Garrett tightened his arm around her. "Let it go. You've been holding it inside too long."

Tears spilled down her cheeks. The tighter Garrett held her, the faster the tears ran. She couldn't stop them.

Breath rasped through her throat, coming from deep within, and suddenly an upheaval of emotion let loose in her and the tears were released in a torrent.

Christie couldn't stop the sobbing. She gripped her hands tightly and held her arms between her knees, her shoulders shaking with the force of the anguish trying to get out. She touched her forehead to her up-drawn knees as spasms wracked her.

Vaguely she knew Garrett's arms continued to hold her close. Christie released the pain she hadn't given voice to since the death of her sister. She had never grieved. The dam of emotion, the unspoken abandonment had remained hidden, bottled up and waiting to rupture. Christie tried to take deep breaths, but the choice over controlling her emotions had been taken from her. For the first time in her memory, Christie abandoned herself and depended on another person to keep her safe.

∞ Chapter Eighteen ∞

ELLEN WAS DEAD AND Christie was very much alive. It was a fact, something she couldn't run from any longer. She had tried so hard to avoid the hurt, but like a runaway train she had found the end of the track and now she lay in a crumpled, smoldering heap.

After a while, the sobs lessened, and Christie sat up, pulling away from Garrett. Shakily, she accepted the handkerchief he pressed into her hand. She felt incredibly weak.

"God, I'm sorry," she muttered unsteadily, gulping. She wiped her burning, irritated eyes with the cloth. She gave a small laugh, but it sounded like a hiccup. "I'm a mess."

"That's been stored up a while." He tipped her chin up with a finger, took the handkerchief back and wiped her cheeks.

Feeling vulnerable, Christie said, "It's kind of

scary, getting hit like that. I couldn't stop it."

"You've got to vent your emotions. Especially someone as strong as you, Christie."

"Yeah, right. I don't feel strong." She held out a shaking hand for him to see. "Right now I'm as weak as a baby."

"You supported your sister and nephew, offered them all the love inside you. You should be proud of what you've done. A lot of people would have run from that responsibility."

"I did run away," she admitted in a low voice. "Don't you see, Garrett, I failed. I promised Ellen I'd give her my bone marrow and she'd get better, but it didn't work. We tried so many treatments; holistic, vitamin therapy, acupuncture, but her illness was too far advanced. I promised her I'd take care of Eric as if he were my own, and I couldn't do that either."

"Christie, you did the best you could. I didn't have to be there to know that. In the end, it wasn't up to you. It was her time. Eric is with Darrell, and you know that's where he should be."

"Yes." The admission had always been difficult, but now a bit of peace stole into her.

"I'm not making excuses, but I'll bet any psychologist would say those thoughts of despair near the end were natural. A culmination of trying to hold everything together and being so tired. We all have crazy thoughts from time to time but we don't act on them. You wanted your sister's pain eased and you knew death was the only way. You have no reason to be carrying this guilt. You're a caring, nurturing woman. Your sister knew it. All that's left is for you to admit it."

"It's been haunting me and I didn't even know it. I blamed Darrell. I controlled my life, every aspect of it, but I couldn't keep her from dying."

"It's not your job. You're not God."

Christie felt as if breaking that damn of emotion had released her in some way.

"You don't have to leave, you know." He touched her cheek with his hand. "Let's talk for awhile."

¤¤

The next afternoon Christie lifted the slip dress from the bed, the one she had worn to Garrett's party. She wriggled into it, smoothed it over her hips and stepped into the matching sandals. Slowly, methodically she pulled her brush through her newly washed hair. Walking across her apartment, she stood at the large window overlooking the house and parking area.

Sadness touched her. Darrell and Eric had not come back and it was almost four o'clock. Was this to be their final goodbye; angry, bitter words? Had she so alienated him that he wouldn't come back to say a last farewell to Ellen? Emptiness gnawed at her. She had jeopardized her relationship with her brother-in-law, and therefore Eric. How could she have been so selfish? Should she just have dropped the whole idea of scattering the ashes? Maybe if she had there wouldn't be a rift between her and Darrell now.

She lifted Ellen's keepsake urn and thoughtfully ran her fingertip along the wooden edge of the book. The time had arrived to scatter her sister's ashes, but she looked outside again, hoping to see Darrell.

Clasping the book close, Christie left her

apartment and walked outside. The air was comfortable, not too warm or cool. The sun was moving low in the sky and it felt like the right time to say goodbye.

She found Garrett and Hannah waiting for her outside. He had showered, she could see damp, curling tendrils of blond hair along his collar. He wore a dark gray shirt and dress jeans as black as the boots on his feet.

"Ready, Christie?" he asked quietly as she walked over to him. He stood beside his truck and opened the door. "Hop in."

Christie shook back her hair. "I'd like to walk, Garrett."

He closed the door. "Sure. I'll keep you company."

"Me too, Daddy." Hannah took Christie's hand.

Christie smiled at her niece, squeezing her hand lightly. They followed the path that ran beside the paddocks. There was no hurry. The moment had finally arrived, a chapter of her life so long open, now about to close. A final goodbye to her little sister.

"Are you okay?" Garrett asked.

"Yes." She looked up at him. "Your Kentucky is so beautiful, I know Ellen would have loved it here. This is the perfect ending." She hesitated, then blurted, "Have you heard from Darrell at all? Has he called?"

Seeing the compassion in his eyes she knew the answer before he shook his head no. "He did say he'd be back today."

Christie looked at the path ahead. "Today is

almost over."

"Give him a chance," was all he said.

With sudden clarity, Christie knew that was the answer. "You're right," she said. "I've never given Darrell a chance. I never considered how he felt when Ellen got sick. I jealously guarded my pain and my sister. I shut him out." She put her head down. "I wish I could tell him I'm sorry."

When they reached the meadow she and Hannah sat in the grass interspersed with the wildflowers. She needed to sit quietly for a moment and think about this last goodbye. Did she recite prayers? She had never really been one for praying. Was it necessary to say a few words before she scattered the ashes? She didn't know the proper protocol, but something told her to speak the words in her heart.

Christie looked up at Garrett as he stood patiently nearby. While she had been preoccupied with her own thoughts, he had picked a small handful of flowers. He held his hand out to her now and Christie grasped his fingers, glad of his strength as he pulled her up from the grass.

Garrett held out the bouquet, a solemn look of caring in his eyes. Christie was reminded of the other time he had presented her with flowers. She stepped close to him and stood on tiptoe. He bent his head and she placed a chaste kiss on his lips.

"Thank you," she whispered, blinking quickly to keep the tears back. This man touched her as no one else ever had. She clutched the bouquet and met his steady gaze. "I'm ready now."

"Am I too late?" Darrell asked behind them.

Christie turned quickly, a cry of relief escaping

her. Darrell had come. She handed the book with her sister's ashes to Garrett and closed the space between her and Darrell. Eric was with him also. Christie embraced Darrell, feeling the sting of tears behind her lids. He gave her a quick hug and then Christie reached out to Eric and urged Hannah closer, then hugged them both as a love of family rose up within her.

"We're here, Aunt Christie," Eric said simply, giving her a beautiful smile.

She smoothed his dark hair and squeezed Hannah's hand. She looked up at Darrell. "I'm very glad of that."

Darrell shrugged. "Yeah, well, I thought it might be a good idea for Eric. It might give him some of this closure they talk about. Maybe it will help all of us," he added simply.

"Thank you, Darrell." The words came from Christie's heart, which felt full to overflowing.

She moved back toward Garrett. "We're all ready." She took the book with the ashes and moved to the top of the knoll. As she stood there, the warmth of the sun touched her, heating the air and releasing a sweet fragrance all around them. She opened the book and then looked back at Darrell. "Would you like to scatter the ashes?" she asked.

Emotions chased across Darrell's face. She could see the fear and uncertainty as he hesitated. Eric slipped his hand into his father's and Christie saw a change come over Darrell. He looked down at his son with an almost calm acceptance on his face. Then he nodded and took the book she held out to him.

"Goodbye sweetheart," he said quite simply. A slight breeze moved around them as he tipped the book upside down. The breeze carried the ashes across the meadow, scattering them like fairy dust.

Christie held her breath and closed her eyes as a wonderful peace settled on her. She could almost hear her sister's exuberant laugh, she could envision her wide smile and the devilment that had always danced in her eyes. "Goodbye Ellen," she whispered, squeezing Eric's shoulder. "Goodbye Judith."

"Mommy is in heaven now?" he asked.

Christie looked down into Eric's sweet face. She nodded, that was all she could manage.

"Yes," Darrell said, squatting beside his son.

"She'll never be sick again?" Eric asked hesitantly.

Darrell ruffled his son's hair. "Never."

Eric smiled. "Goodbye Mommy," he said solemnly, and he leaned his head against his father's shoulder.

Christie absorbed the emotions surging around her. Darrell and Eric seemed held together by a bond stronger than any she had known with her nephew. The right decision had been made, keeping Eric with his father. Perhaps she had been slow in coming to that realization, but now she knew it was the truth.

A knot of emotion that had been lodged in her for what felt like forever slowly loosened and slipped away.

Christie felt the weight of an arm across her shoulders. She looked into Garrett's eyes and read his concern for her. He held his daughter close on his other side and she felt included in their circle of love.

Garrett's eyes seemed to promise her more caring than she'd ever dreamed possible. Her breath caught in her throat. Was she seeing something she wanted to see?

"I need to talk with Darrell," she told him.

"Eric can come with me and Hannah back to the house," he suggested, looking at Darrell.

"Sure," Darrell said. "We're leaving tonight so it might be a good idea to say our goodbyes now." Darrell put his hand on Eric's shoulder. "Go on with Garrett. Christie and I will be along soon."

"Okay, Daddy."

As Garrett and the children walked over the knoll of the meadow Christie turned to Darrell. "You're leaving tonight?"

"Yeah, right after dinner. There'll be less traffic traveling at night. We'll get into New York tomorrow."

"Thank you for coming back." She swallowed with difficultly, but knew the words had to be said. "I'm sorry for the terrible things I said to you. I know you loved Ellen, and she knew it too, even at the end she knew you loved her. She understood better than I did what her illness did to you."

Darrell looked away, his jaw clenching. "I'm not excusing what I did, but Ellen had a sixth sense about a lot of stuff."

"You're right, she did. I'm ashamed of the way I treated you, but I have to deal with my own demons. I wouldn't admit it, but near the end I couldn't handle her being sick any more. I cracked. Just like when the judge awarded you custody of Eric, I knew it was the right decision, but I felt like I'd failed."

"We both know you kept everything together."

"I've made a lot of mistakes."

"I made my own."

"I'm sorry for the pain I've caused."

"I was worried about you Christie. That's one of the reasons I came here."

"I know. It's like I've told Garrett, it's hard to believe someone wants to look out for me. He doesn't understand it takes some getting used to."

"I know your background Christie. I know you've always been the strong one. But now you've found someone who cares about you the way a man should."

"He wants me to stay."

"Then I guess you should. Maybe I was being selfish. It's not so easy caring for a kid. Sometimes I worry I'll make mistakes with Eric. Maybe that's part of the reason I came after you. I don't want to mess him up."

"Eric is happy."

"Thanks." He squeezed her shoulder. "This is your chance at happiness, don't let it slip away. Life is too damned short."

"Sometimes I wonder if I can get past my background. It's weighing me down."

"Have you told Garrett?"

"Not everything."

"Don't you think you should?"

"Yes." Christie rubbed her palms together, suddenly cold despite the sun overhead. "The last time I told anyone was Allen and he walked out on me."

"Ellen said he was a jerk, so you can't go by him." Darrell gave her a half smile. "Good luck Christie. We both know you're strong enough to do whatever you want with your life."

It seemed quite natural to go into his arms. Christie hugged him tightly, closing her eyes and biting her lip as all the old hurts between them fell away. "Thank you for caring." With tears filming her eyes she stepped back. "I do know one thing, Darrell, Ellen would be proud of the father you've become."

¤¤

Dinner that evening turned out to be a festive occasion. Garrett sat back and observed the happy faces around him. Randy and his Mom had joined them and a big surprise had been Sam's announcement that he and Ruth were going to be married.

Garrett marveled at the changes in life at the farm in less than a month. His glance lingered on Christie as she talked with his Mom. Christie had been the catalyst. Each day he found her more amazing. He no longer searched for comparisons between her and Judith. Christie was her own person.

"What do you think about if we have the wedding here Sam?" Garrett said now. All eyes turned to him. "Well, why not? Unless you have somewhere else in mind."

"I think it's a great idea," Christie said, smiling at him. She looked at Ruth and Sam. "And I would love to help."

"Of course I would lend a hand also," his mother

said, throwing Christie a conspiratorial smile.

"Me too — me too," Hannah said excitedly.

"I know we can depend on everyone here," Ruth said in her usual forthright manner. "But we'll see what the future holds before there's definite plans made. Who knows, there might be a flurry of activity at the farm in the near future." Her glance at him and then Christie was full of meaning.

Garrett watched Christie and they shared a smile. They had all the time in the world. He was not letting her go.

¤¤

Darrell and Eric left immediately after their early dinner. Christie knew she would miss Eric, but she felt at peace saying goodbye, knowing he was in good hands and that they would be keeping in touch. She made Darrell promise to call when he arrived home.

Afterward, everyone helped clear away the dinner dishes and they'd gravitated out to the terrace. It'd been fun to sit and just talk companionably. Christie liked to hear Sam and Garrett discussing strategies for the farm, the progress and setbacks. She and Hannah had finished playing a board game when Ruth and Sam decided to leave, citing the cool night air as the reason.

Caroline yawned and nudged Randy, who had been uncharacteristically quiet the entire evening. "I'm ready to go home also," she said.

"And it's your bedtime, young lady," Garrett told his daughter.

"I guess I'll call it a night, too," Christie said.

"But it's only nine!" Ruth declared. "I remember

when I was your age, I'd be out dancing into the morning hours."

"That's what we were doing last week," Sam grumbled, but his glance at Ruth was teasing.

"Ruth's right," Garrett said, his glance lingering on Christie. "It's early. Why don't you stay longer?"

"I have to get a sweater though."

"I'll get Hannah into bed," Garrett said.

Randy reached down and scooped Hannah up into his arms. Hannah squealed and clasped her arms around his neck as he swung her around. "Good night, kiddo."

Hannah kissed Randy, then held out her arms to Caroline.

When everyone moved out to the driveway, Hannah stood on the back porch steps beside her father. "Christie?" she called.

Christie looked back at Hannah.

"When you come back can you say goodnight?" she asked shyly.

Christie felt a burst of happiness. "Of course I will."

Christie walked out to the cars to bid everyone goodnight. Randy was the last to leave. As she moved beside him she wondered at his preoccupation all night.

"How are you doing Randy?"

He looked up, smiling automatically.

"How's Ally?"

"We had a fight. I told her about the place I'm buying and asked her to marry me. She thinks I'm moving too fast." He put his hands in his pockets.

"Well, you haven't been going out that long."

"We've known each other our whole lives."

"It's not the same."

"That's what she said. I just don't want to lose her."

"You won't." She touched his arm reassuringly. "She needs some time." She paused. "Why don't you suggest a long engagement?"

A spark of hope lit Randy's face. "Hmm, maybe hope you're right. Thanks Christie, I gotta go."

After he left, Christie hurried toward the barn, wondering if the excitement she felt showed on the outside. Surely her feet weren't touching the ground. She felt as if she fairly radiated with happiness.

She entered her apartment, hugging herself to ward off the cool night air. She wanted to be close to Garrett tonight, feel his hard arms around her. She had an urge to cover his face with kisses.

Christie retrieved her sweater and hurried back over to the house. As she entered the semi-dark kitchen she saw Bo Peep watching her from her dog bed by the door. Christie moved over to the dog and bent down to carefully stroke the golden head. "You're a good dog, Bo Peep," she whispered. Bo Peep's tail thumped the floor.

Christie ventured down the hallway. Peeking into Hannah's room, she saw she was already in bed. Christie stepped inside and crossed the room to the bed, then bent over to place a gentle kiss on Hannah's smooth forehead.

"Night, Christie," Hannah said in a drowsy voice. "Eric's okay for a boy," she added, almost as an afterthought. "He's a pretty good cousin too."

Christie stifled a laugh. "He thinks you're pretty

cool too. Sweet dreams," she told her.

Christie continued down the hall to the living room. Only one light was lit, leaving the rest of the room in shadow. Country music played softly as Garrett sat in his oversize recliner.

She rubbed her hands up and down her arms, suddenly feeling nervous after her heightened anticipation of being alone with him. "It's getting cool outside." She carefully rolled her sweater cuffs back one turn.

"Why don't you sit down?"

Christie perched on the edge of a chair across the room, kneading the material of her dress with her fingers. She felt unaccountably nervous.

"Are you okay with Darrell and Eric leaving?" he asked quietly.

"I've finally made my peace with Darrell." She gave a deep sigh.

"So there's nothing immediate pulling you back to New York?" His voice sounded husky. Christie felt the start of goose bumps along her legs, recalling the night they'd made love. His voice had been husky then, too.

She rubbed her palms over her knees. "There's no reason to go back. I feel like I'm getting a fresh start here, and I like that idea." She wiggled her toes in her sandals and then bravely looked up at him. "You asked me if I'd consider staying, Garrett, and I want to do that."

He held out his hand.

Without hesitation Christie moved over to him. He urged her down so she sat on his lap sideways. Garrett pulled her close. "This is where I want you to be," he murmured. "What do you have to say about that?" He pushed aside her hair and brought his mouth close to her neck. Her stomach muscles tensed in anticipation but still his lips didn't touch her.

A groan of pleasure built in her chest. "I say yes," she muttered as her fingers worked their way up his shirtfront.

His mouth finally touched the sensitive skin of her neck and she started in surprise and longing. She felt his hot tongue on her skin. Christie lost her grip on his shirt and closed her eyes, concentrating on the sensation of his mouth as he worked his way along her sensitive skin.

With shaking fingers she pulled the buttons of his shirt open. She wanted the material off his shoulders so she could feel him against her. She kissed his mouth, swirled her fingers through his chest hair, aware of his quickened breathing. Christie felt his reaction to her in the tightening of his arms, the strength he'd never use against her.

Their lips met and an immediate heated reaction coursed through her body. She craved Garrett's closeness, her memory crystal clear of the one and only night they'd made love. Taking the initiative, she eagerly touched his mouth, grazed her teeth along his whiskers, enjoying their sensual appeal. This strong man wanted her. His breathing, now as erratic as hers, told her that.

Christie nipped at his lips, wound her fingers through the fine hair at his nape. She wanted nothing more than to stay in his arms all night.

His jaw clenched. "If this goes on much longer,"

he growled, "we're going to end up in my bed. You won't get out until morning." He tightened his arms around her. "Maybe not then."

Christie shivered with anticipation. "I'm prepared to face the consequences," she whispered recklessly, provocatively.

His long fingers threaded gently through her hair. "You keep giving, Christie. I've never known anyone with such a big heart. I want to try to give back some of what you've given me." Garrett placed his hands on either side of her hips, their heat burning through the fabric of her dress. "If you'll give me the chance, I want to make up for the hurt I've caused."

Christie closed her eyes tightly, savoring his touch, the words he had spoken. Her eyes flew open a moment later. "We still have to talk about my background."

"I know." He cupped her cheeks with his palms. "But maybe your past isn't as important as you think it is. Maybe it should stay in the past."

Christie moved her head jerkily, confusion filling her. "That's what I've been doing my entire life, trying to bury the past."

"You have a knack for talking at the wrong moment." Garrett touched his lips to hers, rubbing gently, the friction escalating the heat between them.

Wanting to believe a future waited for them, Christie ignored the warning jangle at the back of her mind. She wanted to laugh and to cry she felt so keyed up. The freedom to love Garrett was only a small step away and she intended to grasp it with both hands.

Fiercely, she pressed up against him, aware of his body's reaction to her closeness. She pressed kisses along his chin, let her lips trail across his. Her gaze met his as his fingers splayed across her neck. In an agony of feeling, she pressed her cheek to his chest, turned her nose into the skin, allowed her tongue to trace and swirl, wetting sensitive spots. "You don't know how many nights I've wanted to do this." She didn't intend to wait another moment.

He murmured her name, his voice hoarse. His hands tightened on her arms and he surged to his feet, bringing her with him.

Christie stood on her toes, gently bit along the cord of his neck, then found his mouth, hungrily assuaging the bone-deep ache inside. Again, her body remembered the exquisite loving; their one night of passion.

Christie wanted that closeness now.

Garrett took her hand and she allowed him to lead her down the hallway and into his room. The door closed and for some reason she didn't mind the closing of that door. Then they were beside the bed and with one hand out behind him, Garrett lowered them onto the mattress, his fingers moving to splay over her belly. Her breasts, threatening to spill from her dress, ached for the touch of his lips. Christie wanted them there. The sensitive skin invited his tongue, his exploration. All of her body quivered in response to his journey across it. Christie pulled her legs up, her hips thrusting against him, her hands around his back now, pulling him down onto her. His weight made her shiver and crave more.

Fleetingly, her vulnerability scared her. She contemplated the hurt she invited. When you loved someone, you became defenseless.

"Christie," he whispered. His voice caressed her, deep, vibrant, full of promised delights. "Come back to me."

Strength and joy infused Christie as realization struck. No, not defenseless. When you loved someone you were empowered.

She watched Garrett's mouth move over her skin, her body reacting erotically, wanting again the feel of him inside and filling her. This man completed her, helped her realize the woman she was meant to be.

Strong hands caressed her skin, cupping her breasts, encircling her, pulling her into him. Christie clasped his hips with her legs, letting her head fall back, just letting herself feel all of him.

Garrett didn't have time to think of anything but Christie, sweet, trusting Christie, and the way she filled him with desire. Caring for her, he felt whole. She was a light in his life, in Hannah's life. At moments like this, he couldn't imagine her being like Judith, who'd been unable to shake free of the demons that pursued her.

Lifting up on his elbows, he watched her, the passion in her half closed eyes, the breath escaping past full red lips. He wanted her. He dropped his mouth once more to those lips, loving their fullness and texture, the way she opened up for him.

They were face to face with barely a breath between them. Her dress hung off one slim white shoulder and the sandals were still on her feet.

Garrett leaned over her and cupped an ankle. He slid the sandal off one foot, then the other. He gently ran a fingertip over her finely arched foot, then moved both hands up over her calves, traced her knees and pushed her thighs apart. He moved closer, kneeling between her legs as she gave him a kiss certain to blow his remaining control.

Maintaining eye contact, Christie trailed two fingers down to his stomach, stopping at his jeans. She circled the jeans snap and then slowly undid it. The zipper slid down, the metal click . . . click the only sound in the room. Breathing hard, he stood and shucked his boots. Impatiently, Garrett jerked his jeans off and kicked them away.

Dry mouthed, he watched Christie lift her dress and pull it over her head. He swallowed quickly as she sat up on the bed, clad only in sheer underwear. The pale skin of her hips drew him, tantalized him as they curved into her rounded bottom. Unable to resist the temptation he cupped her with his hands and pulled her against him.

He felt the shivery breath she took and he dropped his mouth to hers, taking that breath, giving it back, tracing her exquisite lips with his tongue. He could devour her and not get enough. Garrett made himself go slow and savor her closeness. There was no rush, until the torment of her smooth, slim body was suddenly against him.

Christie closed her eyes and gave what sounded a murmur of satisfaction, her body trembling against his. She gripped his waist, moved her hands along his back. Garrett felt the groan building inside. He shook with mixed sensations of wonder and giving, taking and sensation. Stumbling back, he dropped to the edge of the bed. Spreading his legs, he pulled her up against him, letting her nestle against his thighs.

With a small laugh, Christie pushed him and he let himself fall backwards. He lay on his back waiting, hardly daring to breathe as she studied him curiously. Christie pressed her palms flat against his chest. Climbing on top of him, she moved forward until she sprawled erotically and shamelessly wriggled against him.

Garrett ran his palm up the inside of her leg, his fingers feather soft, drawing small circles on her tender flesh. His eyes met hers and he saw desire in her pupils, large and black.

She brought her face close and touched his mouth. She took his breath for her own.

∞ Chapter Nineteen ∞

Garrett woke slowly, stretching from head to toe. Opening his eyes, he saw the clock on his bedside table. Nine-fifteen. He couldn't recall the last time he'd slept so late.

Instantly, he thought of the night he and Christie had shared. He rolled over but she was gone from the bed. He ran his palm over the still warm sheets.

The bedroom door opened. "Hi, Daddy."

He caught Hannah as she jumped onto the bed. "Good morning, Hannah. You look very nice in that blue dress."

"Thank you, Daddy." She gave him a tight hug. "Me and Christie are making breakfast 'cause Ruth isn't working today. I didn't wake you, did I, Daddy? Christie said to let you sleep."

Garrett grinned. "I'm not tired anymore."

"I'll tell Christie." After giving him a kiss, Hannah jumped off the bed.

"Hannah?"

She turned her wide blue gaze on him. "Yes, Daddy?"

"You like Christie, don't you?"

"I love her," she said solemnly.

Garrett smiled at her. "Me, too." He stared at his daughter, and it was like a light bulb flashed in his head. He did love Christie. He patted the sheet beside him. "Sit down a minute. We have to talk."

His daughter sat on the edge of the bed.

"Do you remember when we talked about the accident? I want to make sure you understand it was never your fault."

She nodded.

"I also want you to know that ever since I saw you peeking at me from behind your mom, you've always been my little girl." He wanted there to be no lingering doubts in her mind that he wanted her. Hannah threw her arms around him and hugged him again.

"Oh, Daddy! I love you even more than Albert."

Garrett laughed, but a great relief washed over him. He finally felt like he had a handle on his daughter.

"I have to go help Christie," she said, and ran out of the room.

Garrett heard Hannah's excited chatter all the way from the kitchen.

In the shower he planned what he would say to Christie, how he'd ask her to marry him. She had to say yes. She loved him and he loved her. It was that simple and the time was right for the three of them to be a family. He didn't expect everything to be easy, but he and Christie had a good start.

Exiting the shower, Garrett knotted a towel around his waist. He reached for the bathroom doorknob but the door opened toward him first. Christie stood in the doorway. With a lift of his brow and a leer, he advanced on her. "Since you're here I have every intention of taking advantage of you."

Christie put up a warning hand. "Keep away from me, Garrett McIntyre. I came to tell you breakfast is just about ready. I have other news also." Christie smiled slightly. "Hannah informed me she loves you more than Albert."

"Ah, the highest compliment."

"Ruth was here for just a few minutes. She's taken Hannah with her into town. I imagine she'll have her hands full with the way Hannah's been running through the house," she said. "And now it appears we're all alone."

Garrett began to smile. "Sounds like a conspiracy to me."

"If it is, I vote we should play along." Her smile told him to come and get her. She pretended to evade him by backing out the door but Garrett shackled her wrists in his hands and closed the door. Gently, he pinned her against the wood and put his hands beside her head. "The rule starting today is you can't leave bed until I'm awake. I think you were looking for an excuse to come back in here," he murmured, running his mouth down her neck. "And I'm not letting you go until you admit it."

Christie tipped back her head and closed her eyes. "I'm not admitting to anything," she declared, her palm flat against his chest.

Garrett heard the distant ringing of the phone. "Let the machine get it."

"It might be Darrell," she murmured, "He promised to call."

Garrett closed his eyes and groaned. Christie burst out laughing, no doubt reading the disappointment on his face.

"The bacon's probably nearly burnt anyway," she observed, slipping away from him. She gave him a teasing smile. "See you for breakfast."

Garrett walked into the kitchen a few moments later. He'd let Christie off lightly with a few kisses, but he intended to make up for it later.

He wrinkled his nose and reached over to turn off the griddle. The bacon strips were definitely charred.

"Christie?"

He also flipped off the gas under the teakettle as it began to whistle shrilly. Where was Christie?

Garrett walked back out into the hallway and spotted Christie in the living room. She stood at the French doors, staring outside. The phone was in her hand but Garrett could clearly hear the constant beep of a disconnected line. He felt a sudden chill, seeing her standing there so still.

"Christie, is everything okay?"

As he approached she slowly turned. She fumbled with the phone and then put it down on the table behind her. Gone was the carefree woman he had kissed five minutes earlier. Now her eyes looked deep and haunted.

Telling himself to remain calm, he touched her arm. "Christie."

She started to speak several times but was so obviously upset she stopped. Garrett's gut twisted at the resignation and pain.

Finally she managed, "There's something I've heard Buddy say, about being dumber than a box of rocks." She lifted her eyes to him and the bleakness hurt Garrett, it dug down deep inside him.

"Tell me," he said urgently.

"I must be dumber than a box of rocks to think I could pull this off."

"Pull what off?"

She flung her arm out in a sweeping gesture. "Any of this. You — Hannah, the talk we had about me staying here like we're a normal dating couple. How could I think I could get away from my past? Judith knew it, but I thought I could win. It's always been there waiting to jump on top of me." She lowered her head. "And now it has," she whispered.

"You're not making sense." Garrett gripped her arms and made her face him. "Christie, tell me what you're talking about."

Her eyes looked like liquid chocolate. "That call was from Darrell. He got in early this morning. There was something in his voice — he didn't want to tell me but I knew something was wrong. Apparently my mother's been arrested again. Her name is all over the news." Christie pulled away from him.

"Your mother? What does this mean for you?" Garrett asked.

She spun around and stared at him incredulously. "It means what it's always meant. My family is bad news — lying — stealing and we're drunks who don't care if the whole world knows it."

Garrett put out a hand. "Christie, that's not you."

"It's my family, so it is me," she said, her voice thick with pain. "There's more you should know. My father's been arrested countless times for driving under the influence. My mother's been in and out of jail my entire life. That's why Judith left. She wanted something better." She looked up at him. "She found something better, you, but she couldn't handle it. She couldn't handle normal."

Christie's eyes were dark with wounds he might never understand. He felt as if he'd been hit between the eyes. He needed just a minute to think, to make her see it was her that mattered. "What's important is the trust and understanding we've given each other these past weeks. I care about the woman you are," he said urgently.

"You don't know the woman I am. When your life is a sordid secret, there's nowhere to hide. Eventually the truth comes out, but you wouldn't know anything about that. You're a well-respected businessman, you serve on committees and actively participate in the community. People look up to you. Your life is an honest, open book." She looked at him and then went on deliberately, "I was engaged about six years ago. He was an assistant district attorney with a bright career ahead of him. He told me he loved me. When I told him about my family, our relationship ended. He dropped me cold."

Garrett knew the next few moments were crucial to their future. "I don't care about your family," he said. "It's you I love."

Christie frowned and stared out the glass doors.

"You have no idea what you're saying. I can't stay. I was a fool to try and forget who I am." She turned to face him and there were tears on her cheeks. "I'm so sorry, Garrett." She pulled the door open and ran out onto the terrace.

Garrett stood there, his brain working, trying to see his way through this nightmare. An intensity of emotion gripped him. He couldn't lose her. He wanted to fight for her but he wasn't sure how. All along he'd had his own doubts about her past, but right now the only clear thing in his mind was he didn't want to let her go. Despite what she'd said, she wasn't her sister.

∞ Chapter Twenty ∞

CHRISTIE STOOD ON THE terrace, trembling all over. The sun touched her head but it didn't warm the cold place inside — the place she had run from her entire life. Her past. Her upbringing. The guilt and shame she'd tried to keep hidden, sometimes even from herself. *Judith, I understand.*

Now Garrett knew all the secrets about her messed up family. What right did she have to love Garrett or any man? She'd seen the look on his face. Maybe he was already having second thoughts. *He said he loved her.*

She thought of the way she and Garrett had loved each other last night. It had felt so right.

"Had a little spat?" asked a man's voice, a familiar voice.

Christie turned around and reached for the terrace door just as Les Doyle muscled in close to her and pushed her across the terrace. Christie lost her balance and fell against the edge, gritting her teeth as her knee hit the stone. With dread, Christie realized she and Garrett had been right all along about Les.

"Too bad about your fight," he said. "I guess this means you're finally leaving."

"Why are you here?" she demanded.

His mouth twisted in a mockery of a smile. "You ruined my life, now I'm going to ruin yours." In his hand he held a small handgun.

Terrified, she edged away from him. "This isn't necessary." She looked at the closed terrace door, praying Garrett didn't follow her out. "You have to get help, Les, for yourself and your family."

"Why bother? Kim swore she'd never come back." Christie recognized the stark pain in his voice. "The way I see it, all of this started when you weaseled your way in here."

"No," Christie said. "Kim left because she was afraid for her son. You're not yourself when you drink."

His eyes shifted and she saw a shadow of pain. "You don't know anything about it."

Christie planted her feet. "I grew up in an alcoholic family. I know the signs, I know what it does to the people who love you. It's an obsession you can't kick on your own, no matter how much you think you're the one in control." When he didn't say anything, she pressed her point home. "Think carefully, Les. When you drank, long before I arrived here, what happened?"

"Move off the terrace," he snarled, waving the gun left to right.

"You're afraid to admit it, aren't you?" she said slowly, sympathy filling her. "It hurts like hell to think someone you love doesn't want you anymore."

"Les!" Garrett's voice was behind them. Christie turned back toward the terrace doors, heart racing with fear. Garrett stood in the doorway. "I'm the one that hired her. This isn't her fault."

"Garrett's right, isn't he?" Christie said to Les. "You know it's not my fault or Garrett's. You need to look at yourself Les. You're a good looking guy, you've got a wife and a beautiful baby boy, but you're so far down in that bottle, you can't remember what it was like when you and Kim were happy. A job is just a job. There are other ones, better jobs. But Kim does have a job to come back to. Don't do something you'll regret and pay for the rest of your life."

Les' laugh sounded desperate. "It's gone too far already." His hand with the gun pointed down to the ground.

Christie took a half step closer. She could see the sweat beading his brow. "Stop now before someone gets hurt. You'll go to jail and what will that do to Kim? This next moment will decide the rest of your life. How do you want to live it?"

Christie saw something in his eyes, either desperation or fear, and she knew part or all of what she'd said hit home. As if his feet had been yanked out from under him, Les suddenly collapsed to the stone floor, the gun in his lap. "I didn't mean to start a fire," he said, his voice cracking. "I fell asleep. They've been looking for me everywhere, I couldn't go home."

"Have you been hiding at the ranch, Les?" Garrett asked.

"Yes," he said starkly. Les looked up at Garrett. "The night of the fire it was moonless. I used my lighter to see, but I dropped it on the bag the painter's had in the corner. It started to burn and I thought I stomped it all out, but I woke later and the room was filled with smoke. God, it was choking." His shoulders began to shake. He pushed the gun across the stone, away from him. "Call the police," he said to Garrett. "I'll turn myself in. Right now, I have nothing to lose."

Garrett picked up the gun.

Christie's heart went out to Les and she carefully placed a hand on his shoulder. "We'll get help for you, Les."

¤¤

As Garrett called his brother and explained what had happened, he marveled that Christie had stopped Les in his tracks, maybe even saved his life by dealing with him calmly and rationally. When Randy arrived Christie spoke with him about the different substance and alcohol abuse programs available and Garrett's admiration for her went up another notch. However, they all knew the most important part was up to Les.

When Randy and Les finally drove away in the patrol car, Garrett pulled Christie into his arms, needing to reassure himself that she was okay. "Christie, sweetheart. How did you know all that information about the help that's available for Les?"

"I've worked in the court system for years and my own father has been in various rehab programs."

She looked away. "I've always been afraid," she admitted, lifting her chin. "They say it runs in families. I've never had a drink, not even a taste. I didn't want to find out if I had it. I know what it does to the people you love. So many times, my father promised to quit, but he couldn't. My mother, well, she was in and out of our lives - a lot of it's blurred."

"That's your parents, but it's not you."

She nodded in understanding. "You're right, but I've wasted a lot of time being ashamed of who I was."

Garrett moved across the room and gripped her shoulders. "Your upbringing made you the woman I love." Tenderly, he cupped her face. "Something beautiful came out of the ugliness. You."

"You know all the secrets," she said simply, feeling a tremendous release.

"Marry me."

Christie threw her head back as a smile pulled at her mouth. She lifted her shoulders and a great well of love rose up within her. Tenderly, she smoothed her fingers through his hair. "I love you so much, you're everything to me."

"I won't let you walk away," he said gruffly, "especially now that we're both finally talking some sense. How could I have doubted for one minute we were meant to be together? You're not Judith. You've risen above your past and don't ever forget it."

"We've been too stubborn to see what's so obviously in front of us." She kissed his cheek. "I hope you're interested in kids when we're married," she teased. "I want a brother and sister for Hannah."

His smile was slow and full of promise. "We can get started anytime."

∞ Epilogue ∞

"CHRISTIE JENKINS MCINTYRE."

Christie walked onto the stage and accepted her diploma with a smile. She moved over to the podium and felt very calm as she looked out over the vast sea of faces. Assembled before her were her classmates and peers, family and friends: the people who mattered the most to her.

She clutched the diploma in her hand and held it up in the air, surprised by the applause that continued for several moments.

She smiled down at her family sitting in the front row. Garrett held Katherine, the baby's small dark head nestled against his shoulder, and Hannah sat beside him, the big sister proudly in charge of diaper bag and baby essentials. Darrell and Eric had flown to Kentucky to be here today, along with Trina, Eric's new mom. Behind them sat Garrett's mother, Ruth and Sam with Buddy, Ally and Randy, who had finally married only last month. They all cared about her and in the last several years they had all shown it as families do, in one caring manner after another.

She had practiced her speech for today in front of her husband, but suddenly, she knew she had to share her knowledge in a different manner than she had planned. When the applause died down, she began.

"Friends and classmates, I had planned a different speech today for these graduation ceremonies, but I would like to share a story with you." She lifted her chin and knew without looking at her husband that Garrett was proud of her. "I would like to share with you a story about following your dreams to find the gold and allowing yourself the strength and wisdom to overcome any obstacle, real or perceived. The real truth to success lies not in your past, but what you build for your future."

∞ *THE END* ∞

Excerpt Once and Always

Memory could be gentle. At other times it left scars.

Anna Barlow had read those words this morning and somehow they felt like a reflection of her life. She stared out over her ranch's fields now, trying to shake off the cobwebs of old memories.

Newly warmed earth and northeast temperatures collided, creating ground vapor as the sun fought its way through heavy clouds. She shivered, brushing at the cool morning mist that settled in her hair. Her mare stood unmoving beneath her, her nostrils blowing gently from their run. Anna patted Spirit's neck, wishing she could forget she was barely hanging onto the ranch. . . her home.

Every tree, stick and grain of dirt of the Double B Ranch belonged to her. The barns and dilapidated fences . . . the makeshift corral. She couldn't walk away from her only real home. Her grandfather Martin Barlow had brought her here at the age of fourteen. Now, everyone she'd ever loved was gone. Martin. Tyler.

Restlessly, Anna nudged her gray mare toward a well-worn dirt path that led down to the barns and house.

She'd survived worse. Somehow, she'd get through this too. Anna touched her right cheek and curled her fingers against the scarred flesh, her fingers tracing the faint ridges almost absentmindedly. Her face had once been her biggest asset. Now it brought her only anger and at times self pity. She hated feeling sorry for herself, but God Almighty she was only human.

Giving in to a reckless edge of emotion, Anna urged her mare into a bone-jarring trot down the hillside. When they reached level ground, the spring wind tore against her as they loped across open pasture. She inhaled the clean air into her lungs, reveling in the familiar thunder of hooves beneath her. Gradually, the sting of failure lessened. Self-absorbed and prideful these last two years, she'd allowed the fire that ruined her face to take over her life.

She had to live with her mistakes, but somehow she'd find a way out of this mess.

¤ ¤

Excerpt Heartstealer

Jacie's stomach churned as she stared at the ground two thousand feet below. What insanity made her put herself through this punishment — just to prove she wasn't washed up as a stunt woman?

"Just do it," she muttered. "You've done it thousands of times before. Get your foot out the door and jump."

Automatically, she ran her fingers over her knee support and then the pull ring on her parachute harness. Lastly, she braced the toes of her boots against the door lip.

She had to jump. Skydiving was her life. It had always defined who she was; a member of her family's business, Aerial Antics. Her brother Con would pull her off this job if he thought she wasn't ready. She couldn't go home with her tail between her legs. Her family would try to put her back in cotton wool. Again.

How long did she have to pay for one dumb mistake — two — if she counted the one she'd made thinking Brad loved her.

With a low growl of impatience, she stepped out and an updraft pulled her up and away from the plane. As she plunged downward, a flashback to her parachuting accident thirteen months ago at Angel Falls came dangerously close. She could see again that mountainous ledge of rock, nothing but water and uninhabited jungle below her, the glorious release as she began her freefall, and then her parachute failure. . ..

Her chute opened. Years of training took over and the tightness eased inside her chest. Of course she could do this, she'd been jumping far too long to stop now.

As her feet touched solid earth a gust of wind lifted and pulled her forward, past the camera crews, past the gathered crowd. She caught a glimpse of surprised faces and then she came to a dead stop as her body lightly impacted with another. She had a fleeting impression of a hat flying through the air and they both fell to the ground in a tangle of arms, legs and billowing parachute.

Excerpt Wishing on a Rodeo Moon

Someday, that bull would kill someone. Tye Jenkins just knew it. She straddled the top rail of the bull chute as old Hit Man moved restlessly from side to side.

Tye let her gaze roam the rodeo yard. Her heart jumped like a young colt on a brisk morning as she stared, transfixed, at a dark-haired man. Jake Miller. He stood close by, a cocky look of assurance on his lean face. He was a head taller than most of the men around him, a stranger in business clothes among mud-spattered cowboys. His suit looked expensive, not the most common attire down by the pens. She had never before seen him dressed like that, yet he carried it off with nonchalance and elegance. He stood, feet planted on ground churned up by countless boots and three days of rain, his dark head bare to the falling mist. Tye didn't try to stop the smile spreading across her face. Only Jake could pull off a suit at a rodeo in the drizzling rain.

She hadn't seen or heard from Jake in ten years, not since that terrible night she'd left. He'd showed up now, the night she planned to remember for the rest of her life — the night she'd make the rodeo finals. With the bittersweet knowledge of the past firmly in her mind, Tye sensed it was fitting Jake should be here to see her triumph.

He had changed, matured, yet something in his eyes remained the same. How long had she loved that strong face with its wide cheekbones, no-nonsense jaw touched by the faintest shadow of beard and deep-set eyes of the lightest blue? Her seventeenth summer she had loved him with a young woman's vibrancy. They'd spent endless time together, planning, talking, dreaming. Back then, Tye had thought Jake could do no wrong.

Thanks for purchasing **Echoes From the Past. Visit www.GraceBrannigan.com** to read all my contemporary, time travel, faerie stories and short romantic stories.

www.ingramcontent.com/pod-product-compliance
Lightning Source LLC
Chambersburg PA
CBHW061316170626
46817CB00001B/207

9 781939 061287